George
dismou

He sa
suppose

He found the heavy door of the house fastened; he had to knock. It was opened by a young maidservant, and he pushed past her, drawing his sword. She screamed and the sound echoed through the quiet house.

Richard, sitting dozing in the library, had been roused by the screams and shouts. He got up quickly, in time to hear the clash of steel. But James was on the stairs, hurling himself down, drawing his sword as he came. He pushed his father back into the library with a sweep of his arm.

'Down, murderer!' he shouted and drove his blade into George's chest.

JOSEPHINE BELL

In the King's Absence

Collins

FONTANA BOOKS

First published by Geoffrey Bles 1973
First issued in Fontana Books 1976

Made and printed in Great Britain by
William Collins Sons & Co Ltd Glasgow

CHAPTER ONE

At dusk one evening in October of 1651, the lamps were lit in three rooms of the 'George Inn' at the small fishing village of Brighthelmston lying to the west of Beachy Head on the Channel coast of England. The fishermen tramping in from the beach, where they had drawn up and secured their boats, saw the cheerful glow from the inn windows as a welcome, encouraging them to drive their weary, salt-sprayed limbs across the sliding shingle at a good pace to reach their own glowing firesides and the suppers their goodwives were, they hoped, they expected, at this moment preparing for them.

At the 'George' there were two suppers in progress in two separate rooms, which accounted for the abundance of light and bustle there. In the larger of the two downstairs rooms Colonel Gunter, who had arrived alone in the early afternoon, was entertaining two merchants who had arrived some three hours later than himself. Master Barlow, fair-haired, loquacious, apologized at considerable length for their later arrival. His friend, very tall, dark, reserved in manner, added little to the conversation.

Supper was served to these three gentlemen, and they had scarcely begun to eat when a second party arrived: two men; a Master Mansell, known to the innkeeper, and with him the skipper of a coaster called *Surprise*, also known at Brighthelmston, for she sometimes came to the wharves at Shoreham nearby, where he filled his vessel with coal from the Kentish minefields, in order to carry it to Poole Harbour, west of the Isle of Wight.

These two were also expected by Colonel Gunter and though late in starting their meal, settled down to it as soon as Master Smith the landlord and his kitchen staff were able to serve it up. They made such good progress, their appetites being vastly superior to those of Colonel Gunter's earlier guests, that all five gentlemen finished the meal at about the same time. Whereupon Mansell and the skipper of *Surprise* retired to the second room, smaller and very snug, with a good fire to keep away the autumn chill that had grown with nightfall.

In the supper room, having called for warm drinks, Colonel Gunter explained the situation. Master Barlow and his friends were merchants who had business across the water. Master Mansell was bargaining with Captain Tettersal for his price to take them across the Channel at the start of his next voyage and in the course of it. Master Smith must show discretion because trade abroad was frowned upon by Cromwell's Council of State and he had seen himself, that day, an unusual number of the New Model Army in Arundel, guarding the castle and bridge over the Arun river. Also ships lying offshore.

'They say the Lord Protector sends his army to seize the Channel Island of Jersey, where –' he paused and went on in a whisper – 'our murdered King did send his Queen and the two Princes, as they were at the time.'

'You know this?'

'From Carisbrooke –' the man began, but Colonel Gunter stopped him with a gesture and a look in which anger and anxious fear intermingled.

But in the next few seconds these looks changed to one of open horror. For Smith, seeing the taller of the colonel's visitors rise from his chair near the fire, where he had been sitting with his back to the table, and begin to move towards the uncurtained window of the room, moved quickly towards him, dropped on one knee, seized his hand and kissed it.

'My house is honoured, sir, by Your Majesty – by your presence. May God prosper this voyage.'

As Colonel Gunter sprang to his feet, exclaiming aloud, the landlord went rapidly from the room, closing the door carefully and silently behind him.

Charles, for it was indeed the King, lifted his hand to check the Colonel. He was perfectly calm, quite in control of the situation.

'He knows me and I know him. He was at one time in my father's employ. He is faithful. He will not betray us. But we should perhaps draw the curtains in this room, now darkness has fallen. My Lord Wilmot will help you, Colonel.' He laughed gently, lazily. 'I'll see to this small casement myself and take a breath of sea air in the doing.'

He pushed open the small window at the side of the inn parlour and stuck his head outside, only to withdraw it in an instant, all lassitude gone.

'I' faith, the wind hath gone round while we were wasting

our time at table. We have an off-shore breeze. We should be gone!'

'Captain Tettersal spoke of tomorrow morning, sire. I – we – Mansell at least was careful to avoid an appearance of haste, any kind of desperation.'

But Charles was already at the door, striding across the narrow passage outside, to that other room where Mansell and the captain, who by now was uncertain of the wisdom of his proposed venture, were making very heavy weather of the bargain.

When the King flung open the door, both men started to their feet, in alarm rather than reverence. Charles waved them to their seats but himself remained standing.

'Captain,' he said, controlled but forceful. 'We have a fair wind to clear the land. Should we not sail tonight?'

'Not possible, sir,' answered the seaman bluntly. 'Fair wind, maybe. 'Tis usual to have an off-shore breeze of an evening. But the tide does not serve. The ebb is running fast. *Surprise* is berthed in a creek by Shoreham. She is ready loaded and will sit pretty on the mud as she dries out. I had a mind to go off with the start of the next ebb, when I may warp out if the wind falls.'

Charles did his own calculations, having always taken a great interest in navigation and looked for practical experience in boats when he was in the Isle of Wight and again in Jersey.

'I would prefer we go aboard tonight if that is still possible. Then we may sail at high water or even before if the wind be still in the north.'

'As I hope and expect it may,' said Tettersal. But he looked at Master Mansell as he spoke and added, 'My crew have come into the town here to sleep. Also I have my own gear and certain stores at the other inn. I think the price cannot remain at the figure – '

'Enough,' Charles said, seeing Colonel Gunter had now joined them and was looking so angry at this confusion of times and prices he might at any moment attempt to switch the business to some other ship, a dangerous move to attempt.

Captain Tettersal thought so too and with a few half-hearted mutterings and complaints of being treated less as a ship's master than a peasant farmer, he agreed to Master Mansell's latest figure for conveying the gentlemen from thence.

'My companion, Master Barlow, will be much relieved,' the King said gravely. 'His business in France is urgent, but not looked upon here with any great favour.'

A loud laugh from the door of the room brought all heads round to it again. Lord Wilmot or Master Barlow as he called himself was, as so often during the last month, on the point of spoiling the current plan with his ill-timed mirth. There was a very dangerous pause in the room.

'Henry,' the King said, with a careless laugh but no mirth at all in the glance he directed at his friend, 'you are an incorrigible clown and knave! Go pack your bag again. I'll come with you. We leave here just as soon as Colonel Gunter and Master Mansell have brought up the horses and the good captain has mustered his crew men.'

Colonel Gunter and his servant took the horses down to the beach where they and the travellers mounted and began to move off along the shore, above the tide mark where the shingle was soft and filled the dents of their passage almost at once as they moved. They reached Shoreham before the captain and his crew joined them, but there was still time for all to go on board, except Colonel Gunter and his man who waited, with the horses, in a little sparse wood just above the shore proper.

When they had climbed on board, Charles and Henry Wilmot went aft at once, to stretch themselves on the bunks in a very small, damp, smelly cabin beside the captain's own hardly more spacious quarters.

They had not been there long when Tettersal knocked at the cabin door and entered. He went straight to Charles's bunk, knelt beside it, took the King's hand and kissing it said fervently, as the landlord of the 'George' had done earlier, 'Forgive me, Your Majesty, I dare not disclose my knowledge before. But I recognized you, sir, from seeing Your Majesty with the Prince Rupert on board that brig of the Dutch fleet he brought in to Harwich, but put out again when Cromwell's men rushed through the town to seize you both.'

'Where were you then, captain?'

'Mate on a coaster, like this one, but not exactly a sister ship. Oh, sir, I swear I'll bring you safe out of this country or sink my ship in the endeavour.'

'Safe over to France, captain, if you please. I swim better than my friend here, but not so far as to Normandy.' Captain Tettersall grinned at this sally, but said no more.

Charles slept peacefully until seven o'clock the next morning, when the sounds of action on deck roused him, though he stayed in the cabin when he had dressed and forbade Wilmot, too, to show himself.

In the coppice above the beach Colonel Gunter watched and waited all night with the horses, growing more anxious as the preparations seemed to take so long. He began to fear an interruption or even the arrival of soldiers.

But all went well. The little coaster's sails flew out at last, taking the light breeze that still held from the north, and when the anchor came up and the ship began to move, the colonel raised an arm in salute to her and her good fortune.

When *Surprise* left the mainland behind the northerly breeze grew firmer and she sped along at a good pace. But at the same time the farther she passed from the lee of the land, the larger the swell grew under her though the waves were scarcely white-tipped as yet. And still the King remained hidden in the cabin, eating now a hearty breakfast while Lord Wilmot, who had risen and dressed at the same time as his master, left the table to return to his bunk, unable to face the sight and smell of food.

'You are no sailor, Henry,' Charles said. 'With a sea so little troubled as this I marvel at your condition.'

'Which will be worse before very long,' Wilmot told him, groaning as *Surprise* rolled gently and ran on through growing waves, whose hissing as they struck her sides could be heard plainly in the cabin.

'How wonderful it is,' Charles said, with calm interest in his voice, 'to remember we have but a row of timbers between us and the restless waters. Was it not our great Shakespeare that said somewhere "Trust not the rotten planks!"? The character who spoke those words was a landsman like you, Henry.'

'He spoke good sense,' Wilmot gasped. His face had grown very green, with drops of cold sweat beading his forehead.

Charles, who was both observant and far from callous, got up, opened the cabin door and called for that member of the crew who had brought in the breakfast tray.

'A basin, my man, for my friend, Master Barlow here, who is not accustomed to sea travel.'

'At once, sir,' answered the young man disappearing but returning with a receptacle just in time to receive Lord Wilmot's first vomit.

Charles waited until the spasm was over, the exhausted victim temporarily relieved, lying quiet again, the basin's contents removed and the basin returned to the sufferer's side. Then he left his seat, beckoning to the crew man to go outside the door with him.

'I think you were not with Captain Tettersal when he mustered his crew upon the beach at Shoreham,' he said gravely.

'No, sir. I joined ship later.'

'How much later? I was given to understand we should be on the mud very shortly with no danger of any boarding during the rest of the night?'

'I came off in a coracle used for fowling. Flat-bottomed, sir. They push them over the mud with poles, where they know there is shingle underneath.'

'*They*? Who be they?'

'The natives hereabouts, sir.'

'Of whom you are not one? So wherefore did you come secretly and for what purpose?'

As with the innkeeper and the captain the young man broke down in the presence of such high authority, so keenly and forcefully bearing upon him. He went down on his knees, took the King's hand and kissed it, but dared not speak or raise his eyes to the royal face, so high above him and so lately dark, frowning, understandably suspicious.

'You know me,' Charles said, withdrawing his hand, but making no move towards his waist, where, under his coat, he had both a pistol and a dagger ready for use. 'Tell me your name and who employs you and for what purpose? I think I know your face. Where have I seen you before?'

'I am Alan Ogilvy, Your Majesty,' the youth said, standing up again, as straight as he could, but still wanting two inches of the King's height. 'They say I am like my father, Colonel Francis Ogilvy, who was at one time presented to Your Majesty in Holland.'

'That's it!' cried Charles. 'He was commanding in the army of the Prince of Orange, my brother-in-law. My late brother-in-law, alas.'

Young Alan bowed his head, not knowing how to answer these remarks. But he saw he was not expected to offer any but answers to direct questions and he saw too that Charles, with his quick wits and instant grasp of a situation that concerned him personally, had no need of further information.

'So the captain of this vessel has been in touch with your father, the colonel, to develop any possible plans to aid my safety,' Charles reflected aloud. 'I think this was not known to Colonel Gunter or to Master Mansell. But I take it you are here to act as cabin boy for my needs.' He smiled and added, 'Or shall we promote you to equerry?'

Alan ventured a smile, but the King had already become grave again.

'Is there any further plan prepared? Where is Colonel Ogilvy, your father, at this present time?'

'In France, sir. Waiting to assist Your Majesty when we arrive.'

'But where? The coast of France is long and there are many enemies waiting, patrolling those coastal waters.'

'I have my orders to serve you, sir. They have told me nothing more.'

Charles clapped him on the shoulder.

'Rightly so, my lad. Go find me Captain Tettersal. Tell him I would speak with him. The merchant, poor sick Master Barlow's friend would speak with him. I will go on deck now, for air, tell him. I will meet him there. Alan, did you say your name is? Then take up the breakfast tray, Alan, and go find the captain afterwards.'

Alan went back into the cabin. Through the open door Charles heard poor Wilmot retching and gasping and the boy trying to comfort him. He hesitated, but with a shrug of his wide shoulders turned away and made his way to the starboard side of the deck where he moved to the wooden rail, looking back with interest at the fast-disappearing mainland, the wide horizon ahead and on their starboard hand the nearer contours of the eastern coast of the Isle of Wight.

When Captain Tettersal appeared beside him the King turned, lifting a hand to prevent formal greetings between them.

'We are fortunate in our wind, captain,' he said, smiling. 'I think it may hold for the rest of today, but fall light towards evening. I have seen you use it to the best advantage, but should we not alter course for France now we have the Island well on the beam?'

'That was a thing I had in mind, sir,' Tettersal answered. 'My crew expect me to round away to the west. I carry a cargo of coal to deliver to Poole. Already they have wondered I did not make into Spithead when we were past the Owers.

But my mate agreed we should do best to have the Island to wind'ard and work in the lee of those steep hills rather than beat through the Solent. But I gave no hint we planned to cross the Channel before ever we made for Poole.'

'But they know you have passengers aboard.'

'Two merchants, avoiding the Protector's fettering laws. Nought else.'

'You fear they may object?'

'I do indeed, sir. My mate, Richard Carver, is a Quaker, very firm for truth in all matters.'

'And for that reason persecuted by the Roundhead fanatics,' Charles answered at once, with a quick flash of anger in his dark eyes though his lips still carried a half smile. 'Shall I go speak to them? Put our case, our business being in the interests of our country's prosperity?'

'If Your Maj – if your honour would so condescend – if – '

'Peace, fellow,' said the King, still good-humoured but beginning to lose patience with the other's clumsy hesitation. 'Call them together on the deck and make me known to them as an English merchant you have agreed to carry from England. I'll do the rest.'

Which he managed with such ease and condescension, such humorous display of his ignorance of their craft and such poor knowledge of seafaring that even before they had agreed to divert their voyage's purpose they were explaining, arguing and almost quarrelling over the exact spot on the shores of France where they would bring in *Surprise* and set him and his friend, Master Barlow, 'God mend the poor gentleman by morning', on shore.

'Which should be at Fécamp or thereabouts, Dick,' Captain Tettersal said, speaking for only the second time since the crew had gathered at his call. 'Come with me now and I'll set the course. So go about your business, the rest of you.'

Carver, a giant of a man, a full three inches taller than the King, and twice as wide, shouted a few orders. Tettersal added a couple more and then the two seamen turned away while Charles, after standing silent for a few minutes while the crew set about their given tasks, went quietly to his cabin, where he found Wilmot in an exhausted sleep, pale, but clearly recovering from his ordeal.

Charles did not wake him, nor did he go out on deck again that day. In the afternoon, *Surprise* turned off on her fresh course, the light failing and the wind still in the north, but growing feeble as expected. Alan brought food to the cabin, a plain but sufficient dinner, with apologies for its lateness. Having been on watch all night outside the cabin he had been overcome by sleep and only waked when Captain Tettersal shook him and drove him to the galley. But he did not explain this to the King. Nor did he ask any questions, except to know if he should wake Master Barlow.

'Leave him,' Charles answered. 'He is better sleeping. If that lasts till we make land, so much the better. If not I'll call you to bring him some warm broth. But you and I may be sleeping by then. We had little or none last night.'

Alan bowed, but again avoided explanations.

In the little wood at Shoreham Colonel Gunter saw *Surprise* still just in view off the Isle of Wight, alter course and disappear into the gathering darkness. The King had gone, the horses would not be needed for any crisis, for any desperate, hopeless attempted rescue. Gathering up the reins, he and his servant ended their long vigil and rode off home by tracks and hidden paths among the Downs.

A few hours later, when darkness had quite fallen, a small posse of soldiers came to the creek at Shoreham, asking if anyone had seen a tall, 'black' man with a few followers, perhaps on horseback, riding or walking and asking, perhaps, about the shipping in those parts. But no one could help them.

CHAPTER TWO

Surprise continued her voyage. The travellers slept until two in the morning, when Lord Wilmot woke with a raging thirst, crying out he had been abandoned on the field of battle and cursing those unfaithful mercenaries who had left him helpless.

His cries woke Charles, who at first confused sprang up seizing his pistol.

'Cease that coward noise, Henry!' the King shouted. 'Would you disclose yourself to the whole ship's company? You came near to having my bullet in your guts with your screeching!'

He opened the cabin door and listened, but all was quiet in the captain's cabin, the only noises being distant sounds of wind and water and an occasional muffled shout from those men who were on watch. Alan Ogilvy, however, came to attention as Charles opened the door.

'The broth, Alan,' the King ordered, 'and a fair basin full for me as well and for yourself if you fancy it.'

He went back into the cabin, where Wilmot sat on the edge of his bunk, looking white and miserable, but no longer seasick.

'Safe on shipboard, man, no battlefield, this time,' Charles told him.

'Empty as a dry well,' groaned Wilmot.

'I have sent for the wherewithal to fill you . . .'

Wilmot shuddered.

'I dare not.'

'You will do as I order you and find yourself restored.'

Wilmot was too weakened to protest. He forced himself to take a couple of spoonsful of the excellent broth Alan brought them and after all three had scraped the bottoms of their bowls they lay down again and slept until first light.

Again the King dressed while his friend went on sleeping. He found his cabin door unattended, but Tettersal's cabin was open and the captain came out to join him immediately.

'Land in sight, sir,' he said. 'No vessel to be seen in the offing, thank God. The fair wind holds. I shall keep our present course until we make a more exact landfall.'

'How far off do you reckon us to be?' Charles asked, turning to go on deck.

'Ten miles, on a rough guess,' answered Tettersall. 'We hold our five knots and have done this last hour.'

'Tell your men Master Barlow and I would land where convenient, be it harbour or open coast. We were delayed in England. Our business is urgent. The sooner we reach France, the more grateful we shall feel.'

Captain Tettersal understood the last remark to hint at actual rewards, so he relayed the message to his mate, Richard Carver, who spread it to the rest of the men.

Charles retired again to the cabin. In a couple of hours, God willing, they would have arrived. It had been, in the end, the easiest of his long pilgrimage to safety.

But there was one more threat of danger and that as they came near to the land, with the little harbour of Fécamp actually in sight. A vessel, looking like a Dutch hoy, had come into view about an hour before, sailing coastwise. She seemed to follow their movements, for she went about and shortened sail so as not to pass them, but wait for their coming close. She was of about equal size to *Surprise*, her pennant was a pale blue plain stripe, but she carried two flags, one of the Spanish Netherlands, the other of Holland.

By this time Charles and Wilmot, with Alan Ogilvy in attendance, were all on deck watching.

'She could be an Ostend pirate or she means to mislead us, though friendly,' the captain said, puzzled.

'She could be French, attempting a clumsy disguise,' Wilmot suggested.

Charles turned to the captain.

'Can you deliver us here upon this open beach before us? Can we go ashore in the cock-boat?'

Tettersal was clearly relieved by the suggestion. He went to look at his chart, then came back on deck to give orders where and when to anchor. Meanwhile the hoy turned away to sea, but presently went about again and sailed fussily back.

'Like a hen with one precious chick,' Wilmot said, laughing.

'Or a hawk ready to stoop,' Charles suggested, grimly.

Surprise rounded up into the wind, the anchor ran out on a long, stout rope, the cock-boat was lowered and the two supposed merchants with Alan, the mate Carver and another seaman, got down into it. The King and his friend sat together in the stern of the little boat with Alan on the floor boards at their feet, while the seamen rowed and very soon covered the couple of hundred yards to the shore. But they grounded in the shallow water and for a few seconds while the rowers steadied the little craft with their oars pushed into the mud, they all looked over the sides at the bottom, some nine inches below.

Inshore where they were, there was hardly a ripple on the water. In fact the wind from the north had dropped right away during the last half-hour and though the landing party could not feel it, a fresh breeze was getting up from the south-east and *Surprise*, as they noticed when they looked back, had turned right round with her bows pointed at them. The hoy, too, had gone about again and was now making out to sea.

Carver stood up and stepped into the water. He held out a hand to Charles.

'We must land you as quick as may be, sir,' he said. 'Captain Tettersal would be off again with this change of wind. Get you on my back, sir, and I'll keep you fine and dry till I have you on French soil.'

The King protested but Carver insisted. The broad back received him, the great hands folded under his thighs, he clasped the giant's bull neck and was transported at speed but with little splashing to the top of the beach and let down gently on that foreign soil.

Charles began a speech of thanks but Carver held up his hand.

'I am a Quaker, Your Majesty,' he said, slowly. 'That so-called Protector of ours hath not protected my fellow Friends. He persecutes them, he cuts off their ears and stands them in pillory, he throws them in prison. There be many now that say he and his kind must go, but who be there to replace them but Your Majesty?'

'None,' said Charles, firmly and solemnly. He put out his right hand and took Carver's great fist, holding it as he spoke, 'I swear to you, Richard Carver, that when I come into my own, when I return to England as rightful king, I shall not have forgotten you. Your conscience is your own. So shall be all those of your sect. You preach peace. That is a good thing. When I am King of England again, no man shall suffer for his religion – except those who would plot against the Crown and the Constitution. Believe me, you shall be amply rewarded.'

Carver bent his head to kiss the King's hand that still grasped his own. Then he fell on his knees and in a loud voice thanked God for sending them a fair wind and a clear voyage and for allowing him to take a humble part in that success.

'Amen to all you say, friend,' Charles told him gently, much moved.

Shouts from seaward brought them all standing again, looking at *Surprise*. The wind had grown to a stiff breeze; she was swinging at her anchor, the cable drawn out stiff, nearly horizontal. Tettersal stood at the rail, bellowing to Carver to come back before disaster overtook the vessel.

The giant bounded through the water to the cock-boat where the second seaman had an oar ready to push off the mud. Alan and Wilmot had waded ashore just behind Carver, so there was no delay when the mate reached the little craft and almost at once it was leaping out to sea to rejoin *Surprise*. Eager hands snatched it up from the water as the two sailors climbed aboard. Captain Tettersal set all hands to pull up the anchor but the wind was by now too strong to make this possible and after a brief struggle he ordered Carver to cut the cable, while the sheets were hauled close. *Surprise* turned away and soon was bounding off towards England with a following fair wind, just as she had so lately travelled in the opposite direction.

'Carver said God sent us our north wind yesterday,' Charles said slowly, his eyes still on the retreating ship. 'I think He is still in charge of this voyage, for with this wind they will come into harbour at Poole, with their cargo of coal as they intended and none need know where they went before coming there, nor what cargo they carried to the foreign shore.'

Wilmot roared with laughter at what he considered a prime example of his master's wit, but young Ogilvy, seeing the King did not jest, said with a puzzled air, 'The ship's mate knew you, sire. Will he keep it to himself?'

Charles shrugged.

'Does it matter? Except that the so-called New Model Army will be relieved from its searching for me.' Seeing the young man was still anxious he added, 'I think our good captain, who knew me all along, will have hinted at the truth when he put Carver in charge of the cock-boat. A man to admire that, Alan. A great soul in a great body.'

A voice hailed them from the bank behind the margin of sand and long spiky grass. Alan said quickly, 'It is my father, sire. Colonel Francis Ogilvy, of the army of his late Highness of Orange.'

Charles, whose hand had gone swiftly to the belt beneath his coat, let the hand drop and drew himself to his full formidable height.

'A fellow countryman the first to greet us in our exile. Very fitting. Go bring him to us, lad. We would learn the reason for his presence so direct upon our arrival.'

Alan presented his father as ordered, watching with awed admiration the latter's easy manner and full control of that strange royal interview.

The King was wearing the tattered, grey, servant's livery he had worn on and ever since the long ride with Mistress Jane Lane sitting pillion behind him. The soldier was in uniform, a cuirass his only body armour over a leather jerkin, a short cloak, and instead of a helmet a wide black hat with a knotted ribbon about its crown.

After a brief and respectful greeting Colonel Ogilvy explained that the hoy had indeed been patrolling that coast on the lookout for Charles. He had been expected for some weeks past.

'Why here?' demanded Charles.

'We had news, sire, that Your Majesty escaped to the south but turned east. The prevailing winds in the Channel being from the west – '

'Yes, yes. But why Fécamp?'

'A likely port. Easy to watch from. A seafaring folk, not hostile to Englishmen. A poor, hard-working people, no temptation to pirates of any nationality.'

Charles nodded.

'You have horses?'

'A troop of ten. Will it please Your Majesty to follow me?'

Charles gave up the royal manner instantly. He called to Wilmot and Alan, who were standing a little distance away, to come forward quickly, then dropped a hand lightly upon the colonel's shoulder.

'Lead on, sir,' he said cheerfully. 'The land here may be foreign but it feels familiar to my tread, though scarcely comfortable. But that, as you have no doubt noticed, is due to the state of my shoes.'

This was, indeed, as deplorable as the rest of the King's clothes, though the fact that his feet were dry made their appearance less squalid than poor Wilmot's broken-down boots which were covered with muddy sand and oozing black water from their numerous cracks and holes.

In fact when the colonel had led his master to the group of horses waiting at the corner of a field inland from the beach, the men stared in amazement, not recognizing the two tramps their colonel had produced from the sea. So surprised were they that Ogilvy had to shout an angry order to them to dismount in the presence of the King of England.

They obeyed him quickly enough. Most of them were men from the Netherlands, big fair-haired Flemish mercenaries, speaking their own dialect, in which the colonel had addressed them. Their faces still wore a look of astonishment, but they sprang from their saddles briskly enough and stood at attention as Charles walked down the line with Colonel Ogilvy beside him.

'I think I have seen these men before, have I not?' the King asked. 'Or others like them. At the Hague. Where I recollect seeing you about the Prince of Orange's guard, do I not?'

'I thank Your Majesty for that gracious remembrance,' Ogilvy said, saluting again and moving forward to take the bridle of a horse, held by one of the troopers, but saddled and bridled more richly than the rest.

Charles swung himself up with easy grace. He looked round to see Wilmot mounted, then said briefly, 'And now?'

'To Fécamp, sire,' the colonel said. 'Where you may rest and eat and – ' He broke off, embarrassed.

'And clean ourselves and burn our lousy linen for new, you would say,' Charles finished for him, laughing heartily. 'And find extra mounts, for I see your son goes pillion and two of your troop as well, to supply my Lord Wilmot, for which I pity the nag that has to suffer their combined weight.'

'It will not be easy, sire,' Ogilvy told him. 'We must promise to return any beast we can secure and push on to Rouen as soon as may be.'

But Charles had had enough of taking orders for his conduct. He was no longer on the run. The great burden of secrecy, danger, urgent movement, that had lain upon him for the last six weeks was lifted. He was an exile, the local peasantry scarcely knew who he was, certainly cared little for his predicament, but they need not be feared.

'If there be an inn at Fécamp, we will rest there tonight,' he said. 'Let us be off, Colonel. Rouen may wait till we have washed and eaten and slept upon an unmoving couch.'

At Fécamp the villagers came out to see the strange travellers but stood silent and disapproving for a few minutes, then turned away. No excitement, no drama, no emotional exchange or thanksgiving as could be expected from a near escape from death. Not from the sea: they were accustomed to its terrors. But it had been a peaceful night and a fine morning. Ideal for a voyage. Not from the Dutch or the Ostenders: there had been none in the offing. Only from this tall, worn, tattered young man and his fellow countrymen. The soldiers called him a king, but that must surely be a lie. They had indeed never seen their own king, who had been a young child when he came to the throne and was even now only a boy. But as they discussed all they knew of royalty that evening, and it was not much, they came to the conclusion that the visitor was certainly not a king, even if he had been born a king's son. Moreover he was not likely ever to become a king. Why, he had no luggage with him, not so much as a clean shirt, the innkeeper had said.

Their opinion was unaltered the next morning when the party rode away, the arrivals from England still in their rags, only partially cleaned and mended. At Rouen their reception was much the same, but the town did manage to provide a change of clothes for Charles and Wilmot and Colonel Ogilvy found and hired a coach in which the two men were to set off for Paris, accompanied on the box, by special request of the King, by young Alan Ogilvy.

'I would have your son with me, Colonel,' Charles had explained when the final arrangements were made the night before. 'For he hath shown himself attentive, intelligent and resourceful. I do not know how I may be situated in Paris, but I go first to my mother's Court. Until my household be set up, your boy would be very useful to me. His mother, my Lady Anne, your wife, lives I am told at The Hague, whither you, doubtless, will make your way when this service is ended.'

Colonel Ogilvy bowed, murmuring formal expressions of consent and gratitude. He knew why the King had spoken of his family, for Lord Wilmot, who was about his own age or a few years younger, had met and known him in the army of the Prince of Orange. They had talked the night before, after the King had gone to bed. Ogilvy had heard the details of the long escape after the battle of Worcester, though Wilmot had not stressed the many near-disasters of that adventure, due mainly to the impetuous mistakes he had himself made. No doubt Lord Wilmot had told the King all he knew of Ogilvy's family, his wife who had been Lady Anne Wolmer, daughter of Lord Aldborough, his two surviving sons of whom Alan was the younger and three daughters, still mere children.

The colonel spoke to Alan about the King's command, which, he explained, must be accepted.

'If your brother had been in England when these events were in train I would have set him on to serve His Majesty in the last stage of the rescue,' he said. 'But he was with me in Paris on a message from the Princess of Orange to the Queen Henrietta Maria, her mother. There we had news the King had not been taken at Worcester. Poor Gordon is bitterly disappointed he has had no part to play. He is a soldier like his grandfather Ogilvy.'

'And you too, sir,' Alan protested.

'Maybe. But the will to it did not come at birth as it has with Gordon. You have more the spirit of your great-grandfather, old Doctor Ogilvy of the Charterhouse.'

Alan laughed.

'I may have been set on scholarship because my lady mother would have me at Oxford with my great-uncle Richard, but I can tell you now I was very greatly pleased to have your orders, sir. Oxford is a sad place these days. Sad and fearful since the great wickedness of the Royal Martyr's death.'

The two men bowed their heads. The shock and horror of that end was still, two years later, fresh in their minds and hearts. But they parted in contentment and hope, for Alan was only nineteen, young and strong and romantic, as his father had been when he devoted himself to the exiled Queen of Bohemia.

He sat beside the coachman of the hired vehicle as they clattered out of Rouen, his master, the King, chatting merrily behind with his admired, fond friend and fellow adventurer.

CHAPTER THREE

Luscombe Manor on the outskirts of Oxford lay peaceful, very quiet, almost as if deserted, on the day in early November when the two Ogilvys, Alan and his father, passed through the open, iron-wrought gates at the entrance to the long drive.

A low sun sent its orange rays flickering through the branches of the trees, turning the dying leaves to flame. Upon the weathered brick of the buildings a still deeper crimson-red showed where a strange creeper from the new settlement in West Virginia, sent as a cutting from that distant land, had taken root and prospered, a matter of wonderment to all who saw it. The sun lighted it too and flashed from the many windows of the house as the two horsemen drew close.

As if to welcome them, Alan said wonderingly, uplifted by the beauty of the scene.

'Or to warn us of our peril,' his father argued, for he was tired after two days of hard riding from Bridport, where they had landed from a Dutch fishing boat, with no questions asked.

The colonel drew up at the front door of the house and took his son's rein while Alan dismounted to pull the long iron bell chain beside the carved oak door. He tugged it vigorously and was soon answered by the creaking of bolts drawn back. Half the heavy door opened to disclose a white-haired, stooping old man.

'Is Sir Francis at home, if you please?' Alan asked politely.

'He be in Oxford, young sir,' the old man said. 'Her ladyship is within. Is that not Colonel Francis Ogilvy I see mounted yonder?'

'Your eyes are as good as ever, William,' the colonel answered. 'Here, Alan, take the horses while I go in to pay my respects to the Lady Leslie. Will my son find grooms in the yard, William?'

'Two lumping boys, sir. My eyes grow dim, begging your pardon, for I did not recognize Master Gordon.'

'This is Alan, William, not his elder brother.'

'God's mercy, but he grows apace, he doth indeed, sir.' Raising his voice to a shaky treble he called out, 'You may take the horses to the yard, Master Alan. The lads are there to serve you, for I saw them at work on some harness not a quarter hour since.'

Alan moved away, leading both horses. He had not been in England for over a year before his visit in connection with the King's flight. And then had spent a mere week in London to hear a true account of Worcester and the latest news of the King's whereabouts before hastening back to Holland. For the flight itself he had spent but one night in Brighthelmston. But in the untroubled years of his childhood before the Civil Wars there had been several visits to Oxford and to his maternal grandfather's great house near Banbury. So he knew his way to the yard at Luscombe and having handed over the horses to the boys he found there, and taken the luggage from behind their saddles, he made his way into the house with it to find his hostess.

Lady Leslie was pleased to welcome the visitors. She had loved Colonel Ogilvy when he was a little child, abused and tormented by his mother who had been her husband's first wife. She had grieved for him when he was sent away to the Leslie family at Kilessie near Falkland in Fife. She had done her best to reconcile him with Sir Francis when he had to be told of his bastardy, with all that it meant in social shame if not degradation. His later success in arms and service to the ex-king and queen of Bohemia and above all his later adoption by Colonel Arthur Ogilvy, his natural uncle, had brought the families together again, while the colonel's marriage to a daughter of Lord Aldborough, former friend of the great if dastardly first Duke of Buckingham, put his social position, a matter of the greatest importance in those days, quite beyond doubt.

'Sir Francis should be here within the hour,' she said. 'I trust you are in no manner of haste?' Seeing them hesitate she added, 'Doubtless you intend to visit your uncle the Doctor, Francis. Has he made the acquaintance of this – I cannot call him boy, for he hath all the appearance of a man – ?'

'If it please you, my lady, call me Alan, as always,' said the young man, blushing.

'And so I will, Alan,' answered Lady Leslie, with a very sweet smile.

'But my Uncle Richard is in London, is he not, my lady?' the colonel said. 'Has been, I believe, since before Worcester.'

'But is now returned these ten days. You had no news of this?'

Colonel Ogilvy laughed.

'I – we – Alan and I, have had little time to pick up *foreign* news these two weeks and more. Have we, Alan?'

'That is so. At sea one is spared the news, good or ill.'

His father frowned at him.

'You confuse my Lady Leslie. And border on dangerous matters.'

'Not here in my parlour,' she protested. 'William is most careful, though he does grow old, alas.'

Not wishing to alarm her Colonel Ogilvy said no more about his doubts. Besides, almost directly afterwards Sir Francis rode in from Oxford where he had been lecturing. The surprise caused by the visitors' arrival was gone over again and the guests were pressed to stay at Luscombe as long as they could.

'I hear that Doctor Richard is returned from Paternoster Row,' Colonel Ogilvy said.

'Lucy's mother begged him to stay,' Sir Francis replied. 'But he insists upon his true legal rights here. He hath been mixed in no ploys or schemes to restrict the usurping powers of our present Masters.'

'But they drove him out of the University for being a Royalist, did they not?'

Sir Francis turned his head away, but Lady Leslie explained in her quiet voice that this order was made because Doctor Ogilvy's eldest son had fought at Naseby, two more sons were under arms, but concealed their whereabouts.

'That is not the root of the matter,' Sir Francis interrupted, turning with some bitterness. 'Cynthia, your cousin, Francis, was like to be betrothed to my eldest son, George, Kate's son. But Cynthia preferred a fellow member of that Parliament George was elected to. He hath never forgiven her for that injury. He still seeks to be revenged by persecuting any member of her family.'

'Or his own, for that matter,' Lady Leslie added sorrowfully.

The colonel made no comment and the subject was allowed to drop.

The next day Alan and his father rode over to Doctor Richard's house. They found it sadly changed from the days before the Wars, when Uncle Richard's cheerful energetic wife was still alive, still caring for those surviving members of her large brood of children, one of whom, a daughter, was still unmarried, being of rather feeble mind. There were also there, very often, Cynthia's children, brought up on those natural lines followed by Celia with such marked early success. Four of them still lived, but the whole family had stayed in London when the Civil Wars began and had never been to Oxford since.

So now the house was quiet, the garden neglected. As with Sir Francis Leslie's establishment the serving men in house and garden had gone, some as soldiers to the wars, some to the growing trades in mills and cloth weaving. Many were used to the fashioning of uniforms for the New Model Army of Cromwell and his generals, many to armouries to make swords, cutlasses, muskets, pistols, together with the ammunition, bullets, powder, shot and cannon-balls. Not forgetting the furnishing of horses, stirrups, spurs, bits, bridles, saddles, reins. There was no lack of a good position for any man to serve the rebels and little, it seemed, to be found among the loyal gentry, except defeat in battles, followed by poverty, harder work for less reward in the old domestic jobs upon estates and in houses that might at any time be taken from their owners and themselves turned out of doors, with a taint upon them, too. There was little incentive for young men to develop loyalty: only the old men clung to it.

Doctor Richard was sitting by himself in the library. There was no fire though the day was cold with a chill east wind. An untidily dressed middle-aged woman had opened the door to the visitors, taken them to the library and left them to announce themselves.

Doctor Ogilvy was a few years younger than Sir Francis

Leslie but looked now very much older. He had little to say to his nephew the colonel and hardly seemed aware of Alan's presence. Unlike Sir Francis he asked no questions at all about the reason for their visit to Oxford at the present time, with winter coming on and few students in the colleges. He did not speak of the King at all, but his black clothes showed he was still in mourning for the Royal Martyr and was still very much a Royalist. But when Colonel Ogilvy remarked, a little reproachfully, that he had hoped his Uncle Richard would continue to live in comfort and security at the house in Paternoster Row that had belonged to his schoolmaster grandfather, Doctor George Ogilvy, Richard lost his sad listlessness and answered almost angrily, 'Comfort! Security! What use have I for either? What right to them? What pleasure in them, with Celia gone these ten years and the boys – all gone – '

'Surely Thomas and James have but wisely hid themselves?'

'I hear nothing. I believe them dead. I am alone.'

'You have Sarah. Then Sir Francis sees you often, surely?'

'As often as his son, that snake, that devil, that servant of murderers!'

'George Leslie. He was a friend to all of us, was he not, until his suit for your Cynthia came to nought. I had great sympathy for him then, because I thought his love deserved to prosper.'

'And so did I. But she chose his friend, Cromwell's man, God forgive her! I overlooked it until the wars started but not now – not now.'

'I have no sympathy with George now, but can you not forget him, uncle? Why come back to Oxford where he continually lurks, hoping to do us all injury?'

'Further injury. You know that he bore false witness against my Cynthia's husband, so that he was suspected by Cromwell's Secretary of State, Thurloe, the spy master. And had difficulty in proving his loyalty to his misguided party.'

Doctor Ogilvy looked so enraged that the colonel hurried on.

'But Sarah? I thought she was your housekeeper?'

'She prefers to live with her sister. In that nest of rebel traitors!'

'Then why are you here? Why endure this life, alone, uncared for, when old Mistress Leslie would make you most comfortable in London?'

'Because this is my life, this place of learning. Without my old friends and the new young minds, I am more dead than alive. You are a soldier, Francis, not a scholar. You do not know, maybe, that we have that original, John Wilkins, the only good fruit of that dire pruning of our ranks in the so-called Visitation? Or that others are here, men of great brilliance, Christopher Wren, Robert Boyle and the rest. They are in process of making fresh, astonishing discoveries. In this awful continuing holocaust, this darkness of bigotry, this ruthless hunt to destroy everything of joy, of beauty, simply because they are excellent and give pleasure, our circle of scholars, a rampart against total savagery, is my only light and I would hold to it if I may.'

The old man spoke with such passion that Colonel Ogilvy was again anxious for his uncle's health. They left the house in a state of depression, very much alarmed for Doctor Ogilvy's future. Which feeling was in truth shared by Sir Francis Leslie who deplored his eldest son's bitter resentment, that really dated from the introduction of his gentle stepmother to Luscombe.

On the way back from Doctor Ogilvy's house Alan asked his father for the true facts about George Leslie's behaviour. The colonel was reluctant to bring up the sad past, but he remembered how shocked he had himself been when the story was first told to him at the age Alan had now reached. It was many years since he had felt any bitterness himself and George was less than two years his junior.

'I have told Gordon the bare bones of the tragedy,' he began. 'I think I need not repeat them to you for Gordon will not have hidden them up. He showed no grief when I told him, but rather relished the tale.'

Alan could not control a wide smile, remembering his brother's bawdy version of their grandmother's lapse from virtue.

'My mother betrayed Sir Francis,' the colonel went on. 'But he brought me up as a Leslie, even with his own first name, though in Scotland at the house of the laird of Kilessie, his father. In gratitude or fear or to conceal her true nature, my mother bore Sir Francis two children, a boy, this George, and a girl, Kirstie, who died in childhood, poor mite. I never saw her. But George survived the dangers and diseases he encountered and when his mother fled the country, but took the plague and died miserably at sea, he was a healthy, lively schoolboy of between seven and eight years old.'

'It was then – as soon as Sir Francis became free, that he married the present Lady Leslie?'

'That was the trouble with George. When your grandmother ran away from Luscombe, disappeared from the country, in fact, they had to tell George that his mother had gone abroad to stay with friends. They could not tell him she was proscribed, in danger of being found guilty of conspiring with the Lady Frances Howard to poison and murder a poor prisoner in the Tower.'

'I know the story of that infamy,' Alan said in a grave voice. 'But I think they did not pay the full price for it, though their hired accomplices all did.'

'They paid well enough, those evil Somersets. Banished to a country estate and forbidden to go above three miles from the house. They lived in mutual hate, in miserable boredom, above ten years, I think.'

Colonel Ogilvy fell silent, unwilling to pursue these old criminal acts any further. But Alan wanted to hear more of George, so after a few minutes he asked, 'What then, of this half-uncle of mine? He did well at school, at his college, did he not? What then?'

'He had looked for his mother's return as I told you. When his father married Lucy Butters and brought her to Luscombe he learned that his mother was dead, had died during the voyage overseas. He knew this step-mother, daughter of Mistress Butters who looked after the London merchant, Angus Leslie, a kinsman of Sir Francis, and later married to the old man. As Lucy Butters George had found her kind and gentle at Master Leslie's big City house. But his mother, he remembered, had despised her as a menial, a servant of the household, which she most certainly never was. Though Sir Francis had not understood it, George had adored his beautiful mother, her uncertain temper and frequent cruelties matched his own temperament. Alas, I think I have had it too, in some part. Though they tell me my quick temper comes from my true father.'

'So George began to resent his father's new wife, his new mother? It is natural, but I cannot think my Lady Leslie is in any way to blame.'

'Nor is she. But George hath never relented. Sir Francis and his greatest friends in Oxford, the Ogilvys, were always Royalist, by custom until the troubles started, by conviction when the late King was in peril. Doctor Richard, as you have seen, puts himself in peril continually. Sir Francis buries himself, as always, in his books. He never troubled his head with affairs of state. His second family have been unremarkable; a divine, a schoolmaster, two daughters married into commerce. I think by minding their own business they look to passing though this hideous upheaval untouched except by increasing poverty, which they will bear with meekness but a tough fibre of spiritual strength. An irresistible combination I would have you note, Alan.'

This time Alan laughed aloud and his father allowed himself a rather guilty grin.

'I do not mean to disparage them,' he said. 'And I feel a grudging admiration for their steadiness. Besides, there was another boy, a true rebel, who left Luscombe before the Wars to go into Scotland and has not been heard from since.'

'So there was a modicum of wildness after all?' Alan said. 'A pity we know nought of it. But George. You still have not told me his actions, only his state of mind and his expressed feelings.'

'He found his way into the Parliament. He joined the factions for reform. He was always against the King. Always supporting one sect or another, against the Anglican religion, against the bishops, certainly for the New Model Army and when Cromwell rose to the top as a military commander of genius, a fervent follower, though never a soldier.'

'And now?'

'And now,' said Colonel Ogilvy, slapping his horse affectionately, for the beast was walking more and more slowly and seemed to be going to sleep as it moved, 'and now my half-brother, I believe, hath taken work from that Thurloe, Secretary of State, who boasts that he knows every move of our new true king, Charles, and will overcome him in God's good time.'

'They are very certain, are they not, that God is on their side and fights for them day and night? You are telling me that George Leslie is Thurloe's spy?'

'One of many such. I have no proof. But George was appointed a Visitor when Oxford was purged of Royalists and Sir Francis was in great danger for a time. George would have delighted to bring about his own father's fall, but had little success at that time. He had to content himself with ending his Uncle Richard's work in the university.'

'I think they watch Luscombe still,' Alan said. 'In the stables when we arrived there was one ran off at once, as if with news that must be carried.'

'You saw that?' Colonel Ogilvy's eyes shone suddenly with a light his son had seen often when a prospect of action was before him. 'I ask because as I waited at the door of the house I saw a lurking figure in the shrubberies come to inspect me.'

'You made no move to accost him, or to tell Sir Francis?'

'I would know him again. Accost him? At a fitting time, my son. When I shall dispose of him.'

The colonel laid spur to his laggard horse as he spoke and the pair of them cantered on up the approach to Luscombe, leaving behind the man who had waited in the bushes beside the gates and had managed to hear the last remark Ogilvy had made, as the colonel, who had seen him there, had intended that he should.

CHAPTER FOUR

The next morning Colonel Ogilvy and his son rode away from Luscombe. Their next visit was to the great house near Banbury where Lord Aldborough, young Alan's grandfather, still lived, suffering yet one more setback in his long, confused life.

Thinking matters over in these late years of his age he used to wonder why he had seemed to be picked out for misfortune while all the time doing his best to please and serve. First there had been his good breeding and poor fortune. Then came the opportunity to marry much sought wealth, together with a cousin of that wealth, no less than the great Duke of Buckingham, the first duke of that name.

But this dizzy height did little for him, since when the great peak fell to the assassin's knife, he fell with it. Charles the First wanted none of him when Steenie was gone. But he had remained loyal to the monarchy, saving up the wealth he had gained, his sons for a time joining the Royal army, though they did seem to fade out of the battles after the First Civil War and sent no messages to him. However, his daughter Anne still gave him news of their further careers in Germany.

And now, however much he tried to sink from Parliamentary sight near Banbury, harassment still threatened him. He heard the jangle of harness and the scraping of hooves before the house and trembled inwardly as he heard it.

'Do not look from the window, sir,' he ordered the man who was with him. 'Whoever it may be we must not appear to be alarmed.'

'The two without do not raise matter for alarm,' the black-frocked man said, turning from the window with a smile. 'For it is Colonel Ogilvy, your son-in-law, and one of your grandsons, I believe.'

'Bold, rash man to come thus openly!' Lord Aldborough cried distractedly.

'Surely not, my lord. He holds his command from the Prince of Orange. He has no part in our English quarrels.'

'But he may have soon. The Prince is dead, the Princess is the Martyr's daughter – '

But the parson was already at the door of the room and motioning for caution.

Lord Aldborough was pleased to see the visitors and have some news from abroad, though Colonel Ogilvy knew his father-in-law well enough not to entrust him with any very vital items. Though it was by now guessed that Charles the Second had escaped from the country, the method used and those involved were not yet known. In fact Charles himself already and for many years after his Restoration, forbore to give the correct details for fear of betraying his friends. The colonel had said he came to England to see his son in Oxford, but finding him able to do little study and so to be wasting his time, had decided to take him back to the Low Countries with him.

'But first, my lord, I bring you fond messages from Anne and the younger children. My elder son, Gordon, sends you affectionate respects. He will make a soldier too, sir.'

'I have never thought otherwise, Francis,' Lord Aldborough agreed. 'Grandfather, father and son. What of you, young man?' he asked sharply, turning upon Alan.

The young man was not confused.

'I think I may take after my great-grandfather, Doctor George Ogilvy, my lord. He was a schoolmaster.'

'A schoolmaster? In these stirring times? Have you no higher aim?'

Alan reddened, but with his father's eye on him did not attempt an answer aloud. The parson, however, came to his rescue by leading him away to look at some fine books in Lord Aldborough's library.

'We must not all be soldiers,' he said kindly to the young man. 'You are right to follow where your heart leads.'

'I think it is less my heart than my head,' Alan said bluntly, for he was angered by Lord Aldborough's comments which seemed to him both out of place for one of his family record and also basically stupid.

'Both in balance, is best,' said the parson, serenely.

Alan apologized.

Some of the books were very fine and the finest had been sorted out and placed by themselves.

'They are to be given to the Bodleian Library in Oxford,' the parson said. 'I have persuaded his lordship to give them that protection. They will find it with Master Wilkins, Cromwell's brother-in-law.'

'Will they need protection?' Alan was horrified.

'Indeed they may. My Lord Aldborough is – indiscreet. If his house here by ill chance be sequestrated I fear those puritanical soldiers will have no respect for any book in a Royalist house, Church of England or Catholic.'

They went back to the others in time to hear Colonel Ogilvy accept hospitality for the night, but explain that he must be on his way to Harwich early in the morning, while Alan would return to Oxford and make some attempt to continue his studies there.

They boy said nothing more then, but after they had left Lord Aldborough to make ready for the evening meal, Alan asked why he had changed his plans and that so soon after he had told his grandfather he was not going back to the university.

'Nor will you,' the colonel said. 'But we will go severally in the morning and that early. Then you must turn a short ways off and make for the river. Leave your horse near the bank; it will be found. Some will think you drowned and so much the better. Work your way south from there to the coast. The drover roads would be best. Take ship from any small port.'

'I am to take off your spy from you, then?' Alan asked with a laughing gleam in his eye.

'Unmannerly lout!' his father cried, giving him a hard slap

on the shoulder. 'Nay, seriously, it is to save yourself. So far afield I think George may have been superseded, but they try always for news of the escape.'

He whispered the last words and they did not speak on that subject again that night.

They met briefly the next morning, before Lord Aldborough was stirring, as they thought at first. Colonel Ogilvy came to Alan's room with a small pair of hand shears, the same that he used on his own locks. He had always kept his sons' hair trimmed. As a soldier he had followed his uncle, Arthur Ogilvy, in this, purely for comfort under the helmet of the day. Therefore he had imposed it upon his own boys until Alan went to Oxford to study.

'We had those locks trimmed for your service to the King,' he said. 'You'll need to look a proper peasant again if you are to reach the coast safely.'

Alan submitted easily enough. He was not vain. Besides, his own hair, unlike his elder brother's that was the same bright chestnut his father's had been before it faded with a too liberal dusting of grey, was of a very usual brown, neither thick nor thin, neither curled nor yet perfectly straight.

They finished their business quickly. The colonel deliberately made an uneven job of it, to fit Alan's impersonation of a working man when they should break company. They took up their bundles and went to the staircase. There they stopped dead, confronted by two unwelcome things, a sight and a sound.

In the distance, coming out of the morning mist that lay across the entrance to the drive before the house, a troop of Parliament horse trotted steadily forward. From below stairs, coming up from the closed door of the library, rose the sound of prayers, the parson leading, a mixed male and female response.

'Good God!' cried Colonel Ogilvy. 'They will be discovered!'

He rushed down, flung open the library door and addressing Lord Aldborough cried, 'Hold, my lord! There be visitors at your gates. Disperse! Disperse, with no delay at all!'

For the small gathering seemed to be frozen with horror and incapable of action. They stumbled to their feet, but stood with white faces, staring from one to another.

All except the parson, who was gathering up the sacrament

into a bag, wrapping the wine vessel in a cloth and preparing to make off with both.

Ogilvy stopped him.

'I beg you wait, reverend sir,' he urged in a whisper. 'Your pardon, my lord. Military action needed! Bid them disperse about their usual business.'

Lord Aldborough did so in a shaking voice. There were not more than eight present, five old weathered retainers and three young half-wits, Alan decided. All loyal but liable to confusion and breakdown if pressed. He waited for his father's plan, hoping it might succeed but feeling a cold knot in his stomach as the moments passed.

When the family was alone Colonel Ogilvy swept those separated books from their place at the end of the long table, the books destined for the Bodleian Library. Then he took the communion bread and wine from the priest and disposing them at the other end of the table sat down there, directed Alan to a place beside him with Lord and Lady Aldborough and the parson, now stripped of his vestments, opposite.

A loud knocking sounded through the house.

'The door must be opened to them,' Ogilvy said. 'Listen. We are here to dispose of these books. We have been taking breakfast.'

The parson winced, but said nothing.

'We are not Catholics,' went on Ogilvy. 'Besides, sir, you had not consecrated the bread and wine. Crumble some. It will look like an ampler feast, newly finished. Speak little. I will lead.' He turned to Alan. 'Go find one of the old men. Now, or they will knock in the door. Bring their captain to us here.'

It was old Lady Aldborough who said, 'We will support you, Colonel. It is a way, please God.'

Alan found the old man struggling with the bolts on the great door and joined his strength. They opened it so suddenly and fully that the front rank of three dismounted soldiers fell forward, one to his knees. An ugly snarl rose from the rest, but they fell silent when Alan said in a loud voice, 'Produce your captain and state your business with Lord Aldborough who owns this house and lives here at this time.'

It was not an expected reception but it was heard by the leader of the men, who was a sergeant in the New Model Army, with some training and a great deal of self-importance in his new rank.

'We seek a spy, known to have travelled to this place or nearby it.'

'Then I think you are mistaken,' Alan said. 'But come within and you may speak to Lord Aldborough.'

After a short discussion with his next in command the sergeant ordered the rest of his troop to dismount before the house but not to disperse. He then followed Alan to the library where the latter found the group exactly as he had left them, Colonel Ogilvy drinking from a beaker he had pulled out of his own bundle and Lord Aldborough taking a shuddering sip from Alan's mug.

The matter of the books explained the presence of the parson. No foreign priest, this, just the village incumbent, of help to the lord in his library, now church services were suspended. The full complement – much reduced – of servants were about the house. The two visitors, relations of the family, explained themselves, with papers to prove their identity, produced at once by Colonel Ogilvy. They were just about to leave but were at the sergeant's service with advice if asked.

The sergeant had a very strong sense of something rigged, something far far more innocent than was humanly possible, but he was up against the natural limit of his sturdy imagination, the blank wall of his lack of learning. He was barely literate so he did not even know if these books were really valuable. He felt very strongly that Lord Aldborough was not a clever man, not even a strong man, but he knew the lord was not a physical coward, that he was watching him now as a great lord should, as he had been brought up to expect a great lord to look at him. It infuriated him, but short of physical attack, useless, perhaps reprehensible, he had no redress. He did not know how to bully any other coward but a physical coward.

So he listened to Colonel Ogilvy, who was clearly a fine military man whom he understood.

'I would be very much obliged, Captain,' the colonel was saying, 'if you could relieve the Lord Aldborough of these fine books which he wishes to present to Master John Wilkins, the warden of Wadham College at Oxford. If you return there from any false trail you have travelled in this direction you may in fact find considerable praise for making this present over to Master Wilkins.'

The hard light in the colonel's eye was unmistakable. The sergeant knew where he was with Ogilvy. He was not on

he had not eaten all day.

As he moved cautiously downward he thought he heard a moan quite near him. A child, lost in the wood? It had been too low a sound for a child. An injured peasant, man or woman? He called.

There was no response. It was as if the silence was imposed by force. Force of will? An injured person stifling his own pain? Or worse, an injured person stifled by his injurer?

His father would creep by to continue his own planned escape, Alan thought. Much as he admired Colonel Ogilvy he knew already that his life had hardened him, that he would never have survived his upbringing had he not looked first and always to his safety and those of his men. But Alan knew that it was not in his own nature to follow his father now. He began, slowly, carefully, silently, to search.

This was a game he and Gordon had perfected in the years of their childhood in Holland, in Germany or the United Provinces. In woods far thicker and more complicated than these elegant sweeps beside the Thames. As he drew nearer he was guided from time to time by repeated little groans and gasps, a muttered appeal to Jesus, even to the Virgin Mary. A man, Alan felt sure, with a broken leg, a fit of the ague, not, please Heaven, the smallpox or the plague!

Now he could see, through the screen of a bush, the broad back, a leg crumpled behind, a hand holding a long knife ready to throw, a face darkened and distorted with rage and pain.

And the other two limbs – that distortion of torn clothing and blood and yes, metal! The other arm and leg were together between the merciless jaws of a badger trap, itself fixed into the ground. The unfortunate creature, like the man, was meant to fall between those grinding jaws, that would close on its soft body and transfix it. But in this case the victim must have stepped on the trap, perhaps stooped quickly to help his leg back but not quickly enough before the jaws were sprung, gripping him in this agonizing position, helpless, alone.

Alan saw the poor creature was nearly mad from his sufferings. He must remove the knife first; crippled, imprisoned though he was, he was dangerous. Using another childhood's ploy Alan picked up a couple of stones and carefully tossed them to the far side of the trap. The man's head went round, he stared intently. Alan was upon him, had wrested the knife away and jumped back before the man could even look round.

'My poor fellow!' said Alan with great compassion. 'Will you lie back and let me see if I can get this devilment from off you.'

The man did indeed lie back, but Alan saw that it was because he had fainted away. So much the better, the young man decided and got to work immediately while the wretched creature's limbs were slack and he was insensible.

The wounds were deep in both leg and arm but had not penetrated any vital blood vessel, though at least one bone in each was broken, perhaps more. Alan bound each limb with some of the man's own clothing as a temporary measure. Then he waited for his patient to recover, which took some little time and was slow in completing.

At first the poor fellow thought he had died and lamented the fact, because he was free of his torment and yet not fully out of pain.

'You are still of this world, friend,' Alan said. 'Full relief still awaits you.'

The man began to wail again, to curse his rescuer for keeping him for hanging instead of putting him out of his misery like a dog.

'Many would have done so,' Alan told him, 'had they been owners of this land where we both trespass. But I am as guilty as you, though I do not hunt for game.'

Presently the man raised himself on his sound elbow and stared intently at Alan. Both had had difficulty in understanding the other's speech. This had not surprised Alan who had managed to make out the peasant's earthy burr, but the latter only knew that the rapid flow of clipped speech betokened a gentleman.

The latter now got to his feet and said, 'I think we had better be moving. Where do you live?'

'In Dorchester, but I have a brother by the ford.'

'Here at Shillingford? Then I must make shift to carry you there. As it is all downhill I might succeed.'

The man protested, said he could manage if he rested, said Alan could fetch his brother to him.

'And show to anyone interested where you may be sold or destroyed? What good would that be to your brother or your wife and children if you have them?'

The fellow began to blubber at that and to explain it was to feed them he had come to these woods to seek game or a lowly rabbit if nought else.

'Save your breath!' Alan told him harshly to stop the wailing. 'We shall need all we have, I'm thinking, to get you down to that brother of yours by the ford.'

CHAPTER FIVE

Alan's success in his compassionate act was both his immediate salvation and later renewed his danger. He brought the injured man to Shillingford to his brother's riverside cottage. There his injuries were unwrapped and inspected and after bathing away the blood the skin of the ankle was found to be torn and the ligaments strained, but no bones broken. The arm, however, was cracked above the wrist in both bones and displaced with loss of feeling in some fingers of the hand.

A messenger was sent to the local bone-setter who found the injury within his competence so he set about treating it without delay.

Alan could have slipped out of the cottage very easily during this time without anyone noticing he had gone. In fact, at this time, he had no wish to help in medical matters, being rather squeamish than otherwise. But night was coming on, he had nowhere to go for shelter and though he knew he must not delay too long, he hoped to be offered a meal and a bed as a reward for saving the unfortunate poacher's life.

So he stayed outside the busy circle about the patient, working out a story to cover his last two days' travel and suggest how he hoped to proceed on his way to London. He did not want to rouse curiosity among these village folk, but it was clear the story of his rescue action would soon spread. It would not do to be a mystery. Already there had been a few who stared to hear his speech. They would suspect an Oxford scholar, so near as this to the university town. It occurred to him to add a Dutch foreign accent which, since he had lived abroad off and on for most of his life, he knew well how to manage. It was entirely successful.

The injured man called to him faintly when at last the surgery was over, the ankle bound up, the broken arm fastened to a wooden splint.

'Go to him,' the woman of the house said, taking him by

the hand. 'He would give you his thanks as would we all.'

'I understand,' Alan said thickly, 'but it was nothing. A chance, a luck, you would call it.'

He heard murmurs begin, 'a foreigner', 'a stranger'; faces closing, stiffening.

'I am a seaman,' he said carefully. 'I come from London on a barge, but it go back without me. I look for another.'

It was a chance, but a lucky one. There had indeed been barges on the river of late, the roads being considered less safe by reason of the general lawlessness. A strong young man who had already proved his strength should be welcome on any boat passing down to Reading and beyond.

'I work my way,' Alan suggested, smiling.

That persuaded them. They wanted to give him food that night, for what he had done, but they could not afford to keep him beyond the next morning. Their poverty was real, becoming desperate, since some of their crops had been ruined by the wars, the actual battles or the conscription of the men. So messengers went out that evening and in the early morning a long narrow boat appeared out of the mist on the river, demanded to see the 'foreign lad' and engaged Alan to keep the boat off the bank with a long pole while another youth of about his own age led a stout horse attached to a towing rope from the bows.

In this fashion the narrow boat was conducted to Reading. Alan was given food in reasonable quantities but had to sleep on deck. He expected no better and was content to exchange very few words with his master. The man's wife stayed below for the whole voyage, handing Alan's plate up the hatch to him at mealtimes. The youth with the horse was her son; he was invited below to the table, but he joined Alan on deck at night and the horse was led across there too, over a plank, while the vessel was stood off the bank by means of three sunk barrels to which it was secured. Clearly the people suspected thieves or attackers of some sort.

At Reading Alan helped with the unloading of the cargo and managed to be taken on by a larger craft under sail and oar, proceeding towards London. He was asked no questions but he kept his slightly foreign accent and knew from scraps of conversation he overheard that he was still taken for a young Dutchman.

As they neared the capital he began to overhear news of more general interest than the river trade. The great Fairfax had left the military scene and Oliver Cromwell had taken the supreme command. This had not pleased all his rivals, Lambert particularly resenting his rise. The Parliament were said to fear the generals. The Presbyterians wanted to impose their religion upon the whole country, but the Levellers and half a dozen extreme sects were still standing out against them.

If matters go this way, Alan thought, the King will find his throne again when his followers are ready to rise. But he thought of Lord Aldborough and wondered how and when this could be. It was something his father might be able to tell him. No good asking questions. Best to keep quiet and listen to the opinions of those about him.

Apathy, he decided, was the rule. The people had suffered in many ways, without understanding anything that had happened to them, except the terrible death of Charles the First, the Royal Martyr. The shock of that naked exercise of ultimate power had been great indeed. Numb obedience was the result, the lasting effect of that earthquake at the seat of government. They had not been asked to take sides, though the men had been offered places in the fighting armies and being men had seen a possible advantage to be won in action. That was all. They were not asked to resolve the present confusion. Only the fanatics proclaimed their presence; the rest were too confused.

It took Alan nearly a month to reach London. He managed to stay on the river working in various positions on a wide variety of craft until he found himself in the Pool below London Bridge. Then, without a word, he went ashore, having completed his work, and did not go back to the water until he left the country on a merchant vessel bound for Dunkirk.

He walked up from Blackfriars Stairs to Paternoster Row, near by Saint Paul's great gothic church. He had been here several times before, since the small neat Tudor house with its pretty garden behind belonged now to Colonel Ogilvy. It had been left to him by that other Colonel, Arthur Ogilvy, Alan's own grandfather as he had been taught to call him.

He knew he would be welcome in Paternoster Row, for the admirable housekeeper was Mistress Leslie, widow of the Alderman Angus Leslie, whose daughter was the lady of Luscombe.

'I would scarce have recognized you, Alan,' Mistress Leslie told him when he was led, somewhat reluctantly, by an elderly maid into her little upstairs parlour. Hannah had followed her mistress from Gracious Street when the alderman's death brought about the selling of the merchant's big house there. 'But I do know you and you need not stare at him, Hannah, as if you thought he meant to cut our throats! Take him away and find him hot water and a piece of soap while I look out some of the colonel's clothes that he keeps here for use on his visits. Off with you both now and we will dine together, sir, when you be presentable and you shall tell me all your news.'

Most of it he did tell her, for he knew her discretion was absolute and her long life, spent safely in the background of tremendous events, had rendered her by now impervious to their dangers. The alderman had been a shrewd Scot, making the most of all the rapid developments of late Elizabethan times, including the founding of the colonies in Virginia and Delaware and later farther north about Cape Cod. He had been able to increase his trade in salted fish from a competence of supplies caught off the old-established Newfoundland Banks to a great wealth of prime cod from the mainland coasts. Piracy had increased with European competition from the French and the Dutch, though the Spanish kept mostly to the Caribbean and the Portuguese even farther south in their eager search for more glamorous treasure. With these wide horizons before her eyes Mistress Leslie was scarcely shaken by the internal political strife until the violent death of the King shocked her out of her calm ways.

But then only as the consequences affected her life in Paternoster Row.

'I praise God that He took my dear husband before that grievous day,' she said, when Alan paused in his account of his visit to Oxford with his father. 'Doctor Richard was here and sat all day in the library, not eating, his head in his hands. Praying for the most part. We was too far from Whitehall to hear the large groan that went up from the crowd, but the people came back to their homes in silence and shut their doors and the soldiers went to and fro in the streets, perplexed there was no rejoicings.'

'He still grieves all the time, poor old man,' Alan said.

'And lives in his great house with little or no attention so I am told by our regular messenger,' Mistress Leslie answered. 'I tried to persuade him to stay here where I could see to his comfort, but he said the air of London was poisoned by the guilt of our present masters.

'And that he could not bear to be near his daughter that married a Parliament man.'

'Whom he had admired for his good brains and fine ideas of progress in government,' Mistress Leslie protested. 'Which was the reason for him preferring that marriage to the one presumed to be settled in the family.'

Alan smiled. The love affairs of his father's cousin seemed as remote, as amusing, as those of his more colourful, more excitingly wicked old grandmother.

'You need not find mirth in that story,' Mistress Leslie told him sharply. 'They may be old or middle-aged now, but they had the hot blood of youth at the time. Cynthia took her cousin George for granted. They were friends because they had been children together and while Kate neglected the boy, the girl's mother believed in using less formality of manner than was usual, then as now.'

'I crave pardon, Madam,' Alan said, accepting the rebuke, as was proper, but privately agreeing with his father's aunt.

After a suitable pause he said, 'My half-uncle George hath never forgiven Mistress – Phillips, is it not?'

'Hugh Phillips, elected member of the Parliament that tried the King, but not one of those that convicted him with their signature.'

'But not forgiven by Doctor Richard, never forgiven, never to be spoken of, nor his children, either.'

'You know them, madam? You meet with them?'

Mistress Leslie drew herself up.

'I do so, seeing no reason I should not. They have not given up their religion. He is a London man, a merchant in the cloth trade dealing in the new worsteds and serges, an honest man, a good master to his servants and apprentices.'

'But he serves Cromwell.'

'I have never let matters of state into my life,' Mistress Leslie said. 'They are not for women and we be well rid of such passionate fantasies.'

Alan was impressed by the old lady's truly passionate refusal to hold political opinions. But he remembered George, so he told her a little more about his adventures after leaving Lord Aldborough's home and parting from his father.

'In Oxford we were convinced and Sir Francis Leslie also that George Leslie hath great animosity not only against his cousin Cynthia, Mistress Phillips, and all her family, but against his father and Lady Leslie, your daughter.'

Mistress Leslie sighed.

'Yet Lucy showed him always great kindness when he was a child.'

'But also showed him he would do well to find a wife outside both the Leslie and the Ogilvy families.'

'As my father did,' Alan said boldly, conscious that his own natural grandfather had been a great favourite with the old lady when he was working for the alderman.

'George may well be a Commonwealth spy,' she said, ignoring this last remark of his. 'I think he can do no harm to Colonel Ogilvy who hath always been employed abroad. But with Master Phillips it is a different matter. And with you too, young man. What do they suspect you of? Why pursue you? An Oxford student? Or have you given that up? How comes it you are here in London in filthy clothing, off a river barge, instead of at your books?'

Alan laughed aloud. The sudden spate of questions plied vigorously, struck him as very funny, coming from one who had rejected and renounced any interest in politics, theoretical or practical. But he was determined not to disclose the part, minor as it was, he had played in the escape of Charles the Second from the country.

'I think George Leslie be more than a little crazy,' he said. 'But he will not discover anything to my disadvantage.'

'Nevertheless,' Mistress Leslie told him. 'You must not delay to make arrangements for your return to France. Or is it to be Holland? Or have you made them? I can recommend – '

She broke off as Hannah came in to tell them the meal was ready below.

Alan spent the next two days in discovering a suitable vessel to convey him abroad again. This proved to be less easy than he had hoped, for Cromwell's admirals were showing as much energy, enthusiasm and skill in their trade as were his generals in theirs. At this time the French were not openly hostile, nor were the Dutch. But neither, since the execution of the King and the failure of his nephew, Prince Rupert, to overthrow the usurpers, were willing to become open allies of the successor, Charles the Second. The Dutch soon realized that they must defend their trade against the growing Commonwealth power at sea. And so there were markedly fewer foreign ships in the Pool, Alan found, and of these but two willing to offer him a passage.

But again his command of the Dutch language served his

purpose in the end, but not before his presence in London became known in City circles.

This came about on the third day of his stay in Paternoster Row. Arriving back with his good news, he found a coach drawn up at the door, the door open, attended by Hannah, with a sober-suited gentleman ushering two very quietly-dressed ladies into the house.

Hannah, curtseying to these latter, put out a hand to hold him back until they had entered. But the gentleman, noticing her action, stared long and hard at the young man before asking, 'Mistress Leslie in her invitation, hath told us of our relative, a visitor in her house. If this be he, pray inform me that we may make ourselves known to one another.'

Hannah looked quite overcome by this request so Alan stepped forward saying, 'Indeed, sir, I am Alan Ogilvy, second son of Colonel Francis Ogilvy, whose father by adoption was Colonel Arthur Ogilvy, former owner of this house.'

The stranger bowed and answered, 'So you are great-nephew of Doctor Richard Ogilvy, who is my father-in-law.'

Alan bowed in return, they shook hands with marked reserve but neither said anything of the rift in the family relationship and they walked upstairs in silence to join the ladies, by now seated in Mistress Leslie's parlour. More introductions followed, but the awkwardness Alan feared was dissipated entirely by their hostess, who gathered their whole attention together to explain her action.

'It is no accident that you be all here together,' she said. with quiet authority. 'In times such as these we are divided as families should not be divided, by faults in high places. Be that as it may, honest men hold honest opinions and rightly so – '

'The Lord Cromwell denies to no man an honest opinion,' said Master Phillips quietly. 'It is the small groups of fanatical persons – '

'We shall not discuss them,' Mistress Leslie said firmly. 'But there is one causing distress in this family, not by any fanatical beliefs, but from thwarted desires, gross envy, hatred, malice and all uncharitableness as the Book has it. And it hath come to my knowledge that he seeks to bring harm to you, sir, and to Master Ogilvy here, who is son to his half-brother.'

Mistress Leslie looked round at them all, perfectly aware of having indelicately thrown into the open a number of matters that had lain like rotting wood, slowly moving to destroy the house beam.

The Phillips family was both shocked and distressed, each in his own fashion. Alan, glancing quickly at each in turn, saw pale anger set in the father's face, a hot flush of distress on Mistress Cynthia's cheek and both alarm and curiosity widen their pretty daughter Susan's eyes.

Alan's own glance caught this look and stayed with it, both attraction and pity making his usually well-controlled heart beat faster. He had not hitherto taken much interest in girls, though he had met plenty both in Holland and France. The former he found too solid in their figures, too slow in their wits, the latter too acid, too critical of his poor command of the French language, with features too sharp and sallow for beauty. Susan Phillips was the reverse of all these deficiencies, he decided. Though neither he nor the girl ventured to join the formal exchange of their elders they did manage, when Mistress Leslie took her guests into the garden to enjoy the air and sunshine before re-entering their coach, to move together away from the others. In a short stilted exchange they learned the addresses of their respective homes, the number and names of their brothers and sisters, the principal occupations of the men of the families. Those of the women and girls they did not discuss, it being taken for granted that all females behaved alike, at least in public.

When the visitors had gone Mistress Leslie retired to her own room to rest, while Alan, after considering his plans and putting together his small collection of personal belongings, sat down in the library to write a letter to his great-uncle in Oxford. It seemed to him to be of great importance to keep in touch with his new-found, if distant relatives. He described their good qualities, Master Phillips's polite tolerance, the sober virtues of their manner and appearance, the merchant's comfortable success that had nothing to do with politics, in fact all that recommended them as socially desirable. He suppressed any mention of Susan, except to say that they had come with a daughter of sixteen who was as beautiful as her mother. Old Doctor Richard must have his heart pricked by that description, Alan thought. Without presuming to recommend a reconciliation he hoped his letter might at least lessen the gap between father and daughter. He was well aware that his own desires, moving towards that end, had prompted the letter in the first place.

He showed it to Mistress Leslie when they met again at supper that day. The old lady was delighted. This was exactly what she had hoped to achieve. She was sorry the boy must leave England again so soon, but she had been fully aware he had been less than open over his recent adventures, so it was as well she had nothing she could be forced to reveal.

She soon realized the wisdom of her conclusion, though the family reunion still filled her with a kind of euphoria that made her more garrulous than usual with Hannah. Unfortunate indeed when George Leslie called upon her the day after Alan sailed from England.

She recognized him, though she had not seen him for many years. Not indeed since the funeral of Colonel Arthur Ogilvy, which he had attended with his father, Sir Francis Leslie. Chiefly, she had felt at the time, to ensure that Mistress Cynthia Phillips should not meet her father again upon an occasion of softened feelings.

Mistress Leslie greeted him now without pleasure but with an enhanced sense of duty and with that euphoria that proved so dangerous.

'You are welcome, sir,' she said, smiling, 'though almost a stranger.'

'I live outside the City,' George answered, 'since my home is closed to me.'

'By your own choice, I think. Certainly not my daughter's.'

'By the circumstance of your daughter's marriage to my father, madam,' he answered. His bitter feeling was unchanged, even now, in his middle-age, she realized.

She was determined not to quarrel with him. Besides, she did not yet know why he was there. She waited for him to tell her, which he did at once.

'It hath come to my knowledge that the late Colonel Ogilvy's adopted grandson has been seen at this house two days since. I would speak with him.'

'You are blunt, sir. Pray upon whose authority do you convey such an order?' She was angry, but she caught back a counter order for him to leave the Ogilvy house immediately and went on smoothly, 'Yes. Alan Ogilvy was here to call upon me on his way, at his father's request, to join the family in France.'

'In *France*, say you? I was informed the young man studied in Oxford.'

'So he did, but now he is gone to France. As I am sure

you know, your brother, his father, hath always served the House of Orange, but now the Princess Mary is widowed, her son a young child and their future uncertain.'

'It is not the House of Orange, nor the late Charles Stuart's daughter is our concern, but Englishmen that should serve their native country.'

Mistress Leslie made no answer to this, though her anger boiled anew. She looked at George Leslie, sitting upright and stiff and self-righteous in front of her and spoke now with passion.

'And who are you, George Leslie, son of a loving and most patient scholar and gentleman, to speak of service to his country? What have you ever done but seek to sow ill-feeling in your family and in that of your poor misguided mother? Well, you may know I never have and never will take part in such deep mischief, such jealousy, such wickedness. On the contrary, you may know that I count Master Phillips a member of our family for his wife's sake. They were here to visit me quite recently while Alan was here. We were all friends together and so we shall remain. And now, sir, since the object of your visit hath eluded you, there can be no need of your continued presence in Colonel Ogilvy's house.'

George left Paternoster Row in a furious rage, not relieved by a wait of two hours before he was granted admittance to Master Thurloe, who directed, under Cromwell's orders, that very extensive intelligence service to discover and arrest active Royalists.

'I have little of interest from you, Master Leslie,' Thurloe said coldly, when George was before him at last. 'A sad confusion at Oxford and a contemptible charade at Lord Aldborough's place near Banbury.'

Restraining himself with difficulty George bowed his head, murmuring something about untrained militia pitted against the trained and seasoned experience of a veteran of the Thirty Years War.

'Nevertheless when you did eventually trace that young son of the veteran you were too late,' Thurloe went on. 'You have no information, nor can you now secure it.'

'Except this,' George said, leaning forward. 'I know and I can prove it, young Alan Ogilvy hath been in touch with Master Phillips, the clothier of Cheapside and Highgate Hill.'

'In touch?'

'They have met in Paternoster Row. Perhaps elsewhere.'

Thurloe questioned, George Leslie repeated Mistress Leslie's family indiscretions, adding a slant of his own that suggested intrigue and disloyalty upon one or other side, perhaps both. He left much later, satisfied he had broken up, destroyed entirely, the reunion and understanding so proudly devised, so disastrously betrayed, by the late alderman's loving and faithful wife.

CHAPTER SIX

Alan had been back in Paris with his family for three weeks before he and his father were summoned to an audience with King Charles.

The young King had set up his Court not far from that of the Queen, his mother, but had shown clearly from the start that he would not be ruled by her as he had formerly been when he and his brother James left England for Jersey, before the Martyr King's final defeat and betrayal by one faction of the Scots.

Being only sixteen at that time he had no other choice than to obey her. Now, however, he had both friends and councillors, led by the Lord Chancellor, Sir Edward Hyde, and the companion of his escape, Lord Wilmot. He was able to summon the Marquis of Ormonde, who had been driven out of Ireland, the Earl of Southampton, Sir Edmund Nicholas and others.

'His Majesty's court is laudably gay, considering their dire needs,' Colonel Ogilvy explained as they arrived outside the State rooms. 'He hath no money, but his credit at present is remarkable and he is not thrifty, though I believe him to be an honest man.'

Alan, who had cherished a romantic idea of the King since his service to him on board *Surprise*, was shocked by this casual description and showed it. His father laughed.

'You will find a difference, my son,' he said, as they continued to wait. 'Be careful to show nothing but loyal respect. It is very likely he will not remember you, though I was commanded to bring you here today.'

This seemed very probable, for the Ogilvys were not at

once taken into the presence of the King, but instead were led into a small room where Sir Edward Hyde was sitting, with a clerk at a desk behind him. He greeted the colonel warmly, bade him be seated and leaving Alan standing, said, 'So this is your son, Colonel?'

'My second son, sir.'

'Your heir is already a soldier like yourself and your father, I believe.'

Colonel Ogilvy bowed and said, 'While Alan here hath more talent for scholarship and would be studying in Oxford were the times more suitable for it.'

'Ah.' The Lord Chancellor stared for a few moments at Alan, then turned back to the colonel.

'There have been strange reports from England over the activities at Lord Aldborough's house near Banbury. Also in London at your own dwelling in Paternoster Row. A present of books to the usurper's brother-in-law, a visit from a follower of the regicide. And both of you here in some measure mixed up in these activities. I trust I have my information wrongly slanted, sir – misunderstood.'

Alan felt his cheeks burn with indignation; not so much at the vague accusation, but rather because a slur had been cast on Master Phillips, and therefore upon Mistress Susan, whose bright face had been present in his mind both by day and night since he reached Paris again.

Colonel Ogilvy, however, remained perfectly calm and gave a clear, convincing story of his visits to his friends and relations, the true story of the present of books to the Bodleian, the separate return of himself to Holland first, by way of Harwich and of Alan to France from London.

'And as to this Master Phillips, the cloth merchant,' Sir Edward Hyde persisted, turning to Alan. 'You did truly meet the fellow?'

'I did, sir,' Alan said coldly. 'He being a family connection by marriage of the Ogilvys. The meeting was none of my making, but rather of the late Alderman Leslie's widow's wish. A formal meeting.'

He finished lamely, for he did not want to harm Mistress Leslie, nor suggest that he could have an interest in these distant relations. He rather overdid the casual manner, which the Chancellor put down to general shyness, but Colonel Ogilvy found surprising, since Alan was not shy as a rule but took a keen interest in the people he met and showed a humanity that put aside shyness.

Sir Edward Hyde guessed rightly that both the Ogilvys were keeping family matters secret to themselves and perhaps from one another, so after a little more consideration in silence, tapping his fingers on the table beside him, he got up, beckoned to his clerk and saying, 'I thank you for your patience and information, gentlemen,' led the way out of the room with his man, leaving the visitors behind, while he went forward to advise his Master.

He found King Charles listening to a long account of their escape from Scotland, through Berwick, of two former followers of Montrose, after the latter's dreadful and undeserved death. Charles had heard many stories of a similar kind. This was neither new nor well told. It went on and on, in detailed, slow-moving deliberate Scottish accents. The King, nevertheless, kept his interested gaze upon the pair, while he bent his mind upon the remaining session of his audience, one he had already determined to keep hidden from his Chancellor, who would not approve of it.

At last the loyal pair of Scots came to the end of their story, finishing with a plea to the King to return as soon as possible to his kingdom of Scotland where his subjects longer to rise for him.

'In good time, we promise you,' Charles told them graciously. 'Be assured your support finds both comfort and praise from us and our growing band of followers.'

He bowed to them from where he sat; he stretched out a hand for them to kiss. When they had left the audience chamber he turned to Lord Wilmot who stood beside him and said, 'Now for our gallant colonel and his son. We can use the boy privately while placing the father upon that very necessary guard he must raise over our envoys for aid to this and that country among our desired allies.'

'The colonel is no fool, sire,' Wilmot suggested. 'He will suspect the truth, when you see young Alan apart from him, that Your Majesty doth not wish to risk a sermon from Hyde. He will winkle the truth from me if not from the boy himself.'

'Then you shall not hear it either, Henry,' Charles said, lowering his voice as the Ogilvys were shown into the room.

Alan did indeed find a considerable change in the King, whom he had not seen in audience for nearly half a year. He looked in better health; though nothing could change his dark complexion his face no longer wore the old haggard hunted look, his cheek, still lean, was a little rounder as befitted his youth; his hair, long, curled, abundant, was again his own, no longer the wig he had worn when he first reached Paris in his servant's suit of grey worsted, with his locks shorn to his ears.

Colonel Ogilvy, in warning Alan that the King was changed, had meant in his behaviour not in his appearance. For he had served royal persons all his grown-up life and was well accustomed to the manners of the audience chamber. However, he did not expect Alan to receive any attention beyond a mild acknowledgment of his existence. He knew that as far as he was concerned he was there to receive orders, not the details of time and place but the characters it would be his business to guard and the situations he must avoid or overcome.

The colonel was also there to report upon his visit to England and what he found there.

'Alas, sire,' Ogilvy said. 'I found much true emotion, much loyal steadfastness, but little will to act. Pockets of men, planning, hoping, seeking to enlarge their enclaves of political rebellion, but all hesitant, confused, distrustful. I saw no movement anywhere that gave promise of any possibility of success.'

'In other words,' said Charles bitterly, 'we have heroes, we have swordsmen, horsemen, willing martyrs, but no generals, no soldiery.'

'That is how I saw it, sire.'

'The fellow Cromwell hath generals and soldiery. And ships too, I hear.'

'Master Cromwell is a great general himself, sire.'

The King looked very glum on hearing this, but Chancellor Hyde clearly did not want him to be too discouraged.

'There is good news from the ocean, however,' he said importantly. 'The Prince Rupert still takes prizes on the high seas – '

'With his unfailing impetuosity that wins fights and loses battles,' Charles answered. 'We wish our cousin well, but would encourage him to take his unlucky aid farther from England.'

He laughed up at Wilmot as he spoke. His friend laughed back as was fitting and also because he understood that his Master very often considered him reckless himself and also for that reason to have put the King in some danger during his long escape from England.

Colonel Ogilvy watched them, avoiding the Chancellor's eye because he knew he would catch agreement there. But the rest of the courtiers present, some of them Frenchmen who understood very little English, brightened as Charles's mood grew more cheerful. This was the young King they admired, while faintly despising. The poverty-stricken young rake, never satisfied with a single mistress but passing from one to another with astonishing speed and success while at the same time courting the highest in the land for a wife.

The King's mood changed again. He rose to end the audience, spoke a word here and there, bowed to others without speaking. Almost at once the room was empty except for Hyde, the two Ogilvys, Wilmot, a distant pair of gentlemen in waiting and Charles himself.

'Go with my Lord Chancellor, Colonel,' Charles said, passing in front of Alan and so cutting him away from his father's side. 'The journey you will make needs much care in the manner it is done, Our envoys must travel safely to perform their tasks securely. But we would have you observe to the full, that we may compare the news and views our messengers return to us, with the opinions and feelings of the lesser powers in those lands. My lord,' he added, turning again to Wilmot, so that now Alan alone was behind him, 'go you with them to discuss the ways the parties may follow. Colonel Ogilvy and you, my lord, should between you be able to advise my Lord Chancellor.'

The King stood still now, waving a hand to carry the other three forward to the door. As Alan made a quick movement to follow, thinking he had been forgotten, Charles made a slight gesture and murmured 'Stay!' in a voice too low for the others to hear, but filled with that quiet command that had become an easy habit with him.

So Alan stood, wondering. During the whole audience he had been puzzled to know why he was there. After all, he had done so slight a service to the King on board the *Surprise*, when His Majesty was still practising the manner of a commoner, a lord perhaps, at best a mere country gentleman. Never a king. This day he had been fully regal, a monarch indeed. Alan waited.

The King beckoned him forward, then led him to the embrasure of one of the long windows. When he turned to him again Alan saw that Charles wore his former friendly look, his dark eyes were bright, his full mouth widely smiling.

'I told you when you acted cabin boy to my friend Wilmot and me that you might serve me again, if occasion arose. A simple service as that was, but one to be done with discretion, with care, very quietly. Also the news of it brought to me in person, without giving any of it to another soul.'

Alan answered at once.

'I am altogether at Your Majesty's command.'

'Good lad, good lad!' Charles said gaily. 'Just the answer I looked for. No questions, no doubts, no excuses, no *price*! Nay, do not look so shocked. The French are an avaricious race and the English throne is a pauper. Already our credit begins to close up, though our Royal Mother, being aunt to King Louis, has her allowance from him.'

'My father, sir – ' Alan began, trying to explain that he wanted no hire but would serve the King in loyalty.

But Charles waved him to silence.

'Nevertheless, for your own sake, boy, and to give you the necessary access to me again, I propose to engage you – without salary – as a page of the bedchamber, under the general direction of the Lord Chamberlain.'

His proffered hand seemed to imply a formal engagement, so Alan knelt swiftly to kiss it and rose feeling a glow of importance not spoilt by the sardonic gleam in the King's eyes, for he knew Charles's bitter humour was turned upon himself, not upon the young man he had just honoured. There was after all only two years difference in age between them; the tall young King had less than two inches' advantage in height. For a second the eyes of the pair met. Alan longed to speak his full heart in words of comfort and hope. Surely this Prince, so full of courage, good sense and wit, was not doomed to pass his whole life in poverty, in exile. Surely his history would not repeat that of his sad aunt, the sometime Winter Queen of Bohemia, another exile.

But he dared not put into words a closeness of feeling and a condescension of pity no subject might display to the highest in the land. If that subject acknowledged that great one. As at that moment he did with the whole force of his young mind and heart.

Charles's eyes softened, he smiled with genuine pleasure as he always did when he had won a simple allegiance, unblemished by ambition, false pride or vanity. He laid a hand gently on Alan's shoulder and said, 'It is very simple, Alan.

I would have news of my son. He is with his mother, Mistress Lucy Walter, at The Hague. My Lord Chancellor brings me reports. The Duke of Monmouth is well. The Duke of Monmouth has the gripe, hath fallen and cut his knee, hath swallowed a button. But nought of his looks, his general welfare, his friends – the friends of his mother. Will you bring me true news of his welfare?'

Alan blushed violently, more on account of the ribald tales he had exchanged at Oxford with fellow students on the subject of the King's affairs of the heart, than particularly because he was hearing of their first acknowledged by-product from the child's own father.

'I will do so, sire,' he managed to say in a fairly natural voice. 'I ride into Holland with my father before the end of this week, unless his plan is changed following Your Majesty's orders, given today.'

'It will serve, it will serve,' Charles said, suddenly grown impatient. He lifted his arms, yawning widely. 'You may leave us now, Master Ogilvy,' he pronounced, most fully again the King. 'You may admit your new position in our household but tell no one of your errand. We would have the news of our son undoctored, unbiased by our advisors' wishes. You will provide it. We can trust you for that.'

When Alan had gone Charles stayed by the window of the great audience room until his gentlemen came forward. To minister to his wants, it was supposed; to guard his person, it was believed; to protect him from himself, Sir Edward Hyde piously wished, but scarcely hoped. To amuse and interest him, Charles demanded. Just now, his future or rather the possible plans for securing it having been discussed for several hours, his thoughts had turned by way of that early mistress and her boy to more ardent attractions and behind them to that urgent business of finding himself a suitable wife. Openly he still courted La Grande Mademoiselle as she was called, cousin of young King Louis, but older than he. Older than Charles himself, indeed, her eyes upon successful, not exiled princes, so far without success, but she still hoped. Meanwhile Charles courted her, while he loved, or at any rate, desired that beautiful widow, the Duchesse de Châtillon. Should he make her the Queen of England? Would the English, so Protestant just now, accept another French Catholic Queen, or would that marriage extinguish his already dim hopes of a restoration?

Charles pondered these questions until his gentlemen came round him to learn his pleasure and to take him away to find it. At the end of the evening he hoped the lovely Duchess would help to distract him entirely from his many woes and cares and puzzles and grinding want, so that he might sleep in her arms at last a fulfilled and happy man in place of a struggling, exiled king.

CHAPTER SEVEN

It took Alan three months to discover the whereabouts of Lucy Walter. This was in part because he could not make his inquiries openly, but had to find those who had known her, or of her, when she had been the young King's favourite. Charles had met her at The Hague while he was still Charles the First's heir and not yet eighteen. But the King of England was by then a prisoner in his own country and a year later was dead upon a scaffold in Whitehall by the hand of his own people.

So the young Charles's affair, ardent and innocent enough, though the Prince could not even then be considered wholly inexperienced, did not last for many months. King Charles the Second had matters of the first importance to occupy all his time and attention. His first concern from the very beginning of his exile, had been to recover his throne and his kingdom. So Lucy, expecting no better, was neglected during her inevitable pregnancy by the royal lover who had found such joy in her possession. She had hidden herself away with unexpected discretion until the birth of her son. Whereupon Charles, delighted with her, for he loved children, acknowledged the boy as his, named the infant at once James Scott, and made him Duke of Monmouth.

All very well, Alan found, but where were they now and what had become of that youthful idyll? Gone, he decided, as if it had never been, except for a number of sad, scurrilous tales of Mistress Lucy's later behaviour, though none of her exact whereabouts.

Colonel Ogilvy was mildly helpful, but Alan dared not ask him too many questions, especially about matters in the United Provinces and Holland, since the latter had now lapsed into naval war with the English, only to feel at once the immense improvement in Cromwell's fleet under Admiral Blake. The Dutch still had a superiority in the number of ships, but the new English vessels were larger, their armament heavier, their military complement no longer a rabble but well trained, well disciplined and eager to win in the battle of the Lord God, whom they were told was directly instructing his faithful servant, Oliver Cromwell.

This war was a disappointing setback to the hopes of the English loyalists in general. Though Alan, son of a known and much respected figure attached to the House of Orange, did not feel the handicap at first.

He gathered in time that Mistress Walter was still in Holland. Since the Lady Anne Ogilvy, his mother, was at the widowed Princess of Orange's Court at The Hague, he was able to appear with his own family upon suitable occasions, while being perfectly free for most of the time to travel wherever rumour or more solid information led him.

In the end he traced the discarded favourite to Dordrecht and a tall house upon the central quay. Here she occupied three rooms upon an upper floor, with the little Duke of Monmouth and his nursemaid and an older woman who lived with them on familiar terms but provided the food for all three, which she cooked in the kitchens at the basement of the house.

Mistress Walter was at this time twenty-two and her son three. The mother was still pretty though the fresh Welsh pink and white complexion had faded somewhat and the abundant black locks, as dark as Charles's own, were poorly tended and dull for lack of washing and brushing. The little boy, on the other hand, was in fine health, as rosy as his mother was pale and very well attended by his nurse, who took great pride in his royal origin and in her innocence believed he might yet become heir to the English crown.

Alan presented himself at the house, showing the letter he bore to gain him an entrance. He found no difficulty. The elderly woman, hoping for an increase in her salary with this renewal of the King's interest, took the messenger upstairs at once. In her enthusiasm her knock at Lucy's door was brief, nor did she wait for an answer, but began to open it. So Alan was perfectly aware of a certain scuffle within and though he heard no second voice there was a sound of confused movement too great for a single woman's making.

'A gentleman come from His Majesty, madam,' the woman said. 'Did I not tell thee, my love, his neglect would be over just as soon as the affairs of State would allow?'

Motioning to Alan to go forward the old woman turned and began to descend the stairs again, while Alan moved into the room, took two steps forward and bowed deeply and respectfully.

He was not altogether surprised by the servant's familiarity nor by the general air of disorder in the room and also in the person of the young woman who received him in a friendly way but with evident surprise.

'But you are not – ' she began, then bit her lip and turned away, but looked back again and smiled.

'You expected another visitor, madam?' Alan asked politely.

'Yes, sir. That is to say, I have been warned – '

Again she broke off, frowning, but seated herself in an upright chair and waved Alan to another.

'Mother Schik did mention His Majesty. You come to me from him? You have a letter, perhaps?'

'No letter, madam. But my errand is direct from the King.'

Seeing her instant disappointment Alan felt a quick surge of pity for her. So he went on in a gentle voice, attempting comfort, 'His thoughts turn often to the little Duke, his son.'

'But not to me?'

'Naturally to you, madam, through his concern for you, too.'

'As the boy's mother. Nay, I am not bitter. In him that is natural. I have always understood it. You are to inspect us, I assume, and make a report?'

Alan flushed. Her manner was direct, abrupt, almost offensive. It was easy to realize how this would irritate Charles; not to the point of anger, he was too easy-going for that, too sure of himself now, perhaps always where women were concerned. But dangerous to her future unless she mended it.

It was, however, too early in their acquaintance to attempt to explain this to her. Besides, just then Alan felt his own inexperience most acutely. Mistress Walter was older than he, a woman with a child already three years old. Surely he would never dare to speak to her as the King had hinted; warn her to sink quietly into the background, away from all Court connections, all great ambitions, all thoughts of a grand marriage to follow that supreme position she had so briefly held. Already he thought he had confirmed the truth of the gossip he had heard; that she did not lack admirers, probably a lover.

He began to talk about Charles's present Court and those who formed it. Of how his brother Prince James was serving as a soldier with the French King Louis's troops, of how his youngest brother Henry, Duke of Gloucester, had been allowed to leave England and was now with the widowed Queen, who was trying to make him turn to the Catholic religion, but the King would not allow it.

'Yet His Majesty is three parts Catholic himself,' Lucy protested. 'Or was when I was close to him. Though since we were at The Hague and this is an altogether Protestant country, you understand – '

'The King was brought up in the Church of England,' Alan said firmly. 'That is his church and he declares so continually. England is of that church, however much the Presbyterians and all those manifold mad sects rant to the contrary.'

'Nevertheless – ' Lucy repeated, but a knock at the door, followed by a decent interval, brought the arrival of the Duke of Monmouth, pulling against the hand of his nursemaid.

He was a pretty child, with abundant dark curls flowing down over his shoulders on each side. He was simply dressed, but as a miniature gentleman, no longer in the long gown of the very young, though he was not much above three years old. He spoke in part English, part Dutch, which Alan did not perfectly understand. However his harangue, delivered in a loud, autocratic voice, was addressed in anger to his nurse. He ignored Alan altogether. He seemed to be continuing a quarrel, or rather an extended rebuke, begun elsewhere.

The nurse made no effort to control him, but appealed to his mother instead to scold him as he deserved. To Alan's surprise Mistress Lucy merely laughed, calling to the boy to come to her and tell her what had upset him. Which he did, running into her arms and kissing her upon each cheek in turn. After which he caught sight of Alan, standing gravely behind her. He stood away himself, staring now.

'Master Leslie?' he said, inquiring. Then shook his head. 'No Master Leslie.'

'No, James,' his mother told him. 'This is not Master Leslie. This is Master Alan Ogilvy.'

'Why did he say Leslie?' Alan could not help asking. 'Forgive me for asking, but my father, Colonel Francis Ogilvy, is connected in some sort with a branch of the clan Leslie.'

'And Master George Leslie, as you must very well know, is one of that family,' Mistress Walter said, her eyes sparkling with amusement. 'My little son mistook you for a visitor who pays me the compliment of thinking I can give him information about the King and so comes to visit me.'

'George Leslie, the spy!' Alan exclaimed. 'Here in Dordrecht?'

She paled a little.

'You exaggerate, sir,' she said coldly, realizing her indiscretion. 'But little Jamie is right. Master Leslie came here a week ago and I expect him here again.'

She had expected him today, Alan thought, remembering the confusion on Mistress Walter's face when the old housekeeper had announced him. Well, why not? A recent letter from old Mistress Leslie in Paternoster Row had told him how George had arrived a few hours after he himself had gone aboard his Dutch hoy in the Pool. George had been looking for him then. He would scarcely expect to find him here now. They would not recognize one another, never having met. But Lucy Walter would not fail to introduce them, one to another, if only from a kind of malice, because in each she herself did not count for any purpose, any importance, but only as her fertility affected the royal succession or could be made to affect it, to blast it, rather. George Leslie's purpose in life seemed to be aimed at destruction, in whatever direction he moved.

The little Duke of Monmouth, having decided that the strange man was not dangerous, now went up to him and reaching to his belt hauled down his sword scabbard to inspect it.

'Too long for thee to handle, my little lord,' Alan said, smiling down at the child. 'But stand away a little and I'll show thee how the blade draws.'

'Nay, sir, forbear,' Mistress Lucy entreated. 'He'll learn soon enough. There is too much of his father's spirit here to be encouraged.'

Alan laughed and the child laughed with him. In another few minutes they had become friends, chasing each other about the room, while the nurse stood near the door, clapping her hands, only too pleased to have the awkward scene of her arrival with the boy forgotten. Mistress Walter, still frowning a little, moved out of the way of the couple to stand near the window looking down from time to time into the street.

It was while she was doing so that her expression suddenly changed to one of consternation. She exclaimed aloud:

'Go, nurse!' she cried. 'Run to Mother Schik. Tell her to say I am from home. Quick! Go! This visitor must be delayed!'

The nurse girl, obviously confused, turned fumbling with the door handle in her agitation. The little Duke of Monmouth stopped in his game, which now took the form of riding on Alan's back as he cavorted about the room. The child struggled to free himself, fell a few feet as Alan tried to swing him down and let out a great bellow, more of fear than pain.

The nurse paused with the door half open. Mistress Lucy yelled to her to run to Mother Schik; James yelled to her not to leave him. Alan called above the din, 'Madam, why this agitation? Who have you seen? Who is the unwelcome visitor? How may I aid you?'

Her agitation was growing. She abandoned all show of formal manners, which she had sustained with a fortitude that had surprised Alan thus far. She ran to his side and clasping his right arm with both hands said in a breathless whisper, 'Can you not guess? We have just spoken of him. It is George Leslie. It is that second visit he threatened to make to me!'

'*Threatened*! This is different news, madam!'

'I am afraid of him! He tries to force me to give him scandalous news of the King that he may supply it to those monsters in England to turn the loyal subjects against His Majesty!'

'I will hold the door against him if that is your wish,' Alan said.

The lady's agitation, her warm clasp on his arm, her plump bosom touching his side, all had their effect in rousing his sense of chivalry, or so he marked it to himself. At that moment she became a real person to him for the first time, real, feminine and very little older than himself.

'If you do not wish to see this man, madam,' he promised her stoutly, 'you shall not. I swear it!'

But there were voices on the stairs, a man's tones, cold, bitter, insulting; the nurse protesting, the Duke of Monmouth screaming; the old housekeeper from farther off pouring out curses in a continuous bawl.

'It is too late,' Lucy Walter said, suddenly dropping her hands and stepping away from Alan's side. 'Master Leslie must have his way, as always. I must speak with him, but as always I shall tell him nothing. Perhaps with you here – '

'No!' Alan said, not loudly but with great determination. 'He has not seen me since I was a lad. He must not know my face, to denounce me later in England.'

'Where can you go?' Lucy cried. 'They are upon the stairs!'

'Here!' Alan cried, making for that second door he had seen closing at the moment he had entered the room.

Mistress Walter cried out to stop him but he had reached for and found the door handle and though she cried out again he was through it and had turned to close it as quickly and silently as he had seen it move earlier.

He turned again. Facing him, his drawn sword in his hand, stood a man, a little shorter than himself, certainly broader and older, staring at him from steady grey eyes and with a smile on his lips.

'I think that makes a trio of us, doth it not?' the man said.

CHAPTER EIGHT

Alan's sword was out before the man had finished speaking, but only to defend himself if necessary. Astonishment totally destroyed any anger he might have felt in being so addressed.

'I am a messenger to Mistress Walter from the King of England,' he said in a low voice, very civilly.

The man's mouth widened in soundless mirth.

'Not a substitute?' he asked, and seeing Alan flush and his sword hand move again, began coolly to put up his own blade.

From the room Alan had left they heard a door close and a heavy tread across the floor. As Alan turned towards the advancing tread the other man seized his arm, whispered an emphatic 'Hush!' and drew him quickly to a part of the panelling that opened at a touch, disclosing a narrow stair.

'Down!' said the man, pushing Alan into the opening. Together they went quickly to ground level and through a narrow door into a small wash-yard with a central pump, a wide basin round it and various lines from which flapped drying linen.

With a hand to his mouth, demanding silence, Alan's guide went quickly and silently round two walls of this yard, keeping close in to the bricks, so that anyone watching from the windows above would be unlikely to see them. The side walls of the yard seemed to join similar parts of the same or other houses, while the outer wall, higher than these, presented merely the sky.

Alan remembered that the house stood upon the quay at the central square of the town and that Dordrecht City lay upon the junctions of the rivers Maas and Rhine, with a canal system fed from these waters. Beyond that high wall, he guessed, was water and through it a means of exit from the house without disclosing his companion and himself to anyone watching the front entrance.

He was right. In the corner of the little yard another narrow door proved to be unlocked. It opened easily, showing it was in frequent use, and gave upon a narrow pathway that lay beside a little smelly inlet from the main canal. A few yards along this path another joined it at right angles, while the water turned in the opposite direction. A small rowing boat lay in the angle, tied up to a ring at the edge of the path.

Alan thought it was time for some explanation and that they were now far enough away from the house to make this safe. But as he opened his mouth to speak his guide said, 'No!' in the same near whisper, but added, 'The boat is mine. Get in if you would know more. We cannot speak freely here. We can now be watched.'

Alan, who had put up his sword in the empty yard, felt for the short dagger he also wore at his belt. Before he got down into the boat he loosened it in its sheath, noticing that the other man was observing him closely all the time and seemed to be amused by his behaviour. However he motioned Alan to the stern, got in himself and picking up the short sculls sat down on the forward thwart and began to row down a succession of narrow channels where Alan rapidly lost his sense of direction and at last gave up all idea of regaining it.

They stopped at last, after they had emerged upon a wider stream. Here they disembarked and here the guide said, 'My name is Tom Howard. I have known Mistress Walter for some four months. You say you come from the King. I think my Lucy did not expect your visit.'

Alan was shocked by this openly familiar way of speaking, but the circumstances in which he had met this man had made his purpose in Lucy Walter's house quite plain. So he merely answered, 'My name is Alan Ogilvy. My father is Colonel Francis Ogilvy, who has served in the armies of the United Provinces and the House of Orange for most of his life and his father before him. His Majesty hath made me a page in his household and sent me upon this errand to bring him news of His Grace, the Duke of Monmouth.'

'So.' Master Howard stared at Alan with some interest. 'These names ring familiar. But we must not stand here like two old gossips. Come with me to that wine-shop on the quay. There are things – news – you should carry to the King, our Master, that he should know about his former love.'

'About the fellow, George Leslie, would you not say?'

'Not here!' Tom Howard stopped him again. 'Wait till we are sat where none can overhear us.'

There were two rooms in the shop, whose owner seemed familiar with Master Howard. In the outer one, the shop proper, the wine-merchant and a plump woman were serving customers. Behind a hanging curtain of a dirty brown colour, lay a second smaller chamber, an alcove one would have called it except it had a small grimy window, so smeared by dust, cobwebs and fly-dirt that it was impossible to see what lay beyond. At least no one could spy from without.

The wine-merchant greeted Master Tom openly and upon the latter pointing a discreet finger at the brown curtain nodded his head with a cheerful, 'The usual, master?'

As Howard nodded in turn the shopkeeper gave an order to the woman and the two customers stepped into the dark little room where they sat down at a table and on chairs that had been swept clean, even polished, quite recently.

'Hans will see to it we are not disturbed,' Tom said, 'but do not speak until we are supplied.'

He meant the wine he had ordered, Alan thought, but was not very surprised when this turned out to be the strong ale of the country, of a clear deep brown with a shallow head upon it. Alan drew out his purse but Tom waved away the offer.

'You may pay me later when I have set you on your journey safely from this town,' he said. 'Now explain to me this matter of Master Leslie. Of course I know he is a parliamentarian and a dissenter of one kind or another – '

'Of any kind that suits his purpose,' Alan interrupted scornfully.

'Which is?'

Alan explained the self-made feud, compounded of thwarted love, jealousy, envy and hatred that had set his half-uncle upon his present course.

'So he plans destruction upon all sides, doth me?' Tom Howard asked. He seemed not at all shocked nor even surprised, as indeed he was not. For at this time of civil strife it was a common thing to find family quarrels turned to political advantage against private enemies.

'But you and your own branch of the Ogilvy family have no direct part in this man's enmity, I imagine?' Howard went on.

Alan hesitated. It was true his father refused to discover any real evil in George. They had shared the same mother but had no other link. In upbringing, by profession, in opinion, religion, by allegiance, they could be scarcely more different. As for himself, he doubted if he would recognize the man.

'I doubt if I would know him,' he said aloud, 'but it seems he is determined to know me. Why else should he have followed so close to Mistress Walter's house? Perhaps I should not have fled him but the lady was so agitated, eager to rid herself of my presence, not knowing how to – '

'Not knowing how to prevent you finding me in the inner room. Which you were determined to succeed in, or find me already gone, you young dog!'

They both laughed heartily and Alan confessed that he had waited all through the interview for some plausible excuse for opening that door he had seen closing so secretly.

The wine-merchant, hearing their mirth, pulled aside the brown curtain to offer them another tankard of beer. Tom accepted, but Alan refused. He explained that he must take horse and ride to The Hague, where he expected to find most of his family gathered.

'I have promised my mother to give her my news,' Alan said. 'She is very anxious for her father. He lives in the country, very quietly, but his sons are loyalists, as he is too, of course, and one of them hath ill news of the old man, who cannot show discretion, never having truly learned it. They all fear he may find himself in the Tower.'

Tom Howard raised his eyebrows, the wine-merchant his hands.

'The Tower! Who is this grandfather of yours, young man, who may risk the block instead of the rope?'

Alan told him briefly, but added that he understood Oliver Cromwell was against chopping off more heads or even using the rope for purely political views without planned violence.

'You absolve your tyrant then?' the wine-merchant teased him.

'Never! It is not from any wish to spare lives but simply to avoid making more martyrs. George Leslie pursues my Lord Aldborough because my father married his lordship's daughter.'

'He cannot reach Colonel Ogilvy, but might injure him through his wife?'

'Just so.'

'This is but an extension of the civil war,' Howard said impatiently. 'But ill-devised and useless in the present cause of calming the people and giving supreme power over the army to Cromwell.'

'Useless indeed,' Alan added bitterly. 'But spiteful, ill-intentioned. Especially as regards – '

He broke off, seeing how near he was to disclosing his knowledge of George's most marked victim, the cloth merchant, Phillips. He had told Tom about George's disappointment in losing the hand of his cousin, Cynthia Ogilvy, but not to whom he had lost it. And certainly not about the couple's daughter Susan, whose image still came before him very often, though he had long ago abandoned hope of ever meeting the girl again.

Lady Anne Ogilvy was both surprised and annoyed by Alan's report of his conversation with Master Tom Howard.

'You will not tell me how or why you came upon such a fellow,' she complained. 'Nor in whose company?'

'None but my own, madam,' he answered, quietly. 'Surely my father hath spoken to you of my present employment at the King's Court.'

'So you would have me believe you are in Holland upon Court business. Or upon the King's business?'

She had heard the usual stories about Charles's many mistresses, including those relating to the recent indiscretions of his early favourite, but she did not wish to discuss such matters with her son.

As she expected Alan made no answer to her last question. But instead he asked her if she had any betters news of Lord Aldborough.

'Alas, my poor father!' she answered. 'He stumbles into indiscretion ever more dangerously, nor does my mother give him much help in avoiding it, being a Villiers herself, with much of the reckless thrust of that family, though I should not speak of her with such disrespect.'

She smiled at Alan as she said it, for they were close in spirit, unlike his brother Gordon, who showed not only the ambition of a Buckingham, and the military single-mindedness of his father, but the wildness of his earlier Scottish ancestry.

'Can nothing be done to persuade my Lord Aldborough to leave England until the King comes to his own again?' Alan asked.

'Can we be sure that will ever be?' Lady Anne said sadly. 'Or in my father's lifetime?'

They fell silent. It was a situation shared by many well-born families, where an ageing head clung to his native land and estate, struggling to remain where he was born, in a place he had loved all his life and which he longed to hand on to his heir, even if the true heir had already fallen in battle, slain by those he considered rebels and murderers.

Alan stayed two days at The Hague with his mother and sisters. He was presented to the Princess Mary of Orange, Charles the Second's sister, who seemed both depressed and anxious over her little son. The merchants did not approve of her as Regent; they were inclined to rid themselves of the House of Orange. For the Stuart connection seemed to carry nothing but ill-luck with it. That former marriage of James the First's daughter Elizabeth, to Frederick Elector Palatine, had brought disaster through incompetence and gross misjudgement. Now the second William of Orange was dead, a young man, leaving a very young boy for heir and a Stuart widow in charge of him.

'Our inheritance is marked with misfortune,' she said to Alan in a brief audience. 'You are in our brother's service, my Lady Anne Ogilvy tells me. You may tell him we cannot give him any assistance. We have little enough ourself to support our Court. He must continue to rely upon France. After all Louis is his cousin, his mother is the French King's aunt.'

All this peevish complaint made a very poor impression

upon Alan and lost nothing of its character when he relayed it to Charles in private audience upon his return to Paris.

The King flushed angrily as he listened to Alan's careful account of his meeting with the dowager Princess of Orange.

'Our sister hath not gained in dignity or prudence from her life with these shopkeepers,' he said in exasperation. 'You will repeat nothing of this,' he added, staring haughtily at Alan from his large black eyes.

'Your Majesty is the first to hear it,' Alan answered, 'and will certainly be the last.'

He felt sure that the King's anger was as much caused by his sister's disclosure of the whole family's poverty to a mere commoner, a youth even younger than himself, as to her implied rebuff. He felt too that Charles was justified, for young as he was, quite inexperienced in the ways of the great ones of the earth, the deficiencies of the English King's Court were only too plain. So he stood silent, having made his promise, unhappy at the turn the interview had taken. But it was not his fault that Charles had asked first about the Princess, not about Lucy.

As if he understood what was passing in Alan's mind, Charles dropped the regal manner and leaning casually back in the great chair upon which he had been sitting bolt upright he asked, in a very different voice, 'What of your mission, boy? What of his Grace of Monmouth and the whore, his mother?'

'The little Prince, sire –' began Alan, but Charles stopped him with a hard laugh.

'No Prince, Alan, though mine and of royal blood.'

'The little Duke, Your Majesty, is very well grown for his age, most lively, in excellent health and spirits. He is living in the very good care of a devoted nurse. The household is well maintained by a capable Dutch housekeeper –'

'A bawd? To serve the whore?'

'A cook, sire.'

Charles laughed again, not unkindly, simply because he found Lucy Walter's situation comical, so long as it did not affect him.

'Madam Walter is in good health too, sire. I delivered your Majesty's written instruction.'

'What answer did she give to it?'

Alan thought it best to describe the whole story of the end of the meeting, including his escape with Tom Howard upon the arrival of George Leslie.

'Who is this man, Howard? Apart from being Madam Walter's latest lover?'

'I do not know, sire. He seemed to be aware I came from Your Majesty, but of nothing else. I told him nothing but the tale of my family's connection with Leslie. He as good as told me the man is a spy for the Parliament.'

Charles was silent for so long that Alan feared he had spoken too familiarly or too personally. He had in fact engaged the King's interest most keenly, as he discovered a few days later when he was sent for by Sir Edward Hyde, the Chancellor, soon to be created the Earl of Clarendon.

Sir Edward was affable, but grave as befitted his important office. To none was this importance so clear as to himself, Alan had been told. He had read it in the Chancellor's manner and was the more surprised that his interview began so mildly and with a compliment to his father's splendid service behind the scenes in France and his mother's grace and beauty in attendance upon King Charles's widowed sister.

'And now His Majesty informs me of your personal attendance upon him in the matter of his young bastard son,' Sir Edward went on smoothly. 'The child thrives, you found?'

'Yes, indeed, sir. And Madam Walter too, if I address her correctly.'

'Madam or Mistress, young man, and the latter with more certainty, perhaps.'

The irony soured the conversation. Alan sighed.

'The lady seems to live most moderately, to judge by her establishment and her attendants,' he said.

'But most immodestly, from the rumours that concern her,' Sir Edward said severely. 'And that gives cause for great annoyance to His Majesty, who finds they reflect upon his own present reputation, as you may well understand. Nay, hear me out.'

For Alan, stung by this exaggerated reference to his own report to Charles, had flushed and opened his mouth to correct the Chancellor's assessment.

'This man, Thomas Howard, is known to us as the woman's present protector, after her failure to secure another well-born Englishman in marriage. Master Howard is something of an adventurer and hath been very useful to our cause from time to time. His behaviour towards yourself was typical, cool – a trifle reckless, but effective. He spoke to you about the man

George Leslie. Did he disclose this fellow shared with him Mistress Lucy's favours?'

'He did not,' Alan answered, keeping his temper with an effort. 'He implied that my half-uncle cultivated the lady with a view to possible knowledge of His Majesty's plans, or at any rate his intentions. With the purpose of taking information back to England.'

The Chancellor nodded.

'I have been told of his presence in France and also in the Low Countries,' he said. 'I know that he has worked as a Member of Parliament and remains in that body they call "The Rump". Also that he hath been to Colonel Ogilvy's house near Paul's church.'

'Where I narrowly missed a meeting with him after–'

'After parting from your father and most neatly evading your pursuers,' Hyde finished for him. 'And where Mistress Leslie, that admirable old loyalist and warm-hearted liberal family friend, helps to preserve sanity among the modern maniac bigots.'

His controlled passion both astonished and impressed Alan. He had been told that the Chancellor clucked round the Throne like a demented hen with an alien foster-chick. One with webbed feet, some of them said, knowing Charles's delight in boats and navigation. Hyde's next words linked with Alan's information.

'I think you may be of continued service to our cause in England,' he said. 'This connection in Paternoster Row could be most valuable to us. On account of the range of visitors invited there in the cause of peace and friendship in the Ogilvy family, of which you are an important member.'

He held up a restraining hand again as Alan tried to speak.

'*Therefore*,' he said with emphasis, 'you must become a student once more. With His Majesty's permission and under his direction you will receive a recommendation from Sir Thomas Hobbes, the great mathematician, who is presently instructing the King in the science of navigation, to a similar course with a colleague in Oxford.'

'But they sought to arrest me in Oxford, or rather from Banbury.'

'Sir Thomas's word will protect you. Learn your mathematics, young man. Lodge, if you will, if they will have you, with your great-uncle Doctor Richard Ogilvy, or his friend Sir Francis Leslie, and discover all you can of George Leslie, how much he knows, with whom he makes contact, how dangerous his presence here or in Holland could be to His Majesty's plans or even his person.'

'It is a great purpose,' Alan said, but his eyes gleamed with something other than scholarly interest.

'In which you are but one among very many,' answered Sir Edward Hyde, with pinched disapproval of such enthusiasm.

Alan rejoined his friends at Court in a state of confused euphoria.

'How went it?' they asked him. 'A wigging for absence without leave?' For they had missed him from his duties about the bedchamber as a very newly recruited page.

'He talked like a schoolmaster,' Alan answered, cheerfully. 'No wonder King Charles seeks gayer company.'

A week later he was landed from a coal boat on the shores of Studland Bay outside Poole Harbour in Dorset.

CHAPTER NINE

Charles Stuart, as they called him in government circles in London, was bored. Clearly there was nothing he could do to forward his cause at present. A visit to Paris of his impetuous cousin Rupert, so brilliant in battle and at the same time so disastrous, was no comfort to him, nor even a source of entertainment. But at least his usefulness as a pirate on foreign shipping in the Channel had come to an end, for Cromwell's Admiral Blake, established in the Scilly Isles to prevent such action, had altogether supplanted him. The final result of his efforts had been less to battle with the Spanish than the Dutch, thus turning that sturdy merchant race against not only the new rulers of England but also their defeated royal house.

The King's advisers, those elderly wise men, particularly the 'schoolmaster' whose manner Alan Ogilvy had resented, were perfectly right about Cousin Rupert, as they were about most things. But this did not make the prince's visit more welcome, nor afford any relief to Charles's position and his dwindling resources.

'But I plan to go farther,' Rupert announced with all his

usual optimism and flamboyance.

'Farther?' Charles asked with irony. 'Is that possible? Whither, cousin?'

'Have we not secured or at least laid siege to the island of Jamaica? I will go among those Spanish possessions and find treasure to restore Your Majesty's fortune.'

If Charles did not share Prince Rupert's confidence he at least saw a chance of his employment farther afield, where he could do less harm, if not more good, than darting about the confined waters of the Channel, bringing death and destruction to innocent seamen and their cargoes, without benefit to anyone.

Nevertheless the King could not at any time forget his very real helplessness, his lack of an outlet for his own youthful abundant energy except in the pursuit of women, where his success was all too evident. Except in the matter of advantageous marriage.

Here even the exiled Queen, his mother, was no help to him.

'La Grande Mademoiselle, apart from her grand aspirations, is no longer a desirable match, my son,' she told him. 'For she hath joined the wrong cause in this quarrel of the Fronde; we see her no longer at Court. Put her out of your heart, Charles.'

'She was never in it, madam,' he answered her. 'Four years ago she terrified me with her superior learning and seniority and her contempt for my French. Now she wearies me and I her, though I speak good French, do I not?'

'Good enough,' answered his mother, unwilling as were all her race, to praise any foreigner's command of her language.

'Whereas the Duchesse de Châtillon,' Charles went on, 'though a widow – '

'Is not a fit consort. She could never be received as queen in England.'

'If they will ever take me back, I would persuade them to accept the lovely Isabelle.'

But it was no good. Queen Henrietta Maria had been accustomed to have her own way except in the early days of her marriage to Charles the First. And over her religion at all times. So as long as Charles the Second depended upon her financially he had to give way, much as he resented it.

But outwardly and in public he behaved with the dignity and charm he already knew how to exercise and the licence in sexual matters that was considered perfectly normal in France. But it gave great offence to the present rulers of England, who could and did exaggerate his behaviour with all the prurient imagination peculiar to puritan minds and hearts.

One chief consolation came to Charles, however, brought to him by his friend, the newly created Earl of Rochester, formerly Lord Wilmot. Charles had employed him since his promotion in missions to possible allies and patrons, among such people as the Duke of Lorraine and the Elector of Brandenburg. On most of these missions Colonel Ogilvy had charge of their safety, which pleased both veterans.

On his return from one such expedition Lord Rochester was in high spirits.

'There is promise of a subsidy for Your Majesty,' he proclaimed. 'Made at Ratisbon.'

'You may give the detail to the Lord Chancellor, Henry,' Charles told him. 'Good news indeed, for we go hungry here when our credit flags as it doth all too often of late. But I too have good news. They have released the Princess Henrietta Anne, my little Minette. The Queen expects her before the month is out. Her mother will make her a Catholic but that will do her sweet self no harm.'

Rochester nodded. His travels had taken him into those free-thinking, independent lands where he had campaigned in the middle years of the late King's reign. He found they were better informed of events in that unhappy confused country than was the French Court.

'Your Majesty has news from England?' he asked, cautiously.

'Sparely. Such as my wise Councillors will hand on to me. Oh Henry, I think they send you on these missions to keep you from the Council chamber and from me.'

'No, sire, but because I served with the Dutch and understand the Germanic peoples. From them I have learned that Oliver Cromwell is made Lord Protector of England. From being chief among the generals, but still one of them in their so-called Commonwealth, he lifts himself above them. He is a kind of – '

'King,' said Charles bitterly. 'Traitorous, unanointed, self-appointed tyrant.'

'But therefore human after all,' said Rochester, with all his usual gaiety.

'Villain!' Charles told him with an approving laugh. 'I'll have you stay by me, Henry. My lord Chancellor Hyde shall discover to me further news of this Protector and his tyranny. Pray God my sturdy subjects will see his infamy and turn him out.'

But Sir Edward Hyde was just as depressing as ever in Charles's estimation. Not only was Cromwell making alterations in the government of the country but these were largely in a liberal direction. 'More particularly over the minor religious sects,' he explained. 'Those strange growths that appeared like toadstools with the suppression of the Anglican church and the removal of the bishops.'

'I will not have you speak against the Quakers. My brave bearer at Fécamp was no toadstool when he put me dry-shod on the French shore. I shall never forget the motive of his faithful service. To earn freedom for his kind when I shall come into my own.'

'The Catholics are still pursued with rigour and enmity,' the Chancellor went on, ignoring what he considered to be the King's usual levity. 'But there are Baptists who preach against war in any form, so-called Seekers, who find all other bodies imperfect and Ranters who preach against all authority other than their own consciences.'

'So these little messiahs together with the Quakers find tolerance under the Protector, do they? I cannot believe they be of as great assistance to him as his generals, but perhaps their freedom may help to keep those rivals to his power fairly occupied.'

Hyde agreed. Not for the first time the young Charles had shown insight and intelligence while seeming scarcely to listen to what was said to him. Irritated by his own lack of subtlety the Chancellor persisted.

'Even that lunatic band the Fifth Monarchy Men who preach the Second Coming three year hence, no later than 1666, are no longer rebuked or even confined when they show violence to the lawyers and clergy they denounce.'

'They will not threaten Cromwell while they continue to shout their nonsense,' Charles said. He had tired of his adviser's list. These people, as the new-made Protector saw without difficulty, were no true menace to his position nor to the new State.

'But there is one indulgence may work in his favour if only from gratitude,' Sir Edward Hyde said, bringing forward the news he had found the most disturbing, if not shocking. 'The Jews are allowed once more to enter England if they wish, to trade, to use their perpetual skill in the management of money, even to worship according to their native religion and to build synagogues in which to do so.'

Charles leaped to his feet, shocked and astonished.

'The puritan tyrant, the Christian purified, self-styled friend and servant of the Almighty, admits the murderers of the Son of God! He pampers those slayers of his Master, the King of Heaven! He did not hesitate to murder his Master on earth, the King of England!'

The Chancellor said nothing. He could not complain that Charles was indifferent to this news, but he was a little embarrassed by the young man's excessive emotion. He prepared to explain the real significance of Cromwell's action, but was forestalled.

Charles returned to his former seat and spoke more quietly but with great scorn.

'It is easy to understand this yeoman's purpose. Was not his grandfather, or uncle or some such local worthy in Norfolk, of considerable wealth and therefore great repute and respect? I thought as much. So the Jews are admitted in the service of trade, of England's prosperity, in competition with the welfare of his foreign enemies.'

'Your Majesty has a remarkable grasp of events,' said Sir Edward, hoping now to be released from yet another baffling interview. His wish was fulfilled almost at once. Charles relapsed into depression, which lasted for a day or two, until Lord Rochester came to him again, bearing a parcel that contained a handsome, leatherbound and gold-tooled book.

'What have you there?' Charles asked languidly, for literary pursuits were not usual with his lively reckless friend, so boyish in spite of his mature age.

'A volume that has come to me from England, sire,' Rochester answered, putting it into the King's outstretched hand, 'where it hath caused a great stir among all who read or can persuade others to read it out to them.'

Charles turned the book over, saw its title, *Eikon Basilike*, and looked up sharply.

'"Image of a King!" Its provenance?' he asked, in a strained voice.

'They say it is the collected thoughts of his late Majesty, taken from diaries and sundry papers composed in – in Carisbrooke Castle on Wight and other places of confinement.'

The King got to his feet and walked across the room to the window. With his back to Rochester he began to turn the pages of the book, reading now and then, breaking off to stare out at the quiet lawns below and the occasional figures sauntering there at ease or hurrying on some errand about the Court.

At last he clapped the book shut, turned with a look of haggard grief upon his dark face and said hoarsely, near to tears, 'I think this was not composed by my father. His thoughts were simple where these are subtle; agitated, often severe, where here there is much reasoned argument.'

'Nevertheless it is greatly in demand I am told, and read by rich and poor alike, loyalist and rebel. They continue to print it, edition after edition, and distribute it all over the country.'

'Who are *they*?'

'I know not. It was brought to me by a London merchant at Rotterdam, as I passed by that city recently.'

'I will keep the copy,' Charles said, his voice returning to normal.

By the time he sent Rochester from him he seemed to have recovered from the shock the *Eikon Basilike* had given him. It had reminded him, with overwhelming force and an instant onrush of grief, of the earlier book upon kingship written by his grandfather, King James the First, whose beliefs his own father had held with equal obstinacy but less intelligence and far less tact.

That night, for once alone in his great bed, he wept for all that misdirected energy, its tragic outcome and his own plight that had resulted as the inevitable sequel. Not for the first time he promised himself that should his fortunes change and the new-styled Protector be no longer able to exercise that spurious position, he would concern himself less with the pursuit of power than the welfare of those loyal subjects who were proclaiming their feelings and beliefs in the purchase of this last supposed link with their murdered lord and master.

Rochester had been right about the book's popularity. In London it was the subject of much subdued gossip. Alan Ogilvy came across it at his father's house in Paternoster Row when he went from Oxford to London to find Sir Thomas Hobbes and deliver to him King Charles's note of recommendation.

'I was told to find him in Oxford,' he explained to Mistress Leslie. 'The Protector's brother-in-law condescended to read the note and seemed to approve it. As my uncle Ogilvy told us, my father and me, there be many very learned men, philosophers and such, gathered about Master Wilkins.'

'He is Warden of Wadham College, is he not?' the old lady asked. She laughed. 'I repeat this name and style like a parrot for I do not have the smallest notion what they mean.'

'I hope they mean I may settle back to my studies,' Alan said. But he did not explain that he had other work, the King's work, which was to observe and report upon any loyal gathering in the university town that might plan profitably for a hopeful revolt at some future time.

Mistress Leslie produced her copy of the *Eikon Basilike* while Alan was still staying with her. It happened on a day when Mistress Cynthia Phillips and her daughter Susan had come to call at the house. It was also the day when Alan had at last been able to speak to Sir Thomas Hobbes, who received King Charles's note with kindness and interest. He thought the young man had a serious disposition, very young, very eager to acquire some scholarship, particularly of a scientific kind. Sir Thomas was perfectly willing to promote Alan's interest at Oxford with a recommendation to the Warden of Wadham.

This was highly satisfactory, but the interview lasted all too long for Alan, who knew of the expected visit of the Phillips ladies.

On this occasion Master Phillips had excused himself. He had always regretted the break in his friendship with George Leslie since his marriage. He had not misunderstood the cause, nor resented it, for he loved his wife very dearly and it was no surprise to him that others should do the same. But he did regret and even had begun to fear George's hitherto concealed but now declared hatred of himself and all of his family. The civil war inevitably put opportunity for fake witness, lying accusations and suchlike evil in the conduct of family feuds. George had already attacked those loyalist Oxford members of his family that he considered his enemies. What might he not do now that the Protector's army had become so powerful in the land that Cromwell himself, though he had taken supreme power, might not be inclined to protect one who was a merchant and manufacturer above all, a Parliamentary party member still serving in the so-called 'Rump', liable to be dissolved now at any time. But a religious fanatic, never. It amazed Master Phillips to hear some of the twisted interpretation George put upon certain of his sayings and doings at home. The man must have a very morbid imagination.

Mistress Cynthia, however, paid little attention to her husband's misgivings. The house in Paternoster Row had been her grandfather's property; she had a perfect right to visit there as her father did, however infrequently now in his old age. Mistress Leslie had warned her of George Leslie's increasingly frequent appearance. She wanted to know more of this.

'He is insolent,' Mistress Leslie said. 'He speaks as if he owns this house, because it belonged to his grandfather.'

'Through his mother,' Mistress Phillips answered. 'I through my father, though I make no claim, for old Doctor Ogilvy left it to his elder son, my uncle Arthur, and it passed from him to his own adopted son, Colonel Ogilvy.'

Mistress Leslie sighed.

'Another part, that, of this private war Master George wages.'

Susan Phillips, who had heard all this too many times to keep any interest in it, now lifted from the table in the parlour a new minted book with a title she did not understand, but her mother did, for Master Phillips had told her of its unfortunate popularity.

'Put it down, child,' she ordered. 'That is no fit reading for you.'

'But what does its name mean?' the girl asked.

'It means "Image of a King" and purports to have been written by Charles Stuart, the convicted betrayer of his country.'

Mistress Leslie flushed deeply and was about to retort when Alan Ogilvy was announced. He was surprised by the sudden hush that fell upon the room, for he had heard raised voices as he mounted the stairs behind Hannah. But when the door closed behind him, Mistress Leslie, obviously relieved by the interruption, explained his presence to her visitors and asked him how he had fared with Sir Thomas.

'Exceeding well, madam,' he said. 'I may return to Oxford forthwith and have every prospect of employment there.'

Congratulations and compliments followed, the conversation became general. By skilful movement Alan managed to reach Susan's side. She still held the disputed book, so he begged to be shown it, and having seen, told her he knew of its provenance.

'I think it will be proscribed,' he said, 'as lying, traitorous matter. Already I hear the great writer Milton hath been ordered to write a pamphlet, refuting it and the authorship. He will have to comply, but few will read his work. Besides, he is for freedom of speech in his defence of the Press.'

'And liberty of conscience as our Lord Protector declares,' said Mistress Phillips firmly.

Again the growing argument was interrupted, but this time more alarmingly. For George Leslie, eager, aggressive, his face twisted into a mask of spite, burst unannounced into the room, followed by two helmeted guards of the New Model Army.

Alan, sharing the general astonishment, still held the *Eikon Basilike* in his hand. But he felt it taken swiftly from him and heard Susan's gentle voice whisper, 'Deny you have it or have seen it!'

He let it go and did not at once turn to look at her. When he did so, the book had disappeared, but she was holding one full sleeve against the waist of her wide gown.

'You have a traitor in your house, madam!' George said fiercely, addressing Mistress Leslie. 'This young man, son of my mother's bastard, hath brought subversive matter, a scurrilous libel of a book, into your house. I am here to arrest him in the name of the Commonwealth!'

Of all the faces in the room the whitest, the most shocked, was that of Mistress Phillips, but Leslie ignored her presence completely for the whole time he was there. Alan moved a hand to his sword hilt on hearing the insult to his father, but dropped it when the soldiers took a step towards him.

Mistress Leslie, pale-lipped, said quickly, 'I have no book – '

'You engage in plotting with this young scoundrel, who is in the pay of the exiled Charles Stuart.'

'I deny it.'

'The magistrate shall decide.'

Clearly there was nothing to be done, Alan knew, until he was before a magistrate to whom he might show his letter from Sir Thomas Hobbes. He had recovered from the shock of George's appearance, so he bowed the women a polite farewell and left between the two guards.

As they reached the gate upon the street, just beyond the door, Alan caught sight of a large passing figure. He called, 'Master Carver! Master Richard Carver!'

The man turned and at once came back, staring until he recognized the caller, when he smiled and held out a hand. But George Leslie behind cried, 'Out of the way there! I have this fellow under arrest! Out of the way in the name of the Commonwealth!'

Carver paid no attention to this order. He clasped Alan's hand, while his bulk prevented the soldiers from moving through the gate.

'And how be thee, young sir?' the seaman asked, 'since thee crewed with me in that crisis we met on our way to Holland?'

He laid emphasis on the last word and smiled again. Leslie repeated his order in a still more furious voice. People in the street began to stop and stare. The bells of Saint Paul's rang out the hour, but still Master Carver, mate of *Surprise*, held Alan's hand and asked in his great voice above the noise around, 'Be thee in trouble then, young sir?'

'They are making a grave mistake, master mate,' Alan yelled back. 'But they take me to a magistrate, none the less.'

'Then I will come with thee, friend,' said Quaker Carver. 'And we will lead the way.'

CHAPTER TEN

George Leslie was speechless with rage, but he saw that he was rapidly becoming a figure of fun to the growing crowd in Paternoster Row. His intended victim was walking calmly forward, still in pleasant conversation with the burly seaman who appeared to be a friend of his. The soldiers had moved on also, to keep in touch with the man they had been ordered to arrest. This left George to bring up the rear, a position he had never dreamed of holding.

However, both Carver and the soldiers seemed to know the way to the local court, for they stopped when they reached the outside of a guarded building and turned about to wait for Master Leslie, who arrived scarlet-faced and panting, his temper imperfectly controlled.

'Of what are thee accused?' Carver asked, seeing that Alan was not afraid, but calm and confident.

'It is rooted in a family quarrel, I think,' the young man answered, 'which doth in no way concern me, as I think I can prove readily.'

'You remain in England?'

'I study in Oxford.'

'He lies,' George broke in. 'Begone, sir, whoever you are. I see by your speech you are a Quaker. Take care I do not arrest you too, for presuming to speak to my prisoner, a traitor, as I shall prove.'

Master Carver turned his back upon the angry man, but as he was on his way to visit others of his sect and had no intention of rousing action against himself or them, he took leave of Alan and walked away towards Cheapside.

The magistrate was less than sympathetic to what he saw at once was a trumped-up charge against Alan. Too many of these private feuds were coming his way now and being a conscientious man with a feeling for justice, he was sickened by them. Also he recognized the man, George Leslie, as an active member of the parliament, a warped scholar, very eager in defence of the new government, probably one of Thurloe's spies, always on the track of improbable plots. Or real treacheries? Magistrate Stringer did not want to know which. His business lay with theft and fraud and petty violence and street crimes of every kind.

The young man before him now did not appear to be criminal in any way. He was not affected by Master Leslie's bitter accusations, merely waiting, it seemed, for his own turn to answer them.

Which he did very effectively by producing his letter from the well-known and much-respected Sir Thomas Hobbes, mathematician and philosopher. Since the letter was addressed to no less a person than the Protector's brother-in-law Master James Wilkins of Wadham College at Oxford, recommending this youth –

'What is your name, young man?' he asked, keeping his hand on the letter and looking up at Alan.

'Alan Ogilvy,' the accused said calmly, holding out his hand for his property.

George Leslie stepped forward to snatch the document, but one of the soldiers put out a stout arm to bar his way.

'I think this is none of your business, sir,' the magistrate said, moving the letter still nearer to himself.

He turned to Alan and began to question him closely about his parentage, his relationship with the Ogilvys, past and present, his upbringing, his early studies in Oxford, his visits to his parents abroad.

Alan was never more thankful than now that his father's career had been so little mixed with the Civil War in England. And even now was not directly involved in the exiled King's movements, nor the latter's plans for the future. The magistrate failed altogether to ask Alan if he himself was, or had been, employed by Charles Stuart, the older or the younger, though George Leslie intervened several times with hints that he knew of some secret activities that proved exactly the opposite of what his half-nephew was saying.

As indeed he did, Alan thought, laughing inwardly, as he remembered escaping from Lucy Walter's house in Dordrecht just in time to avoid the pursuer.

But the magistrate ignored Master Leslie. He found Alan truthful, straightforward, serious, well behaved. He folded the letter from Sir Thomas Hobbes and gave it back to the young man. He dismissed the soldiers, he told George he was mistaken about young Master Ogilvy. He advised him in a cold voice to take more care in forming his accusations. This was not the first time. He remembered a certain occasion when even that worthy cloth manufacturer and merchant, Master Hugh Phillips, had been mentioned as less than loyal to the Commonwealth.

Alan, his letter securely stowed inside his jacket, had been turning away after bowing his thanks politely to the magistrate, when he heard Master Phillips's name mentioned. So he did not hurry away from the court, but waited for Master Leslie to join him at the door. When the latter did so he bowed very politely again and said, 'I trust you are now convinced of my innocence, Uncle George. I go at once with my recommendation to Oxford, where I look to stay with my great-uncle Richard.'

'Where you go does not concern me, impudent puppy that you are,' George hissed at him. 'I neither trust your word nor your intention.'

He checked himself as he was about to say something of his own intentions, muttered a brief curse on the whole tribe of Ogilvy and began to move away, at first slowly, then at a good pace.

Alan started to go off in the opposite direction, his mind much troubled by Leslie's hatred. He had not gone more than a few steps when Richard Carver's large figure joined him and his deep gentle voice said, 'I see thee hath thy liberty, friend.'

'Oh yes,' Alan answered. 'But I never had much fear of losing it.'

He explained everything that had been said after Carver had left the courthouse door and added, 'I am indeed much beholdened to you, sir, for giving me such aid and comfort in my distress.'

As the seaman made no answer to this he went on, 'I was inclined to let my anger rule me under the fellow's continued abuse and had I done so and attacked him it might well have been the end of me. My father hath complained often of our family quickness of temper and how it betrayed him in his own youth. You showed me how it might be ruled.'

'Read thy bible, friend,' Carver said after a pause. 'Learn the rule of God and of his son, Jesus Christ our Lord. It is simple, it is the Way, but hard to follow.'

Alan bowed his head but found no answer. He had heard this sort of thing before, but found it cant of an embarrassing kind. In Carver's mouth and in these circumstances he did not find it cant, but he still had nothing to say.

Presently the seaman stopped and said, 'We part here. I go to visit some of my people who suffer for their Faith because they preach peace and goodwill, and pure faith.'

Alan, looking up, saw they had come outside the prison.

'Is it safe for you to go in to see them?' he asked awkwardly.

'I take them the wherewithal to feed them. The turnkey does not object to share the bodily sustenance and so does not withhold the spiritual.'

They shook hands and Alan turned away to go back to Paternoster Row, much impressed by his whole experience and particularly by the Quaker's deep assurance.

He found Mistress Leslie still much shaken by George Leslie's rude invasion. She burst into tears when Alan arrived, unhurt and unhindered in his plans. She kept exclaiming, 'That wicked man! That cruel wretch! Poor Cynthia! Poor lamb! To wish such evil to her when it was he himself put her in touch with his friend, Master Phillips!'

'So that was the way of it?' Alan said. 'No wonder her

preference has driven him mad with jealousy he has never conquered!'

'Jealousy is his second name! He hates my Lucy, too, because she found the happiness with his father the poor man was robbed of by his mother.'

'I would I had met my grandmother!' Alan cried, half laughing.

'Scurrilous rascal!' Mistress Leslie told him, raising a hand to smack his cheek, but kissing it instead.

For she was thankful to see he had come to no harm, which she had feared all the time he was away. She had not seen his protector join the party at the gate.

Alan now told her about Carver's action and she in her turn described how Mistress Phillips had called for her coach immediately and left with Susan, saying she dared not come again until the young man had left London, if he was fortunate enough to avoid punishment. But Susan had lingered behind and then come quickly back to give her the book she had hidden all this time in her wide sleeve.

'Brave girl!' Alan exclaimed. 'Brave and quick-witted!'

'That she hath always been. She should have been a boy and a soldier, her father says.'

'I would rather she remained as she is, a maiden and beautiful.

Seeing the look in his eyes Mistress Leslie said, 'The book was meant for you, lad, though she did not speak your name. So take it. I cannot keep it in this house for fear George Leslie may pounce again. As I am sure he fully intends.'

'Why so?'

'Because he is trying to secure this house for himself and the rules of sequestration are beyond any ordinary understanding.'

Alan did not press her to explain because he wanted to go to his room and handle the book and think about Susan and press his lips to the cover where it had rested in the crook of her arm. Besides, he must pack his clothes and make arrangements for his journey to Oxford the next day. Having no groom with him or other companion he must find and arrange to join others in like case or a party of coaches with attendants. The roads had never been safe from robbers, but now with many destitute sometime soldiers at large, as well as dissenters of strange sects, groups of loyalists and other desperate beings, a single rider took his life in his hands if he passed even a mile or two from the city, or at night even within its bounds.

In this he was successful, though he had to wait another full day and night before the cavalcade he had news of was ready to leave.

The journey went smoothly, the weather was kind, the roads dry, and with little wind the dust lay quiet even under the hoofs of eight horses, for no one was in a great hurry, so the pace was subdued.

As Alan rode over the bridge at Wallingford a man cutting reeds by the river's edge quite near the ancient stonework looked up at the party of riders. His eyes met Alan's and both stared, for they recognized one another. The reed-cutter was the poacher whom Alan had rescued from the trap in the woods by Goring.

Neither spoke, but Alan held back his horse until his companions had passed on, then reined in and looked back. The man had climbed the river bank and after seeing that his former deliverer had stopped, came forward. He limped a little still but clearly got no pain from the ankle and was not gravely handicapped by its deformity. One wrist was stiff, but served.

As he came near Alan said, 'So your leg recovered from your – accident?'

'And the arm. Thanks to you, master. My life as well as my limbs.'

'For your life you should thank God. The ankle too.'

'God did not loose the trap, nor carry me home, though I prayed to Him for help all those hours of pain.'

'You blaspheme, fellow,' Alan said, 'I think it was God sent me to find you.' He was smiling and the man laughed. On a warm impulse he said, 'What is your name, friend?'

'Will Cutler,' the man answered, staring. 'Be you one of 'em, sir?'

Alan saw that he meant was he a Quaker, so he answered, 'I know a seaman who is one of the fellowship. And you?'

'Nay, but there's a parcel of such in town,' he nodded back at Wallingford, 'and they do serve the sick hereabouts – Only – '

'Only they are too godly for such as thou, rascal.'

They both laughed again and Alan gathered up his reins

and rode on, while Will Cutler slid carefully down the river bank again to attack the reeds with more vigour than ever after such a pleasant unexpected encounter with one whom he would always admire and respect as his life's hero.

Alan caught up the rest of his train very soon and the remainder of his journey was uneventful, indeed so dull he found it wearisome and was glad when he parted from his companions to reach his Uncle Richard's house.

He had not been there since his visit with his father nearly two years ago, when they had been shocked by its state of neglect. This was now worse, far worse, Alan decided. The same old servant opened the door to him, but failed at first to know him. When she did so, she greeted him sourly, saying that the doctor would no longer receive visitors.

'Is he ill?' Alan asked, alarmed by her manner.

'Neither truly ill, nor by any means well,' she answered.

'But he is here? He is in the house?'

She agreed, grudgingly.

'Then pray tell him his great-nephew asks the favour of presenting himself, on his return to Oxford to study.'

After predicting total failure, the old woman went away, but came back almost at once with such a gloomy expression on her face that Alan expected to be sent about his business. But the message she brought was quite the reverse. Doctor Ogilvy would be pleased to receive his nephew; the lad in the yard would see to his horse. This sounded promising. Alan followed the housekeeper to the library and went in.

Doctor Ogilvy had aged considerably in the two years that had passed. From being an anxious, indignant old man of considerable vigour and very reckless speech, even to relatives, he was now subdued, shrunken and frail. His white hair had thinned, straggling uncombed about his neck and ears. He kept his seat as Alan went in, but held out a hand to greet him.

'You are Alan, are you not? Or Gordon? Alan is a boy.'

'No longer, sir. It is two years since I was last in Oxford.'

'So you are a man, I see. And they will let you study? Stay in England to study?'

'I was recommended to Sir Thomas Hobbes and have his letter to the Warden of Wadham.'

'I understand.' The old man's voice was bitter. Alan waited. But Doctor Ogilvy did not continue. Instead he turned away his face and after a short silence asked, 'Where will you lodge, boy?'

'I have called upon you first, sir, to ask your advice.'

'Or to seek a free lodging?'

Alan muttered with a red face, 'I would know if there be rooms for undergraduates at Wadham.'

Doctor Ogilvy laughed unexpectedly; a dry cackle that led to a coughing fit. When he recovered from it he said in a more friendly tone, 'I did not suspect you, Alan. You will lodge with me tonight, at least. I have already ordered a bed to be prepared. And you will take your supper with me, if you please. Tomorrow you will consult Sir Francis Leslie who is better able to advise. I am still suspect, though they have cut me off from my work, also from my fellow scholars, except such as remain true friends. You must not risk contamination, nor must I give excuse for their further spite.'

It all came out then. The subtle moves George Leslie made unceasingly, in spite of Sir Francis Leslie's efforts to protect his old friend. The hints, the threats of sequestration, the invented news of his sons, several times falsely reported dead, or again taken prisoner or discovered making plots. All to frighten him, to wear him down.

'I am alone, save for Francis Leslie,' he ended. 'And Lucy, who comforts me for my daughter's loss. I would not have Cynthia untrue to her husband, but it is a sore grief to hear nothing from her, nor be able to send my news to London.'

'There I can help,' Alan said eagerly, 'I will do so gladly.'

He explained his contacts with the Phillips family through Mistress Leslie. Doctor Ogilvy listened, unwilling at first to hear any good of the cloth merchant. But later so grateful for Alan's news that he found fresh questions to keep the young man talking until a meal was served and after it until a late hour when Alan was clearly half asleep and his great-uncle released him to his bed.

The next morning he rode over to Luscombe, where he was made very welcome by Sir Francis and his lady. Here he found a prudent prosperity together with the political neutrality Alan had by now sought refuge in. For himself he still felt a certain degree of guilt, for he had been flattered by the King's favour and by his somewhat indefinite post as a page in the royal household. Besides, he held Charles in sincere regard for his courage, well proved, his wisdom and patience, upheld by his advisers, and above all for his wit and gallantry, all his own and overpowering where Alan's reserved, though far from timid nature was concerned.

On the other hand he had come to admire some aspects of the Protector's administration. According to Master Phillips, commerce had every prospect of success if only the chaotic state of Europe with its old wars continuing and new ones recently begun. The new state in England seemed to be succeeding in the management of finance where the murdered king had failed utterly. So did the New Army and the New Navy. While here in Oxford, in such quiet homes as Luscombe, Sir Francis and others were able to continue their studies and their research with more encouragement than in the past, as he explained to Alan.

'Master Wilkins of Wadham, with the Lord Protector's aid, hath gathered together a parcel of good brains and inquiring minds and firm hearts, the three qualities most needed in the pursuit of knowledge. Use the letter you have with you and present yourself to Master Wilkins. I have no doubt at all he will find a place for you among those who study and discuss the ways of nature.'

'Meanwhile you must stay with us here at Luscombe,' Lady Leslie invited. 'Doctor Ogilvy's position grows ever more dangerous as he rages openly against our new rulers.'

Alan said nothing. Sir Francis gestured to his wife to stop explaining a situation that grieved him very sorely since his own son was responsible for the greater part of it. Richard Ogilvy would have proclaimed his loyalty to the King in any case, but he had been goaded into his major indiscretions by George and that for the purpose of private revenge.

Alan took Sir Francis's advice and found the welcome the scholar had predicted. Among the Warden's colleagues research by experiment held the highest place; discussion, dialectic, argument the second. Sir William Harvey's discoveries about the circulation of the blood had pushed forward great advances in the field of medicine as well as the mechanics of animal and human physiology.

It was in this field that Alan found his main interest. By the following year he knew that he was no scholar; philosophy, even of this advanced sort, was not his aim. But more than ever, his interest lay with man, rather than mankind. The model he would follow was the great discoverer himself. Sir William Harvey had been the late king's doctor. He himself would become a physician, if required a surgeon too. His first patient, Cutler, had proved his innate ability. He could never be a soldier, supporting a special cause by fighting and killing. But a man of healing, supporting men, women and children by destroying the disease or mending the wounds that menaced them.

CHAPTER ELEVEN

For the next six months Alan worked hard and prudently at his chosen subjects, establishing himself in the student ranks at Wadham and making himself known personally at last to Warden John Wilkins through the good offices of Sir Thomas Hobbes, who spent much of his time now in Oxford.

The author of *Leviathan* was no longer welcome in Holland, nor did King Charles consent to any further coaching in mathematics from the great mathematician and philosopher. So Sir Thomas found it necessary to return to England where he managed to make his peace with Cromwell.

In fact the King had used his tutor simply to learn about navigation, for the monarch had never forgotten his earlier experiences at sea. Charles the First had made his son Admiral of the Fleet when he was only ten years old, in the first Civil War. This too the young King had never forgotten. There were times when he dreamed still of winning back his throne by a victory at sea, but he knew very well that Cromwell's new navy and brilliant Admiral Blake made this impossible at present. So when the Dutch drove Sir Thomas Hobbes from Holland, Charles made no complaint. He knew he was no longer welcome there himself. He had spent most of the time since his escape from England in France. But even here his growing poverty made life disagreeable to him. He was already arranging to join his widowed sister Mary of Orange at Spa in the German Alliance, since she too, with her little son, was afraid to stay in the State of Orange.

Alan profited by these moves of his Master. He managed to send news to the King in humble, loyal reports of conditions in London and Oxford, written to his father and mother. These were despatched from Luscombe to London and conveyed abroad from there by Master Phillips, who accepted and respected Sir Francis's apparent neutrality.

Alan was uneasy over this mild deception, but he spoke the truth about his father's employment abroad and the despatches were sent to Colonel Ogilvy, though the whole content was not for him.

In time Alan felt secure enough to make a long-promised visit to his grandfather near Banbury. He carried a letter from his mother, declaring his intention to Sir Francis before he rode away. The latter insisted upon his taking a groom from Luscombe with him.

Lord Aldborough was delighted to see the young man and particularly pleased to read his daughter's letter, giving him and his wife the latest news of Colonel Ogilvy's family. Since his very alarming visitation by the New Army, so cleverly managed by his son-in-law, Lord Aldborough had come to depend upon the younger man's advice. As Lady Aldborough explained to Alan, 'Your father hath been the greatest blessing to my lord. There is no situation we have been forced to endure that we have not surmounted through his wisdom and kindness. I trust you are not come hither, boy, to upset the peace and quiet we live in. Nor excite that evil interest in us that might have thrown us out of our property or even cast us into the Tower for treason or on some other fatal charge. We have feared it more than once these last years.'

'God forbid!' Alan exclaimed. 'But I did consider well before I came hither.'

He explained his work at Oxford and his purpose in pursuing it. He offered to ride back with the groom on the morrow.

'Or we may lodge at the inn here if your ladyship prefers it,' he offered. 'But I think a closer welcome might excite less comment.'

'Seeing you are my grandson,' she said in a sour voice, her Buckingham blood betraying her origin more than she would wish had she been capable of knowing it.

'Why no, my lady,' Alan said, blushing deeply. His mother, still beautiful, always gentle and loving, matched the old earl in her manners. His blushes were not for his own outspokenness but for Lady Aldborough's lack of breeding. In any case the times had changed, he told himself smugly and at once thought of Susan and blushed again, seeing where these grand conclusions were leading him.

Lady Aldborough saw the blushes, was pleased by this sign

of youthful confusion, proud of her rebuke and its effect, as she judged it.

'Nay, my son. You may lodge with us this night and tomorrow. It will be as well you do so, as we expect a visit from certain – from friends of your grandfather – by tomorrow evening. And by then you must be on your way.'

Alan left her shortly after, to find the groom and discover what arrangements had been made for him. The man said little except that both he and the horses had been served and were provided for. The stables were not full and there were farm carts where there had formerly been coaches. But the whole scene was far more prosperous than poor Uncle Richard's grass-grown yard, the cobblestones loose, the wooden doors of the stables cracked, their hinges leaning, the stalls inside broken up for firewood.

He explained his plans to the groom, who led him aside a few paces and spoke in a low voice.

'As soon as may be, Master Ogilvy, sir,' he said. 'The sooner the better to my way of thinking. Those here be uneasy, they tell me. For all it looks so quiet, they know, and the village folk know, there bain't no quiet in the land. The Lord Protector has it all in his big fist these days. And that holds the soldiers too, the big-mouthed major-generals, as they call them. But for how long?'

'Quiet!' Alan ordered. 'I know nought of this, nor want to know, while it doth not come my way!'

The man's mouth twisted in contempt.

'You speak like Sir Francis himself,' he muttered. 'And you but a boy, begging your pardon, sir.'

'You need not do so, since you do not feel it,' Alan said, with a gleam of anger in his grey eyes that altered the groom's expression. 'There has not as yet been any threatening thing that I have not avoided by my own efforts. When it comes to me, I will fight it, never fear.' He added, seeing another change on the man's face, 'And I do not boast, I assure you.'

He turned away without another word and went back into the house. The groom, only partly reassured, rejoined his stable companions.

Lord Aldborough appeared with the rest of the family for the afternoon meal and later took Alan alone with him into his library. Here he demanded all the latest news from France, but Alan, partly because he had little to give and partly because he did not altogether rely upon his grandfather's discretion, made a poor job of it. His lordship was disappointed. Admittedly Alan had worked himself into a position from which he could learn the rebel government's main intentions. But these seemed to be peaceful, placatory.

'The supplanter must needs encourage trade,' he said. 'Learning, too, cannot threaten his position. But he has enemies among his own following. Already his own so-called Council of State begins to fail him. And the first Triennial Parliament, but just formed, will not last out the year. The members dispute together and want alterations made.'

'This I have heard,' Alan said. 'Also that the generals are turning against Cromwell because he hath set himself up above them.

'But you have not yourself been troubled by all this discussion I trust, my lord?'

Lord Aldborough allowed himself such a blatant conspiratorial smile that Alan shuddered inwardly to see it. Worse was to follow.

'Though I live here in great retirement, have given up all intercourse with my London friends, such as frequented the Court in former times, I do have news of them. As I do, they live on their estates, farm their lands for sustenance, which pleases the peasants, hunt seldom, but on well-advertised occasions. At such times we meet where none can interrupt or interfere.'

Seeing his grandson was duly impressed, Lord Aldborough went on to explain his own dangerous involvement in a body of disaffected or as they preferred to be known, loyalist peers and gentry, who called themselves the 'Sealed Knot'.

'Oh yes, we intend to rise when all is ready, all the arms collected, all the branches of our society linked, fully prepared.'

It seemed to Alan that such a loosely knit body of conspirators must come to disaster, but he only said, 'I trust you know and study your immediate enemies, my lord.'

'Ah.' Lord Aldborough spoke thoughtfully. 'That buzzing bluebottle that plagues your family connections comes here at regular intervals. I do not find it convenient to receive him.'

'Is that wise?' Alan could not help asking. He had seen nothing of George in Oxford; he knew that Parliamentary member had been dismissed from Westminster with the other 'Rump' members, but had heard no more during the year and had supposed he had been otherwise employed or had decided to give up his attacks upon the Ogilvy family.

In this he was quite wrong. George Leslie's bitter envy and hatred of his former friend, Master Phillips, burned ever more fiercely as he continued to fail in his attempts to injure him. At the time of Alan's belated visit to his grandfather George was in Whitehall, making reports, both true and false, to his master, John Thurloe, that prime spider at the centre of the Protector's intelligence web.

Master Thurloe had employed George Leslie more regularly since the latter had been removed from Parliament when Cromwell dissolved the 'Rump' before setting up new instruments of government. Master Leslie had come to him complaining of this harsh treatment. Master Thurloe had pointed out that Master Leslie need not complain at the flow of events. He pointed out too that the Lord Protector had made no criticism of his behaviour; he was known to be a loyal parliamentarian, no wild enthusiast, no mad sectarian. He would not be forgotten. As peace and order developed in the land, no doubt a suitable employment would fall to all those loyal members not at present able to represent their constituents. Without suggesting any special field of endeavour Master Thurloe got rid of his complaining visitor; who presently found himself assigned an easy task to compile a list of identities. He fulfilled it grudgingly but fairly fast. He was paid a reasonable sum for his pains. A succession of tasks followed, some in England, chiefly at Oxford, some abroad.

It was not long before he realized he had far better opportunities now for injuring his personal enemies in the performance of his work. He took pride in his ingenuity. Also he had more time to use a certain source that had always been available to him. And with his most recent work in London and near Banbury he had decided he could arrange for some telling blows where they could hurt most.

Master Thurloe's head offices in Whitehall occupied a number of rooms for himself and his chief assistants; the clerks and sorters of the posts, the agents from abroad and where necessary their interpreters. To one like George Leslie, whose work had seldom lain behind a desk, the Thurloe rooms seemed one huge confusion, a sinister ant-hill of secret activity. In reality they held the widest, deepest, most accurate compilation of foreign knowledge that any government in

Europe had ever been able to set up.

'Master George Leslie wishes to make a report,' a young man in sober brown clothes reported.

'Again!' Master Thurloe sighed. He covered what was lying on his table with a large hand and nodded. He was staring towards the door, his hand still flat upon the table, when George was shown in. He remained silent until the door was closed behind his visitor, but then seemed to come to himself, started and said, 'Be seated, sir. You have news for me?'

It was the usual beginning. The silence and the stare had been added recently, meant to hurry up delivery of a report or shake out a complaint or an excuse. Master Thurloe had found them effective.

But not today. Master Leslie produced, in a great many virulent, for the most part malicious words, a mass of detail, relating to Alan's innocent life in Oxford, another relating to Master Phillips's industrious, honest life in the City, a third describing the feeble, pitiful, impoverished existence of Doctor Richard Ogilvy.

'And what do you intend that I should conclude from all this?' Thurloe asked bluntly.

'Why, their overriding guilt!' George protested. 'Young Ogilvy is Charles Stuart's spy. He was in Dordrecht with Stuart's first bastard's mother. He hath been in Oxford plotting with his old crazed great-uncle, received by my scholar father, who cares nought for England, but only for the ancient books of learning. And most recently of all with his grandfather, the Lord Aldborough – '

'One of that "Sealed Knot" who talk together of risings, but are so firmly "Sealed" I think the "Knot" will never be cut,' Thurloe told him.

Master Leslie flushed a dark red but said no more.

'Look you, sir,' Thurloe went on. 'I value your intention, or that part of it that concerns the safety of our country. But I have no inclination or time to pursue family quarrels, nor will I allow it through my office. So I must ask you sort out well your information before you bring it here. Oxford is a sucked orange. Senile dons and young men with a thirst for natural philosophy are no danger. Scotland has risen and fallen again, thanks to General Monck. Whispers are coming from the West country now. You may go to Bristol, sir, and join your former colleagues there. But do not report to me in person again before the winter.'

He rapped on his table to call the guard at the door, turning his head away from Leslie's furious face. When the hired spy had gone he sent for his closest colleague.

'Master Phillips, a cloth manufacturer, late member of parliament discharged with the "Rump". Probable business connections with the Low Countries. I would know these and also his family connections, marriages and so on, children, their ages, activities, friends. Our usual dossier.'

'Phillips,' the other said, thoughtfully. 'No hothead. Absented himself – ill, perhaps – at the time of the execution. But present at the trial. Close friend of that agent you had with you just now.'

'Friend?'

'Sometime friend, I swear.'

'No longer. Bitter enemy now, it seems. Discover why for me.'

The colleague wrinkled his nose.

'Nay, I am not curious,' Thurloe explained. 'But Master Leslie's hatreds impair his usefulness. I may have to dismiss him. Today he wasted my time, except for that hint about Master Phillips. We cannot have a disloyal cloth maker. Far too dangerous.'

'You mean for the necessary trade abroad? These new light yarns – worsteds – I believe they call them. Our broadcloth is too heavy for warmer climes. This worsted makes a new, very acceptable weave.'

Master Thurloe nodded. His highly skilled and disciplined army of agents abroad brought him commercial as well as political news. His net spread very wide and not solely with a defensive aim.

Alan went back to his work in Oxford after spending the inside of a week at his grandparents' house. His surviving uncles did not come there, but Lord Aldborough still expected to hear that they were preparing to rise in the west or in Cheshire, unless they had decided to join the King in Germany. Alan was relieved to find his grandfather had no exact news. So he could give nothing away, the young man told himself with amused satisfaction. He relayed it to Sir Francis Leslie at Luscombe with less than appropriate seriousness.

Lady Leslie was inclined to scold him.

'You speak lightly,' she said. 'But it is no light matter. The country has been quiet for months now. So much the more sure it becomes that this uneasy peace will be broken. Sir Francis fears it and so do I. For the Lord Protector is hated on all sides. The sects detest him, the Levellers would pull him down: they say no man should have more power or wealth than another –'

'Only they do not include the peasant, scarcely the yeoman,' Sir Francis interrupted. 'They would put down, even eliminate, all lords with all the bishops. The former highest and the lowest, who always have suffered.'

'The generals hate his lordship Cromwell,' Alan said, nodding agreement. 'The more so since he has turned the government upside down. He only holds his power through the army, a precarious state, surely. I only wish to continue my work. Men of healing belong to no party, and no sect. I am not disloyal to our real cause, but I bless this uneasy peace and fear its ending.'

Lady Leslie said, 'Amen to that,' but Sir Francis merely shook his head.

Not long afterwards Doctor Richard Ogilvy rode over to Luscombe one morning in a state of pitiful agitation, with news that struck horror into them all.

CHAPTER TWELVE

He rode into the stable yard, shaking all over and grey in the face. The groom could not persuade him to dismount, so he sent the stable lads running to find Sir Francis and the mistress, one or the other or both if possible. The housekeeper, together with Alan whom she had forced to leave his books, came running.

'For Sir Francis and my lady are from home in the carriage, though I expect them at any time now,' she told him.

Alan gave this message to the distraught old man, still sitting his horse in the yard, the groom still trying to persuade him to dismount, while the poor beast hung its head, showing how hardly it had been ridden.

'Uncle Ogilvy,' Alan exclaimed. 'Come within, sir, I do beg of you. Sir Francis and Lady Leslie are in Oxford, but expected home within the hour. Pray let me take you in to wait their coming. Yon beast is like to fall under you for thirst and exhaustion!'

Alan had struck the right note. Careless of his own condition Doctor Ogilvy had never neglected his animals or his servants. So now he allowed his great-nephew to help him to the ground and lead him to the library, where the housekeeper had already set wine and fresh plums from the garden and was waiting for further orders.

The doctor thanked her in a weak voice and when he had seen her close the door behind her leaned from his chair towards Alan and said in an anguished voice, 'The West hath risen! They gained somewhat from the surprise and swiftness of their action, but it cannot last. Already the overwhelming forces of the usurper are pushing them back.'

He closed his eyes and let his hand drop wearily.

'How know you this, Uncle?' Alan asked quickly, dreading to hear the answer he feared.

'James has sent word. Thomas is wounded. They have been forced to hide. If they are found they will surely be lost.'

The old man opened his eyes with such a look of terror and despair that Alan felt cold fear himself.

'How did the message come?'

'I am sworn not to say, but I trust in the truth of it. I think you will be the only help they may find, but I will say naught until Francis advises us.'

Fortunately the Leslies arrived home very soon after this. Doctor Ogilvy had begun to find some strength by then, so he repeated his dreadful news briefly and waited for Sir Francis to give his opinion.

'They must be got out of the west country, that is plain,' the latter said and waited, looking at Lucy. Because it was obvious that young Alan Ogilvy was the only relative of the doctor's family able to help, but was he willing?

Lucy had already exchanged smiles with Alan, so she now nodded to him to offer his services without delay.

He did not speak at once, but when he did he put forward a plan that might have some chance of success or at any rate some prospect of finding the two men. In age they came between him and his father, for they were the youngest of Mistress Celia's nine babies and by the time they were full grown the doctor and his wife had suffered many losses.

These Lady Leslie explained to Alan later that evening. Three of the eldest of the children had died of disease in childhood at the time of an epidemic that had also carried off George Leslie's little sister Kirstie. Later a boy had been killed by a fall from his horse and another had been drowned in the Thames. Three sons had grown to manhood, but one had been killed at Naseby.

'The girls were a disappointment to their father,' Lucy finished. 'Sarah, the younger, is of feeble mind. But only a little so afflicted. Incapable of any kind of learning, but by nature passionate, changeable, difficult. Cynthia, the elder, should have married George, though we may be thankful now she did not. But she wanted his friend and nothing would change her mind. Celia, their mother, had been indulgent in all their upbringing and the doctor had seldom gainsaid her. I think he would have softened towards Cynthia had it not been for the wars and the bloodshed and the destruction. But the husband is of the Parliament side. To that he is totally averse. Also this Master Phillips does truly believe in that cause.'

'But he is no soldier nor any kind of tyrant,' Alan told her. 'Besides, he wishes to be reconciled to his father-in-law, for he hath fallen out with his sometime friend, George Leslie, who will bring harm to him if he may. I would help Master Phillips if I could.'

'Then do you bring those two, Thomas and James Ogilvy, safe out of the fighting in the west and Richard Ogilvy will give you anything you ask of him.'

'Pray God then I be in time,' Alan said, 'for it can only be done as I have suggested. Of that I am very sure.'

He went back to Doctor Ogilvy after Sir Francis had argued with his friend and having calmed his frantic impatience, sent again for Alan to explain his plan further if he agreed to set it in motion.

As Alan explained, he had no chance whatever of finding his way through to the loyalist lines if he travelled by road from Oxford, or by drove road or open moor.

'To leave Oxford by road and towards the west would raise questions at once,' he said. 'But for you, sir, to bring me a message from my father to join him across the water –'

Sir Francis nodded vigorously.

'The boy has sense, Richard,' he urged. 'Take a boat well off shore, Alan, is that it? Then change to some merchant vessel and go down into Devon or Cornwall and go ashore in some fishing boat in one of those many bays or coves or rivers.'

'That is the best way, I am sure of it,' Alan answered. 'If you have any directions for me, sir,' he urged the doctor, 'pray give them to me now.'

Doctor Ogilvy nodded. He had gathered strength since his arrival at Luscombe. He had little hope of full success, but with the promise of aid, though not of the kind he expected, he was prepared to use Alan when no other means offered themselves.

The next morning the young man went openly to Warden Wilkins to explain that his father wished to see him in Paris. This was to help the latter transport his luggage to Cologne where the rest of the family had gone from The Hague.

Master Wilkins knew that Colonel Ogilvy had been employed for many years in the armies of the Reformation countries abroad. He gave his permission, not wishing to inquire too closely into the boy's movements. Young Ogilvy was no firebrand and he seemed to have a real wish to follow the art of healing. He felt that this should be encouraged, quietly and without too many awkward questions asked.

So he gave his permission, together with a little sensible advice. Alan went back to the doctor's house from Luscombe, walking beside the old man's horse. Doctor Ogilvy sent for his groom at once and told Alan to pack a bundle and be ready by the time the man appeared at the house. Which he did with a companion, who spoke with a strange country burr that Alan could barely understand. The three of them set off at dusk on foot, Alan indistinguishable from the other two in the rough clothes he had worn for his last cross-country adventure.

They had consulted together in the stables before they left the house, so they had no need to talk as they went, but plodded on silently like any small group of labourers set upon an errand in the fields. They went down the valley and presently joined the river at a sharpish bend, where the groom, stooping under the poplars on the bend, discovered a flat-bottomed boat into which he climbed first and then handed in Alan. The stranger followed.

Without need for further parley Alan saw the groom safe back to the bank, then cast off the boat, while the stranger took up the oars. When they had floated away the groom loosed his short sword in its scabbard at his hip and went cautiously up the steep bank and after a patient, silent wait at the top while the sound of the boat died away, began a roundabout walk back to the doctor's house.

The two in the boat rowed quietly down to Shillingford beyond Dorchester. There they drew in to the bank and Alan went to find the reed-cutter. As he hoped, the man was willing to keep the boat ready waiting for him if he should come back for it in a matter of weeks.

'Use it as if it was your own,' Alan told him. 'But do not tell a soul how you came by it. Nay, do not ask me either where I go now. But with God's blessing I shall be back. Spread no news. Say no more than you must. I trust I shall be back. I go now from the farther bank.'

'South?' the man said.

'East,' Alan answered, laughing, seeing the other tried to trap him. 'The stream winds sharply here, I think.'

A faint answering laugh came to him but he dared not call out in case anyone was walking down to the ford with a pony or a laden donkey and might be frightened by a shout.

The stranger was waiting on the far bank, nervous and inclined to be angry. So Alan made no explanations, simply tied the boat among the rushes and picking up a strong staff from the bottom of it set off to climb the first range of hills to bring them to the drover's road that should guide them across the Berkshire downs into the valley of the Test where they might pick up another boat to take them on to the sea.

For as it had seemed to Alan that their surest way to reach the west country was by water and he knew that Cromwell had a firm grasp upon the great ports of the English Channel, he should slip away, if he could, from one of those small harbours lying round about Poole or Swanage or from one of the sheltered coves beyond St Alban's head.

It was now that Alan's silent companion came alive at last. He listened to Alan's plan and then offered one of his own. A small fishing settlement where he had once, some years before, floated in on a spar after his boat had broken up in the great race off Portland. He had lived in that bay nearly a year.

So now the story began to emerge. Confident of his wide ranging knowledge, his companions in Penruddock's tragic rising had laid it upon him to set up a rescue of the Oxford regiment of loyalists. So he had brought the message east, but he could give it only to an old man, to one old man, the father of the badly wounded one –

'This you did not say to him,' Alan cut in, horrified.

'What good would that ha' done? To zay there be no 'elp for the poor young feller? Most likely dead afore now?'

And they not a third of the way yet. Alan, exhausted, hungry, decided the whole attempt was hopeless, but he had made too many plans during that night and suffered too much in unwanted physical labour and interrupted studies for him to be able to give up yet. And soon after this they found a small encampment by the river they would now cross but not use in their further progress. Two long boats with horses to draw them were stationed at the bank, the families and crews settling to their breakfasts. Beyond them the river wound through water meadows where bullocks grazed and far away a tall spire showed where Salisbury cathedral guided travellers to the town.

The boatmen gave them welcome and food and fresh directions that sent them on their way with new strength and courage. By the evening they had taken the ferry to the Isle of Purbeck and found the Devon man's friends.

At this stage in their journey two things happened. There was talk of the fighting in the west country, but not excited talk, just interested, a piece of foreign news. And Alan's companion disclosed his name. But indirectly.

Hitherto the man had called him master, or young master. But now the people in the small hut by the sandy beach at the back of the cove were calling him Silas. So without explanation or delay Alan used the name as well, explaining that he was Alan and they should call him that, without title of any kind. They were simple folk and saw no reason why they should not do as he asked, though he grinned shyly when he used it himself.

However, they rested only one night in that place and the following day, after Silas had made a visit to Lulworth, a fishing boat from that village left the cove with two men, its owners, working the gear and the sails. But when they turned westwards after they were clear of the great race at Portland, there were the four of them to fish and sail and keep a look out for undesirable, inquisitive ships on watch for the Lord Protector's enemies.

Alan had not discussed their plans with Silas since the night before, when he had put himself wholly in his guide's hands. He could do no less when it came to finding the boat to take him farther. As the Devon coast came up before them in the late afternoon he moved to Silas and said plainly, 'What now, my friend?'

The man laughed silently. He had a habit of so distorting his face and showing his ragged teeth without any sound of mirth. It had alarmed and then irritated Alan at first. But now he was used to it. The sounds of wind and wave were enough to discourage loud laughter, but to one so used to them as Silas could not destroy his amusement. So now Silas both enjoyed and admired Alan's patient endurance of the last three days, ending in his present understanding of the nearness of enemy country and their need of a good plan to help them to invade it. The young gentleman's eagerness made Silas laugh.

'They sojers has their camp near Brixham,' he explained. 'So we go not into Tor Bay, nor so near Berry Head, neether. Rather into the Dart, is what we aim for.'

'But surely we can't sail into the Dart without catch? They'd know us for foreigners!' Alan protested.

'Who zaid as we'd sail in aboard this vessel? We aim to find Dartmouth boats around sundown.'

'And transfer?'

'Zurelye.'

And so it fell out. The sea along those coasts was full of bobbing vessels around sundown. Depending upon the times of the tides they left the rivers and harbours in a regular rhythm and returned again at the end of the day's work. Silas and Alan, without attracting special attention, managed to transfer to a Dartmouth drifter and having sent their heartfelt thanks to the Purbeck families, kept out of sight while Silas's home friends took him and Alan into the river and on to the fish quay.

The wind had died as night drew on. But the tide was rising, so with the long sweeps out they were able to make slow progress. It was while the two strangers helped in this punishing work that a rough voice hailed them from the water, and a long, wide rowing boat carrying six armed men, four rowers and a leader of some sort came alongside.

'Take my rope, fellow!' cried the one in the stern, turning his musket towards the drifter's skipper.

'Who be you, then?' asked the latter. But he caught the rope as a matter of habit.

'In the name of –' began the other, then gave a slow wink and went on – 'our Lord Protector, God save him!' Putting his weapon down on the thwart beside him, he stood up, with his hands over the gunwhale of the fishing boat. The skipper, staring down at him intently, advanced his own hands close to where those of the other rested.

'Nought but fish, I take it, master?'

'Nought else.'

'Pass, then.'

Stooping, the man drew a cross in red chalk on the bows of the vessel, the skipper called to Alan and Silas, who bent to the sweeps again and the boat moved on upstream, past the little harbour with its wharves and sheds to the wide spreading lake-like bend of the river at Dittisham and on to another smaller lake near Totnes.

As they dropped anchor there and before the vessel had properly settled, a man came from the bushes on the Totnes side, beckoning.

'Go on with Silas, Alan,' the skipper said. 'I think he must have good news, that man, or we should not see him. But I will wait here till morning.'

Silas was now in full charge, on home ground, Alan discovered. It turned out that he was gamekeeper to the owner of Fillingham Hall, a big estate near Totnes, only about half a mile from the river, with an ancient building rather like Dartington, but not so high nor so isolated among housing of a later date. Silas had been in his present employment for several years, since his career as a fisherman had ended with his near-fatal experience on the other side of Lyme Bay. Alan took this fresh instalment of the man's career with reservations. He had found the language of these western parts almost impossible to understand, and though Silas spoke more intelligibly than most, he was not yet so used to his speech that he felt sure of all he heard.

On arriving at the Hall, Silas led the way to a side door in a high wall. It opened easily and they passed through, first into an outhouse and through this down steps to a cellar, from the far side of which they climbed more steps into a great deserted kitchen.

'The two gentlemen from Oxford joined my master last spring,' Silas explained. 'Expecting we should rise first, to be the signal for all about the country.'

'My grandfather has much the same hope,' Alan said bitterly.

'It will take more than one dig and hunt to loosen this fox,' Silas said. 'No cub now. Full grown and heavy. I was to stay here in Fillingham, but render aid of any kind when needed.'

'And that sent you to me in Oxford?'

'My master had disappeared, but young Captain Ogilvy, the elder of the two and stronger, came back walking with Captain Thomas before him on the remaining horse.'

'Like that? In the open?'

Silas gave his silent laugh.

'The moor was covered with them. Still and dead or heaved up on ponies, held there by their friends. To die in the ditches if they did not discover shelter. As this pair would seem to have done even before we came.'

He touched his shirt inside which he had pushed the note the skipper had given him.

'Let me have it again,' Alan said. The note had given directions where the Ogilvys were hidden and finished, 'When read, burn.' It was time they did this, but Silas wanted to keep moving. Also he seemed to be following the directions carefully; they should reach the hiding place within the next few minutes. Even though the kitchen hearth was quite cold. Somewhere in this large, empty house the fugitives had gone to ground. Were they still here in safety or had they already been discovered and a trap set for anyone who sought to join them?

Some extra wish for caution held Alan back when in the end Silas decided to go forward to the room where he expected to find the brothers. It was at the rear of the house, at the side of the big kitchen, where a number of small storerooms housed winter goods in peace time. Since the Civil Wars they had housed bulky clothes, livery and light body armour and had been kept locked, though Silas as well as two indoor upper servants had also been allowed to have keys.

As Alan shrank back into the deep dorway of a larder next to the main kitchen and Silas stepped forward, a voice cried 'Halt!' and one of Cromwell's soldiers appeared in the passage, his heavy pistol raised. He was looking beyond Alan and did not see him. He moved again out of sight.

Alan did nothing. He heard Silas answer, give his name, explain his position in the household; he heard the soldier advance, a key turn in a lock, a door open –

Well, they had moved, that was plain, at any rate. Alan, still undiscovered, still crouched in his doorway, still wondered what he must do next.

But not for long. Cautiously looking out into the passage

he saw Silas reappear at the corner round which the soldier had passed. The gamekeeper beckoned, putting a hand before his mouth to warn Alan not to speak. Inside the room there were three men; two in stained, partly torn clothes, whom Alan took to be his cousins and one, in the uniform of the New Army, stretched upon a bed, seemingly unconscious.

CHAPTER THIRTEEN

There was something wrong in this scene. Alan felt it at once. Where was his gravely wounded cousin? Neither of the two strongly built and active men could be he. And why was the Parliament soldier lying stretched on the bed, senseless, breathing heavily?

Breathing it would seem far too heavily. Alan glanced at him, then at the pair facing him.

'I must beg your pardon, gentlemen, for not knowing how I should address you. For I believe you be my great-uncle Richard Ogilvy's sons, but which is Thomas and which James I am ignorant, for I think I never met either of you when I was a child. I was out of England all those years.'

The shorter of the men hesitated and turned away. The other said, 'I am James Ogilvy. This is my friend – but he would not be known. We forestall the troops – at least – '

'Silas!' Alan cried, springing back to the wall, whipping out his sword as he did so. 'This is the enemy that would trap us! That man on the bed is no more senseless than we are!'

'I have his pistol, master!' cried Silas, at which the soldier who had begun to raise himself, flopped back and lay stiller than ever, while Silas and Alan shot out of the room, bolting the door after them. They left the house by the first outside door they could discover.

Alan was furious. One of his cousins, at least, was a traitor. Perhaps he had been so all along or perhaps he had been bought by the enemy since he moved into the county. At any rate he had betrayed himself very quickly. But to what purpose?

'To save the property, sir. But those two were neither of

them Captain Ogilvy, sir. Cavaliers, may be, come to save Fillingham. These be peaceable parts. We doan't go for to burn nor destroy in these parts. Master Penruddock from Cornwall – that's different. I'd say there's few put theirselves forward that didn't regret it by nightfall that same day.'

'How shall I find my wounded cousin?' Alan pleaded, 'or his dead body?'

Silas, who had guided Alan from the gardens to a coppice and now to the edge of it, disclosed that they were on the edge of the river again at a point where they were high above the water and could scramble down one of the number of steep gulleys to a muddy beach.

'I think if you would go on board again, sir, while I make inquiries, that promises our best chance. I am well known all about here. If my master still lives – even if he does not – it will be natural for me to go about seeking for him and his friends.'

Alan agreed. He was growing more anxious hourly because he had no proof that the tall man in the house was or was not James Ogilvy or had ever had any connection with Doctor Richard Ogilvy. Silas said no, and Silas knew the brothers. But was he to be trusted entirely? Certainly he must finish his mission within the next twelve hours for the parliament soldier's tale of invasion and disturbance, of search and threat, would loose a whole battalion upon the place. There would be every effort made to destroy a highway of escape by sea for fugitives from Penruddock's rising.

He fretted in the smelly shelter of the fishing boat until evening when Silas came back, rowing upstream in another borrowed pram. But he had news. At any rate here he was back. Alan wondered if the whole point of the exercise was to bring him into peril, if not to arrest, as a rebel in his turn.

But Silas had news of the Ogilvy brothers at last. The men they had seen were impostors and clumsy at that. They had gone into the house with the soldier as guard. They had gone to take possession.

'For my master, poor gentleman, is dead!' lamented Silas. 'He was taken prisoner, sadly wounded, three days since and died at Exeter. His men that were with him took him into the town to find a surgeon, otherwise he would not have been taken. Now they too are prisoners and folk say the Parliament major-general is so savage at the rebellion he is like to hang them all.'

'And my cousins?' Alan asked, giving way to his impatience.

'They had travelled on towards this place in haste to find shelter and rest for the wounded one. Rumour has it they are hid by the Diggers along the coast west of the river's mouth.'

'Diggers? You have Diggers here also?'

Alan had heard of this strange sect in the rural heart of England, groups of primitive Christian believers, who tried to live together, sharing all things and growing their food, building their huts, supporting themselves wholly. He wondered how they could manage here upon a rocky coast among a population that lived by fishing, in hilly country rising inland almost at once to bare moors, where small cattle ran sparsely.

'They came,' Silas answered. 'They chose this way and no one sees any need to interfere. If they cannot succeed, they'll go and we shall not have driven them off.'

A hard decision, Alan thought, but he had already decided that these west country people were hard and determined. They lived near the edge of the great ocean: they spent much of their life on it. Visitors must learn their ways or go.

The skipper of the fishing boat gave Silas and Alan a share of his ship's evening meal, after which he pulled up his anchor and began the journey back down river. He would put them off before they reached the town and then drop farther down still to the second bend below the town wharves. If Alan had found his cousins and they were able to travel he would take them on board there to clear the river mouth. But they must transfer to another ship before midday the following morning.

With Silas still in charge Alan was helpless. He had eaten very little during the last five days and except for the night in the cove near Lulworth had hardly slept. He was confused, half asleep on his feet. He began to feel the whole expedition was a fantasy, totally unreal. At any time now Silas would explain there were no Ogilvys in Devon or they were already in their graves. George Leslie was behind this whole extraordinary puppet show. It was not a dream perhaps but it was grossly unreal. George Leslie had made this phantom show. It was intended to destroy him and all his family. The plan would suddenly be made plain, when there would be no escape. But he must go through with it to the end. There was no other choice.

When they left the fishing boat Silas led through narrow country lanes that brought them past the tall cliff at the western side of the river's mouth, where the two small castles stood on either side of the water. Formerly a chain could be hung between them. There was no chain now, but Silas told Alan there was talk of getting one up again. Only the new government did not want to discourage the fishing activities of the port, nor have to rely wholly upon the Torbay fishing fleets between Brixham and Salcombe, farther west.

The Diggers were settled on the flat land between Dartmouth and Start Point. They had been there for just over two years, ten couples and the resulting increase of that time, with the seven or eight children they had brought with them. They had not improved the rough wooden huts they had built to shelter themselves in the autumn of their arrival. But they had taken to the sea rather than the land for their survival. A fleet of small boats lay on the shore above the tide line, constantly attended and worked by the menfolk of the community. Farther inland the pitiful crops of peas and beans showed how little success the women had with a garden, while two goats on tether seemed more of a liability than an asset.

At sight of Silas, with Alan beside him, a group of men came up from the beach, showing a more marked friendliness than any of the cottagers they had passed on the way from Fillingham Hall.

'He lives and improves,' the foremost said to Silas, then waited, staring at Alan.

'Come,' said another and without waiting for introductions the whole group swept the two arrivals to one of the huts and through the open doorway to the hot, dark, smoke-filled interior.

And now Alan did at last find his cousins, barely distinguishable from those who sheltered them, but even the wounded Thomas in better shape than he had dared to hope for. The cannon ball that had killed his horse under him had been followed by a volley of musket fire from the advancing infantry and a shot from this had split his left shoulder as he lay stunned beside the animal.

'James got Silas to heave me up in front of him and he rode off with me,' Thomas said. 'I see we are even more greatly beholden to him.'

The gamekeeper's part in the whole affair now became

plain. He had thought his master's friends would make their way clear of the field of battle and find help at the Hall, for at that time Penruddock's force had secured the success of surprise. It was not until the battle was over by the next day that the result declared itself. Defeat with the master of Fillingham dead and nothing known of the fate of the Ogilvys or any of his other followers.

'I searched at the Hall before the servants went,' Silas told them. 'They wanted no part in the rising, those that were left there. My poor master had begged me to send the gentlemen home and told me where I might find their father.'

'It was a miracle you found me to go with you,' Alan said. 'But once in your own country I think you have good friends.'

He turned away towards Thomas.

'Have you a surgeon among the folk here, that you seem so strong? Or was the wound – ?'

'Less than we feared? Aye,' Thomas answered. 'Also these people washed it with sea water and slaked my thirst with their country wines when I had nearly bled to death.'

Alan was about to suggest he should change the dressing when three of the older men of the group came to the hut. They had serious news, just brought to them from Dartmouth village by some boys that had gone there to exchange fresh caught fish for flour.

The New Army was sweeping across the county, wrecking and burning. Fillingham Hall was on fire. Two thieves and a looting soldier they had captured there had been hanged. Search was continuing in every direction for other men seen leaving the Hall. The fishing fleet was putting to sea at once to avoid being stopped.

'Will they not be stopped by the soldiers who came to us as we went up river?' Alan asked quickly.

'Nay, they were in charge of a friend,' Silas said. 'There has been peace and quiet here for months. The locals have been set over the port. They will all go to ground now. We will have to find some other way to leave.'

'You have done enough,' James Ogilvy said. 'We must look to ourselves.'

Since it was obvious they could do nothing in this respect and that their presence in the commune, if discovered, would mean its total destruction, the only way to escape became clear enough. The fishing fleet from Dartmouth would soon be at sea, therefore their own little inshore boats had better get out there too and if possible transfer the three Ogilvys to some larger craft and so bring them farther off shore to greater safety.

They had no choice, nor was there much time if they were to find any of the fishing boats still within reach as the tide ran out. There was an unnatural silence over the sea and a great darkness where oil lamps usually bobbed and sails rustled as the off-shore wind came over the high cliffs to fill them.

Crouched with three of the young men, one in each of the coracles, the Ogilvys set off from the shore. Alan and James rowed, guided by their boat's owners, while Thomas guided his own rower who kept between his two partners. In this fashion they drew away from the land and moving up the coast towards the river mouth began to see the group of jagged rocks rear up at the edge of the cliff and hear the waves splash over them.

It was a hazardous voyage for the six of them and had it not been for Silas they might never have found the vessel they sought. But once more that resourceful man of many skills resolved their difficulty. As soon as he heard their basic plan and realized that the drifter would leave her anchorage when her skipper heard the army was beginning its punitive sweep of the county, he hurried away, found him about to cast off, but persuaded him to take him aboard.

'I made no mention of you or your cousins,' Silas told Alan later that afternoon as they proceeded, fishing as they went, towards a likely rendezvous south of Portland. 'Not until we was outside the river and tide slack on the ebb. Then I told him you would be waiting for the help he could give an he would. So he called me an old rogue, a proper fox and I deserved to be hanged. Which I would be for sure, I told him, if he took me back in to land.'

'Come you with us, then?' Alan asked. 'We plan for France. At least –'

'I understand you, master. So be it. The Hall's burned, my master's dead, his friends, if they live, will be in hiding from now on. I dare not hazard the good people by Lulworth again so soon, nor are we likely to meet them. Our skipper hath some knowledge he keeps to himself and we must needs trust him.'

Alan conveyed this message to the brothers who had kept

very quiet all day, partly because they did not want to pester their present rescuer and partly because Thomas, who had borne the earlier excitement and danger with great fortitude using his good arm and not complaining when the small boat's movement jarred his wounded shoulder, had fainted away on being helped into the drifter. Alan had attended to him and had quickly found his wound had begun to bleed again. He wished he had seen to it before they set out, but at least there was sea water in plenty to cleanse it again and an assortment of reasonably clean linen pieces among the clothes of the three gentlemen to make a fresh dressing, aided by ship's tow to pad it for comfort. Alan fixed the arm in a sling made from the sash Thomas had worn at his waist. He had taken a hot drink and then slept, on and off, for most of the day, with James dozing beside him.

Towards nightfall the skipper called Alan to him. They were now out of sight of land with the horizon a circle round them and no other vessel in sight. The skipper had lighted a hurricane lantern which he had hung from the stay which passed between his short mizzen mast and the poop. He was still drifting, the great net dragging lazily from the stern. His three crew, members of his family, were asleep under the half-decked part of the bows. A gentle breeze filled the short sail on the mizzen; the mainsail was down but bunched and tied loosely. Silas was nowhere to be seen.

'Young sir,' the skipper said. 'I think you would leave the country. You and those two cavaliers.'

He spoke the word with grim disdain, which made Alan flush.

'They have fought for the King these many years,' he said. 'They would fight for his son, to restore him his throne.'

'But chose a wrong time. Now we shall all suffer for it.'

'*They* did not choose the time. Thomas suffers sorely already.'

The skipper looked at him with interest and liking.

'You must study to heal wounds, I think, young sir.'

'I would become a physician as well.'

The skipper was plainly impressed.

'When Silas told me where you had gone and what had befallen them and you both, I was certain we had heard the end of you. Those mad creatures they call Diggers – '

'Are simple good folk who lack the religion they look for since it hath been put down. So they make their own, after the rule of our Lord Jesus Christ. They generally fail or are dispersed or even destroyed. These have prospered, solely because they have taken to the sea.'

'I was astonished they showed such skill in coming alongside me.'

The skipper stopped speaking. He pointed towards the south, but Alan could see nothing new there.

'If that mast out yonder comes our way, it may be I can arrange a passage for you,' he said.

'All four of us?' Alan asked. He was careful to show no surprise until he heard more.

The skipper's mouth widened in a grin like Silas's own manifestation of mirth.

'I take it you pay for your passage?' he said.

'How much?'

Alan made no move to disclose his purse. He had watched his father's bargaining upon several occasions. The soldier knew how to hire himself as well as others. He kept his money close until the terms were settled.

So it was now. As darkness fell and the other ship, after growing from masthead to sail, to hull, to brigantine, faded to a row of lights as the sky darkened, Alan and the skipper progressed from number to number, from sum to sum and settled, subject to the oncomer's approval, upon an amount that should satisfy them all round.

Silas joined them during this period but did not interfere. It was he, however, who suggested that Alan should give him the purse to hold after they had closed the larger vessel. Silas would make the final share-out.

Alan then went away to tell his cousins what he had done and to have them shade him from view while he slit the seam of his belt to get out the coins he had carried from Oxford.

Before dawn the travellers had transferred once more, to the deck of the Dutch brig and the comfortable cabin where Thomas could stretch out on a bunk with cushions to prop his shoulder instead of the sash. Alan massaged his hand and forearm, cramped by the long hours in the drifter. He changed the outer dressings on the wound but he dared not do more, for the patient was flushed and restless and he feared greatly for the future.

And rightly so. Thomas was in a high fever and delirious before the next night. There were times when they all despaired of his life. Alan was forced to inspect the wound, warned, if only by the foetid smell of it, that there would be greater danger in not doing so. He found decaying flesh and splinters of bone from the wrecked shoulder blade and torn shoulder muscle. But there was no further haemorrhage and when five days later the brigantine came into harbour at Ijmuiden, the fever had nearly subsided and the gaping wound was beginning to close in at the sides.

Within a week from their landing, after they had moved to Amsterdam, messages had reached Colonel Ogilvy, who came promptly to make arrangements for his cousins. The Dutch surgeon who was now attending Thomas was full of praise for Alan.

'Having no exact knowledge he hath used an excellent common sense,' he told the colonel. 'The man is strong and in his prime, but to survive that constant removal from place to place is a miracle.'

Alone with his son Colonel Ogilvy was able to tell him that the King was now staying with his sister, the widowed Princess of Orange, at Spa in the Rhineland. He was living on a small allowance from his potential allies and was beginning to gather about him an increased number of emigrant followers.

'Whom he sees as a future army,' the colonel said, sighing. 'But they are far from any promise of that. I will take James to him, but Thomas must stay here. I think you should go back to Oxford at once. Try to persuade my Uncle Richard to come over to be with him. He must now be in danger again from George Leslie and you too, perhaps, from the same source.'

Alan explained his position in Oxford. He spoke with admiration and respect of Warden Wilkins and the men of science about him. Colonel Ogilvy smiled grimly.

'Do not let His Majesty hear such words,' he said.

'How can I, sir, since I go back to England on your orders?'

Two weeks later Alan was again in London, landed from a Danish ship that had picked him up from The Hague and put him down from a ship's boat off the Isle of Thanet.

He went to the house in Paternoster Row, carrying a letter from his father to Mistress Leslie. She was delighted to see him but he told her nothing of his recent adventures, only that his father had sent for him, that two of Doctor Richard

Ogilvy's sons had reached Holland and wished their father to join them and that he was on his way back to Oxford with that message.

He longed to ask for news of the Phillips family, but though he approached the subject several times Mistress Leslie gave him no encouragement. This he discovered was deliberate when she said to him the next morning, 'Alan, I must know if you will be here this day or if you will be gone by noon, because I have Mistress Phillips and Susan bidden to take dinner with me and perhaps you would wish to meet them again and perhaps you would not.'

She said this with laughter in her eyes but in a very demure voice. Alan blushed hotly.

'I think you know well I have a great regard for that family, though I cannot be of Master Phillips's opinions,' he said stiffly, and then gave up the struggle to preserve his dignity and agreed that nothing would please him more than to see Mistress Phillips and her daughter, whose beauty and charm had never left his mind since he had last seen her in that house.

It was a halting, conventional speech in the gallant manner. Alan had never attempted such an artificial invention before in his life and Mistress Leslie regarded him with pity and amusement, but no unkindness.

'Nay, Alan,' she said. 'Tell me you love the wench an you will. That is honest and true, I think. Nor would Mistress Phillips look hardly upon you, being a sort of cousin. And as for Master Phillips –'

'As for politics,' Alan cried angrily, 'I have lived too much abroad to be aware of our English quarrels when I was a child. Or get embroiled in them as I grew up. I find I owe allegiance to our young King Charles, who is clever and wise and patient and kind.'

'But self-willed and self-indulgent and lazy, they say,' Mistress Leslie protested.

'When there is ought for him to do that can truly engage him, he concerns himself fully in the matter,' Alan answered. 'He loves pleasure, he is very active. I cannot see harm in that. He attracts affection.'

'Particularly the affection of women. Would you model yourself upon his young Majesty's example?'

Alan, reasonable as always, even where his feelings were

concerned, laughed aloud but made no answer in words to his kind hostess.

Mistress Phillips and her daughter came the next day to Paternoster Row. It was two years since they had met Alan upon the occasion of his brief arrest and as swift release. Susan found Alan broader, handsomer, far more assured. He thought her lovelier than ever. Mistress Phillips was most interested to hear that he had been abroad to see his family and that he had found her two youngest brothers in Holland, from where they proposed to join the King in exile.

'I have a letter to bring to the Doctor from James,' Alan told her. 'They would have him join them, since they cannot now return home.'

'I think he will refuse,' she answered. 'He hath never wished to live since my mother died. Yet when we were young we were such a great and happy family.'

She went on in this strain for a time, until Mistress Leslie persuaded her to move to her little parlour upstairs and sent the two young people out into the garden.

Susan was shy, but Alan had lived an undergraduate life in Oxford for long enough to manage a conversation with a young woman to his advantage, apart from wishing to stay with her as long as possible. She got over her shyness very easily in his company, finding as she had before that their minds matched without difficulty upon most topics, so that in the end Alan exclaimed, 'How senseless it is that our two families should be considered enemies, as if we were not related. That poor bitter soul, George Leslie, still seeks to ruin us both, I on account of my father's success, and you because your mother preferred your father to himself. Yet we are friends, are we not, Mistress Susan? True friends, I would have us and more than friends.'

They had come to the side wall of the small garden, near the house, out of sight of the rounded window of the parlour upstairs. Lifting her right hand in his Alan kissed it upon the back and then, more lingeringly, upon the palm.

'I love you, Susan,' he said. 'I dare tell you so, for the times are dangerous and we shall not know when we may meet again or what will happen to either of us. I go to Oxford tomorrow. After that, your grandfather will decide.'

She looked up at him with honest, glowing pleasure.

'I have loved you since we first met in this garden,' she

said. 'But we must not tell my father yet. He would not forgive you for speaking to me of love in times such as these. Perhaps not at all. He is a very strict puritan, though my mother is not.'

Alan's mind and heart alike told him her father was wrong, sadly, perversely wrong. But he understood why the cloth maker had wished to marry the scholar's daughter. Doctor Ogilvy's wife, Celia, had been just such another as Cynthia, her daughter, and now again her grand-daughter, Susan. The same clear beauty, the same gentle, honest, brave spirit. He understood and he was prepared to wait.

'I will not approach him while the country lies under this oppression,' he told her. 'I think the people will not endure it for very long. Cromwell is hated upon all sides. The generals envy him and one another. The Levellers think he betrays their ideals. The common people miss their pleasures, their ale shops, their theatres, their church services. The loyalists want their king again.'

She heard him out, half laughing.

'And you that swore you took no interest in politics,' she scolded gently. 'Tell me about the Lady Anne, your mother, and about the King's Court and the great ladies he favours.'

'I have not seen His Majesty since he left Paris,' Alan answered. 'But if the Doctor will go with me to his sons I may take up my post again in his household.'

He set out for Oxford again the next day and though Doctor Ogilvy was astonished and relieved to hear of his son's narrow escape from death in the failure of the Penruddock rising, nothing Alan could say would persuade him to join them abroad. His house would be sequestered, he declared, if he was not there to be thrown into prison. That Leslie fiend would be at their throats to ruin them all if he got so much as a hint of the whereabouts of Thomas and James. He thanked Alan for all he had done: he wished he could reward Silas. But that must be the end of the matter until the country rose in earnest. And that would not be in his own lifetime, he felt certain.

CHAPTER FOURTEEN

Though King Charles had no body of trained spies to equal in cunning and efficiency Master Thurloe's organization based on London, he did manage to have news brought to him from England and Scotland whenever the indignant peoples there rose against the oppressor. Or this was how it was presented to him. To Cromwell the same news was given by Thurloe as yet another wicked rebellion against progress, law and order.

Colonel Ogilvy begged leave to present his cousin James, with excuses for his cousin Thomas. Leave was graciously granted for an audience.

'We will have the full Council to attend it with us,' Charles told Lord Clarendon. 'We look to hear a true account of poor Penruddock's failure and the whole progress of that calamity.'

'The colonel's son, Alan, brought them off with the help of some local gamekeeper or fisherman that went to Oxford, sent by his master, to bring help into the west country. Young Ogilvy obeyed the call.'

Charles frowned a little.

'Our page, you mean? Who has not attended us this twelvemonth but sends me regular reports, very confidential, yet quite openly conveyed. We would like well to know what Thurloe thinks of them, what he concludes we must think of them, and how much Alan knows of Thurloe.'

'Young Ogilvy has been well advised to stay in England and study at Oxford. He works well there and would follow the great Doctor Harvey in his researches in natural philosophy.'

Charles gave Lord Clarendon a quick glance and nod.

'He hath gone back to his studies, they tell us, at his father's orders.'

'With Your Majesty's approval that would appear the best way he may conduct himself at present. The colonel is here still under military orders, his family, apart from Alan, is with him. And now these two cousins.'

'Who still wait for us to receive them. Pray fetch them in, my lord.'

Charles welcomed James Ogilvy graciously, with kind inquiries for his brother's progress. Thomas was making a slow recovery, James told him. He went on, 'We have been fortunate in having with us our dead friend's personal servant, former gamekeeper, veteran soldier, sometime fisherman, master of many trades and known throughout the west country for his exploits.'

'And named Silas, we have been told,' Charles said, smiling. 'We have had him recommended to us as one who can arrange a passage to England at short notice or a passage from there with little more delay.'

'Indeed, sire, there is a regular trade in these passages with a number of ships of several nations. Silas left us to return to Devon, but comes again to make a full report to Your Majesty of how the people fared after Penruddock's troops dispersed.'

Colonel Ogilvy was astonished by the arrogant tone of this speech. He saw the King's face darken beyond its usual swarthiness and his black eyes sparkle in anger. James Ogilvy was past thirty and so considerably older than the King, but Charles was no longer the inexperienced young man he had been when he finally escaped from England after Worcester. He could not be approached as such.

But with experience of misfortune had come patience. Charles controlled his anger while bringing the audience to a swift end, rather to James Ogilvy's surprise, who thought he had enlightened the exile most profitably.

Enlightenment was on its way. From accustomed sources that brought news regularly to the King, he was told that Cromwell had been infuriated and alarmed both by a minor rebellion in Scotland easily put down by General Monck, now in charge of that province, and also by this latest mismanaged affair in the west. The country must settle, Cromwell swore: it was not enough to defeat rebellion when it broke out; it must not even appear. So he had the whole land divided into eleven regions, over each of which a major-general with effective troops was set. Their duty was to patrol, to inspect, to discipline, to subdue, to punish. The land was become a prison camp, the people groaned in misery.

'The tyrant murderer acts as he would in conquest of a foreign land,' Charles complained. 'As he did in Ireland, in revenge because they would be loyal to my father. It will not advantage him. Already more than half his own army hates him. The landowners hate him. The churchmen deprived of their living hate him. The common people resent his severity.'

For some days the King nursed his distress, refusing all comfort in private and keeping aloof from the public entertainments his Court considered necessary for his welfare. Not that his Council devised expensive plays, masques or balls. They could not afford such things. The royal purse could not always provide enough food to satisfy a young man's appetite, far less his pleasures. But Charles was gay by nature and his present depression was unusual. It came to the notice of his widowed sister, who in turn discussed it with their cousin, the Princess Sophia, youngest daughter of the still exiled Queen of Bohemia.

Mary, Princess of Orange, sent for her cousin, to consult her about Charles.

'My brother is very low, cousin,' she told her, 'since this recent defeat of his supporters in the west country of England. It is time he became reconciled to his fate, it being only four years since he escaped the death he risked by going back to that unhappy island.'

'We cannot expect him to accept it yet,' Sophia answered. 'You are thinking of my father's fate and my mother's astonishing endurance. Charles has a very different nature.'

The Princess Mary nodded. She was sitting in a pleasant ground floor room with tall windows looking upon a terrace above a wide lawn in the mansion she now occupied with her ladies, her little son and those few gentlemen of the late Prince's court who had left The Hague to go with her into exile in Germany until her child was old enough to rule through a Regent. The Princess Sophia was here with her mother because the latter's son, Charles Louis, now Elector Palatine under the treaty ending the Thirty Years War with the Emperor, had gone to take back a part of his unfortunate father's lost inheritance.

'Charles of England you mean, do you not? Or your brother, Charles Louis, the new Elector?'

Sophia laughed. She had a nature as happy as Charles Stuart's could have been in easier circumstances. She liked her cousin in spite of his dissolute behaviour. She was stimulated by his wit as he was by hers. In fact there were times when hints were made in her presence that the young English King admired her deeply. But he never behaved in any way unseemly towards her. She did not know whether to consider this a mark of respect or of indifference.

The Princess Mary could not find it important either way. To her own ladies she explained this.

'My cousin Sophia has a keen mind and a very pleasing nature,' she said. 'But like all that immense family she is wilful and also without any fortune to sustain her wilfulness. With poor Charles a pauper, he must marry a fortune if he can find one. A young wealthy widow who would not be too hopeful of his restoration to his lost throne – '

They ran through the list of his present mistresses, together with their stories of those who had dropped from the royal favour since he left France. But this was all mere gossip and remained so while Charles paid visits to his sister's Court and improved his acquaintance with the Princess Sophia.

Certainly they took pleasure in one another's company, for each employed a lively sense of ridicule, that did not avoid a considerable coarseness, in describing their misfortunes and adventures.

'Ah, Sophie,' the King told her one afternoon, as they strolled about the garden of the mansion. 'You jest like any rough soldier and are not put out when I give you return in kind.'

'Do I offend Your Majesty?' she asked, very smoothly.

He caught her round the waist and moved on, holding her close.

'Indeed no,' he answered. 'In fact, since you stir up my wits, you leave my passions unmoved.'

'This is a doubtful compliment, sire. What am I to say in return? That I am obliged to Your Majesty for due warning of the total indifference your busy fingers impress upon my person at this exact moment?'

They both laughed and she pulled away from him. Whereupon he caught her close again and kissed her hard. But this spoiled the pleasant, easy contact between them. The King released her, became formal in manner and speech, so that the Princess dropped him a deep curtsey and her maid of honour, waiting a little way off across the garden, came forward at a little gesture from her mistress and followed towards the distant terrace.

King Charles stood watching. The Princess was not beautiful, he told himself yet again, but she had a neat figure and a nimble brain. As a companion she could be stimulating and might comfort him. She was not cold. He had not tried to rouse her feelings; such behaviour would be most unmannerly. But he had been aware that his description of his indifference was false and she had been aware of it, too.

What then remained to divide them, to keep them apart? Surely his aunt, the widowed and ageing Winter Queen? And the poverty of that numerous, disinherited horde?

As he walked back to his own part of the mansion, Charles put before himself squarely all those arguments he had invented in favour of a marriage with the Princess Sophia and all those he could set against it. Until he left France he had still hoped for a match with the delicious Duchesse de Châtillon or even with La Grande Mademoiselle. Both these were now impossible. So was a third project, the niece of Cardinal Mazarin, a luscious Italian, but denied him by the whole power of France, the Cardinal himself, the Queen Regent Anne and his own mother, ex-queen of England as well.

He complained that evening to Lord Rochester, who had been sent to entertain his master by an anxious and irritated Lord Clarendon.

'You find us out of spirits, Henry,' the King told his friend, putting on a very regal air. 'What with unresponsive maidens and their suspicious mothers and defeated soldiers with wounded eyes or torn bodies, like hounds finding a superior wolf in the covert.'

'The lady I take to be the Princess Sophia,' Rochester answered calmly. 'There I hesitate to give comfort to Your Majesty, taking into account the life history of that most tragical family. Moreover their persisting poverty.'

'My heart is indeed not seriously damaged in that cause,' Charles said, unbending a little. 'The want of any fortune is a most crying fault in that direction.'

'As for the other, have we not agreed that any rebellion likely of success will take much careful planning and so far nothing useful has been started? There are groups and so-called clubs or associations formed, but there are no leaders, save a few hotheads like the unlucky Penruddock. They indeed have no possible chance of success.'

Charles sprang from his chair with an impatient gesture and took several turns about the room.

'You tell me nought I do not know well already, Henry. Meanwhile that poor Thomas Ogilvy rots slowly in his ruined shoulder, mewed up in Amsterdam, attended by his devoted brother, regretting their exile and haunted by Thurloe's spies, the chief of whom, I hear from Rotterdam, is one of their own family.'

'George Leslie, sire. The Colonel Francis Ogilvy has much to tell of a family feud, that should be trifling but seems to spread as time goes by like green scum on a pond.'

Charles stopped his pacing.

'Rotterdam, did'st say?'

'Aye, Your Majesty.'

Rochester spoke gravely, for he understood the King's sudden interest. Lucy Walter with Charles's little son and her second child, a daughter, born to one of her later lovers, lived chiefly at this time in Rotterdam, passing at frequent intervals from one protector to the next.

'That old crone, Mother Schik, young Alan Ogilvy called her, does she still attend the young whore? Have we news from that quarter?'

'The little Duke is in good health, sire. On the word of one, Master Thomas Howard.'

'We may trust his word? Thurloe is everywhere. There is a rumour that Willis, so far taken to be a reliable informant, may be in Thurloe's pay.'

Rochester sighed. All the rumours found their way to the King however hard his Court and his Councillors tried to keep them from him. They did not allow enough for his intelligence, nor for his easy power over his women, through whom rumour chiefly circulated. So now he twisted his friend back and forth, until at last he understood from him that Mistress Walter was likely to travel to England, to give her knowledge of her first lover's affairs to Master Thurloe's office, on purpose to soil his character and reputation still further. For this she would receive a considerable sum of money and, she hoped, an establishment and an income that would allow her to settle respectably in her native land of Wales.

'So that is the slut's purpose!' Charles exclaimed at last. 'And when will this grand plan come about? Who will escort the lady? Our somewhat clumsy Tom Howard, or that nimble serpent, George Leslie?' He paused and then went on, 'I would my young page, Alan, were less studious. Or less gifted in his chosen calling. He would make a more proper escort for the mother of my eldest son in her visit to the usurper of my country.'

Rochester made no direct answer to this. But he said earnestly, 'It would be most undesirable, sire, that the Duke should go to England with his mother.'

Charles stared. The idea alone of this seemed to astound him. But later, when he had dismissed Rochester with orders to find Tom Howard, he sent for the Chancellor, put the whole situation, as he now understood it, before him, and kept him discussing the probable outcome until Howard was brought in, escorted by Colonel Ogilvy.

'The colonel commands the security of Your Majesty's Court,' Lord Clarendon explained, as he begged leave to retire. Not for the first time he regretted engaging Rochester to rouse the King's interest in current affairs. Matters were taking far too active a turn.

But the colonel received the information calmly. His son had made the whole matter plain to him when the boy had been assisted by Master Howard at Dordrecht to avoid that family ill-wisher and mischief-maker.

'Did the lady come to hear of this?' Charles asked Howard.

'Not from me, Your Majesty. She imagined I had already left the house when she allowed Master Ogilvy to hide himself upon Master Leslie's arrival.'

The King's face grew stiff with disgust at the recital of these unsavoury and vulgar antics. He remained silent for a few minutes and then said to Colonel Ogilvy, 'We would have this matter dealt with discreetly, Colonel, and without delay. First, as to the lady. If she embroil herself with our enemies she must be their responsibility. She shall receive in future no sort of allowance or support from us. Howard, here, shall assist her to cross the Low Countries until she make her decision and it may be Thurloe's man will be instructed to take her to his master. Time will show whom she elects to serve. Next, as to our son. We will not claim him until this uncertain business is settled, but by God he is ours, acknowledged, claimed, entitled Duke of Monmouth. He will be raised as we desire and see fit. Therefore his whereabouts must be known at all times and his welfare attended to and his education in due course.'

'Your Majesty's orders shall be most strictly obeyed,' Colonel Ogilvy said with a very low and formal bow.

Charles's voice trembled a little as he went on.

'We will not suffer damage to our good name and reputation,' he protested. 'Do we not endure hardship enough in our public conditions, without being humiliated, insulted, grossly injured –'

He glanced about the room, meeting blank faces and fugitive eyes. His self-pity was earning him no sympathy, that was plain. And why should it? A pox on them all, he swore to himself. Modest discretion was the chief quality a royal mistress should display upon every occasion. More particularly when her reign was over, and Lucy's had been these many years.

He turned again to Colonel Ogilvy.

'Your son, Alan, sir,' he said, in a firmer voice, 'hath served us well and with a discretion beyond his years. We would not disturb his present studies nor injure him with the usurper's brother-in-law, the Oxford scholar, Wilkins. But we might wish to employ him again in the matter of our son, should the boy's mother seek to favour herself in England at our expense. We would have you inform him of our will in this respect, to hold himself in readiness.'

'It shall be done, sire,' the colonel promised.

When he left the King he sought out Tom Howard, who had been making his report to the Chancellor upon affairs in the Low Countries. Howard had one distressing piece of news that he repeated to the colonel.

'The man Silas is in Amsterdam again,' he said. 'He took ship back to Devon when the Ogilvys had found means to live and Captain Thomas's life was no longer in danger, though he mends deuced slowly. He landed at Salcombe and found to his great distress that the small settlement of those self-styled Diggers was dispersed, two of the elders who gave his party shelter had been hanged, their boats taken from them, several of the young men conscripted into the ruling major-general's forces. He tried to find those to whom he felt himself indebted, but his former friends warned him to give up any such quest, for fear of bringing them not help but final disaster. Silas has come back to the continent, raging and swearing revenge and promising to enlist the King in his plans to assassinate the tyrant.'

'He must not grieve His Majesty further,' Colonel Ogilvy said. 'He has been troubled too much of late and feels his helplessness most bitterly.'

But Silas had already succeeded in his design to report to Charles himself. His story impressed Lord Clarendon as useful in taking the King's mind from his private affairs, so he arranged the necessary interview.

His main object was successful, though Charles had no very

clear idea of what this strange community had been, nor why it had wandered so far from its origins in Surrey. He understood well enough, however, that a harmless, poverty-stricken group of innocent, ignorant, unskilled folk of religious intention had simply tried to help other unfortunates and had been cruelly attacked for it. When Silas had been praised for his endeavours, thanked and sparingly rewarded, the King withdrew into a small room alone and there gave rein to his grief, frustration and anger in bitter tears.

CHAPTER FIFTEEN

Master Hugh Phillips, pacing the business office of his comfortable house near Aldersgate in the City of London, was holding a consultation with various of his commercial friends. They were all cloth makers or cloth merchants and most of them had done very well out of the Civil Wars, in which they had served the Parliament cause from political conviction as well as from legitimate self-interest.

But times were changing. The end of heavy fighting had altered their markets. The growth of intense rivalry with the Dutch in all forms of trade abroad as well as a continuance of piracy with France and Spain made export hazardous, while the home market faded. With the Court abolished, the former wealthy aristocracy fled or in hiding, the gentry in their present poverty living and working to maintain their own lands, the demand for high-grade cloth in the modern designs was negligible.

All this was disturbing to Master Phillips and his friends, though he was determined to find a way in the newly organized State to preserve a modest prosperity for himself and his family. But there was an added anxiety in his life and one that he understood as to the cause, but could see no way to overcome.

His allegiance, his integrity, his devotion to the Cause was, it seemed, once more in doubt. For some weeks now he had been aware of surveillance, not only of his trade, his warehouse, its contents, his workers at their looms, but as well of himself and his family, and particularly of his sad sister-in-law, Sarah Ogilvy, who should have been looking after her aged father, but had refused to stay any longer in Oxford in her neglected parental house.

It had become clear to Hugh Phillips that the elaborate but deadly security exercised by the Secretary of State had reached out to himself again and the news of it had come to his associates, for they had now accused him, demanding explanations.

'I have told you how I am placed with this sometime, but now malignant friend, George Leslie,' he said, for he had indeed discussed this unfortunate connection of his wife's family more than once in the past. He had proved then that George had lied. 'I cannot prove outright that he is Thurloe's spy, but I am made almost sure of it by this fresh action of his in the matter of Charles Stuart's early whore.'

'She that he had in the Low Countries as a mere boy and that bore him a son?' asked one of the older merchants, looking very shocked.

'The same. I am told this fellow Leslie hath brought her to England to lay claim to some moneys she swears the dissolute ex-monarch or some one of her later loves owes to her. But it is a ploy of Thurloe's to cast further aspersion on the tarnished portrait we have here of Charles Stuart and his so-called Court in exile.'

The faces round him, Hugh Phillips noticed, were less sympathetic than he hoped and expected so he fell silent, worried and disappointed by what he saw. One of the more intelligent and well informed of the cloth designers said in a puzzled voice, 'I do not altogether understand, friend Hugh, how you come to hear news so far outside your real interests. The question of George Leslie, now. We all know he is the eldest son of Sir Francis Leslie, that wholly admirable scholar, by his first wife, your respected lady's aunt. But Mistress Cynthia has seen and heard little of him since your marriage to her destroyed his own hopes in that direction. So how comes it you are able to conclude so much about the fellow's activities?'

'Aye,' put in another. 'How come all these suspicions of Thurloe and spying and that notorious doxy with her Stuart bastard?'

Master Phillips's hesitation did nothing to damp the wild flaring of their several imaginations. On the contrary, when he said, with evident unwillingness, 'There is another connection of the Ogilvy family, an offshoot of the sister's branch, that mother of George Leslie, whose half-brother became Colonel Francis Ogilvy – '

'Whose son is that young Alan Ogilvy we hear of and sometimes have seen – '

'And is acquainted with old Mistress Leslie, widow of the late alderman, Angus Leslie – '

The voices assailed him from every side, to drive him up and down his office, holding back the implications, driving off the barbed questions, but understanding quite clearly that Alan, that seemingly reasonable, unprejudiced lad, might be a worse, more cleverly disguised enemy than even George Leslie himself.

'This young man comes from neutral soil,' he insisted at last, to put a stop to the flood of questions and return to matters of business. 'His soldier father has never served in this country, never appeared in any battle of the Civil War. Colonel Ogilvy has never lived here – '

'His wife is titled and her father, Lord Aldborough, is a suspected recusant and a known royalist.'

'Young Alan studies in Oxford and is much thought of by the Warden of Wadham, the Lord Protector's kinsman.'

'And yet is to be seen right often in London at the Ogilvy house which Mistress Leslie cares for.'

Master Phillips groaned aloud. The tone of the discussion sickened him. Either they considered Alan to be an obvious spy and himself a fool to be taken in by him, or they thought he made light of Alan's activities because he was himself partly involved in subversion. In either case he was in great danger of losing their confidence.

He returned to his place at his desk and sat down. Before he had time to speak the venomous colleague said, 'We still have no satisfactory answer to how Master Phillips learned about the whore, Lucy Walter. May we know now the source of that information?'

Boldness was the only means, Phillips decided.

'The information came through Paternoster Row,' he answered steadily. 'I would imagine from Holland, because the woman is known widely to have been living there for several years under the protection of a rapid succession of lovers.'

'From Alan Ogilvy, then?'

'Mistress Leslie has many connections with France and the Low Countries. The alderman was in the fish trade, you may remember.'

'And so have we,' said the youngest and hitherto most silent of the group. 'We have our own sources of information, I think.'

There was silence in the room after this. Until a fresh subject of discussion was put forward that concerned only their home affairs and did not lead to unhappy problems of intention or development.

But the group broke up soon after this and significantly refused both refreshment and any sort of social gathering. Hugh spoke sadly and seriously to his wife afterwards.

'There is a net drawing round me again,' he said and explained the suspicions and hints that had been voiced at the meeting.

'There is nothing secret about that Lucy Walter,' Cynthia said, scornfully. 'But naturally those old sour puritans among you resent her notoriety, while delighting in the cause of it.'

'I think you wrong them,' her husband answered. 'But right or wrong I am in danger from them and I must demand of you that you avoid both Leslies and Ogilvys until this demand for investigation has been dispelled or overcome.'

Cynthia was inclined to rebel at this firm order from her usually mild husband and she carried her complaint to her sister, who carried it in turn to George Leslie. For Sarah, too, had spent much of her childhood in the company of the Luscombe family. Her poor limited feelings and understanding, while making her difficult to train as a child and later to engage in normal adult interests, nevertheless built her into the devoted slave of the man who had used her when he was a boy to secure access to her elder sister Cynthia, at the time he was seriously paying court to her.

Sarah it had been all the time who had provided George with his material for Thurloe and who now, like the maggot in the fruit, was spoiling and eating away the centre of the Phillips family affections, their faith in Hugh, their trust in Cynthia. Also, in fresh spite, Susan's young love and hope for the future, Alan Ogilvy.

Alan duly received the message from Charles to renew his acquaintance with Mistress Walter if she came to England, to bring the King's knowledge of his son up to date and if the woman was not expelled from London immediately to try to secure this or at any rate prevent an unwelcome outburst of gossip about Charles's personal affairs.

George Leslie had made his plan to convey Lucy from Holland to where she could work more active mischief for him. He had acted with some care that the detail of his plan would not be discovered by the other side. He had wormed himself into old Mother Schik's confidence as fully as he had into Lucy's own, though there were times when she still feared and tried to avoid him. He assured them both he did all to right Lucy's wrongs and those of her children and so they must give wrong dates for her leaving for England and settle the children and the housekeeper with the wine merchant Hans in Dordrecht while she was away. But he had reckoned without Tom Howard.

While Alan was considering how best to obey the King's command without drawing undue attention to himself he met, outside the College gates and seemingly quite by accident, a person who brought at once to his mind the most ludicrous adventure of his life up to this moment.

'Master Howard!' he exclaimed. 'What make you here in Oxford?'

'I think you know that already,' the tall man answered, taking Alan's arm familiarly, 'but let us walk on together as friends until we can speak further.'

This they did and when they could conveniently they sat on the bank of the Cherwell in sight, but out of hearing, of any who passed on the towpath some yards away. At first they exchanged casual news of unnamed places and persons until they were quite sure they were unheeded. Then Tom gave him further, more serious information.

When Alan fully understood George Leslie's plan regarding Lucy Walter, he nodded with a face of disgust.

'I have had a letter to this effect,' he said, 'disguised and without names, but the meaning is clear. So they have come, have they?'

'They have come. Leslie has forced himself upon good Mistress Leslie in Paternoster Row, but Mistress Walter is already carried off to the Tower by Thurloe's orders, so I think the villain does not succeed over well.'

'The Tower!'

'From which she will doubtless disappear, but whether back across the sea or forward into her grave we cannot know immediately.'

Alan swore furiously.

'My orders are to discover from her any useful news of the King's son,' he groaned. 'Am I to brave the Tower for that? What construction can our present nest of stinging serpents put on such a request, such an action, even if granted?'

'I think you would have to take her back to Holland if she be released.'

Alan stared at him.

'Why not you, sir? Are you not her friend, her sometime protector? Could you not indeed have saved her from the whole distress and danger of this enterprise?'

Howard laughed.

'Have you forgot the plight we were in at Dordrecht when the lady feared to have our presence discovered by this same Leslie? I work for His Majesty too, my lad. And I have been instructed to see you perform this task and none other. But I dare not appear in public, Thurloe's public.'

Alan argued a little longer, but it was no use. He gave in, with a very ill grace, for it meant leaving his work again, making another poor excuse to join his family abroad, with yet more likelihood that he would never be allowed back to continue his studies in natural philosophy and the art of medicine.

Presently he and Tom Howard walked back into the town, to the simple lodging to which Alan had moved from Luscombe on his last return from Spa. The Leslies had been touched by the young man's careful thought for their safety. His recent long absence had been duly noted in all quarters of power, both university and governmental, and though the apparent protection of the Warden of Wadham was very powerful, the new severity of the law, as administered by the hated major-generals, had been devised to bite. And bite it did, so the Leslies approved while they regretted the need for Alan's departure. They had seen very little of him of late. He did not now warn them of his fresh going.

Tom had put up for the previous night at a small inn on the outskirts of the town. He had his own horse there and when Alan came to him carrying a bundle of clothes and a couple of precious notebooks of his experiments, he found another horse waiting as well and the two rode off together.

Mistress Leslie was thrown into a great flutter by their arrival at the Ogilvy house. Master George had commandeered it in the name of the Lord Protector, she told them. He had produced a paper from Master Secretary Thurloe to that effect. But thank the good Lord he had not brought that brazen whore to the house, for she had been seized as soon as landed at Tilbury and thrown at once into the Tower, from whence all decent folk hoped her next journey would be to Tyburn and good riddance to a false Welsh fornicator –

'I believe the sin was equal in the first instance, madam,' Tom could not help interrupting and Mistress Leslie blushed and stopped a tirade that was quite out of keeping with her usual good temper and kindliness.

But Alan understood her sense of outrage, which was his kinsman's fault rather than poor Lucy's. He said so, whereupon she turned to him and said with tears in her eyes, 'You are right, Alan. Moreover by his evil presence here he has driven away our excellent friends and your good cousins the Phillipses. I have not seen Mistress Cynthia, nor Master Hugh these many weeks.'

'And Susan?' Alan asked, trying to control the fear in his voice.

'Nothing. The whole family, I hear, is in danger now from that devil's hints and lies.'

Tom Howard interrupted again.

'Where is Master Leslie now? Does he still lodge here?'

Mistress Leslie gave a short bitter laugh.

'Think you I would have taken you in had he been like to appear? I am old, I need not fear the future, which spells death before long in any case. But I am not yet so tired of this world I would spring on for death with eagerness. No, he took his things away, looking part angry, part anxious. He gave me no word of thanks nor any explanation, so I cannot tell you if he be still in London or gone from hence. Only I judge he hath not wholly succeeded in his present wickedness.'

Alan and Howard exchanged glances. The latter said, 'Madam, if we may trespass upon your hospitality a few hours longer, so that Master Ogilvy here may rest with you, I will go out and discover if I can how matters lie with regard to Mistress Walter. She came here under Master Leslie's protection, I have been told, to set in order some monetary affairs in her family. In this she was independent of her protector.'

As Mistress Leslie looked from one to the other of the young men Alan added, 'My business is from the King to Mistress Walter about his son. Only that. If I can see her it will be soon and I can return to Oxford.'

She looked relieved and recovered her spirits somewhat. While Tom was away she gave Alan a good dinner and spent a pleasant hour hearing news of his family. But on Howard's return he was thrown again into a deep depression. For there was no comfort for any of them. Lucy Walter was not allowed to pursue any kind of business with her lawyers, family or otherwise. She would not be punished for returning to England without permission. But she would be deported again this very night.

'Alone?' Alan asked, in an agony of doubt, fear and distaste.

'Apparently. I cannot work direct, you understand. If you must see her I could perhaps help you to do so. Whether that contents you and she can give you what you seek must be your own business.'

'By seeing her I fulfil my mission,' Alan argued.

'By seeing her you bring yourself and your family before the authorities,' warned Mistress Leslie.

'And thereby please this vicious kinsman of yours,' added Tom, 'by adding to the sum of errors your family is piling up in serving the Exile.'

'I cannot help it,' Alan decided in the end.

He gathered his things together again, thanked Mistress Leslie and kissed her very tenderly. Whereupon she wept and blessed him for his generous heart and said she would pray for him every day until she heard he was safely away from their suffering land.

'You had best keep over there until the people rise in earnest,' she whispered as she kissed him in return. 'Which they surely will if the present laws prevail.'

'Hush!' said Howard, guarding the door, 'or you will not live to see that happy day.'

Alan, instructed by his friend, presented himself at the Tower as an acquaintance of Mistress Walter, sent to speak to her before her imminent departure. He gave his correct name, clearly familiar.

'You last saw the lady in Dordrecht, sir?'

'That is correct.'

This must be Tom's work, he thought.

'Also connected in kinship with the gentleman who escorted her from Amsterdam, I believe?'

Alan nodded: he could not bring himself to do more. Papers were compared, he added his name to a list. Then he was allowed in and conducted up a narrow staircase to a small room, where Lucy Walter sat, very subdued by her present surroundings.

She jumped up eagerly when the door was unlocked but sat down again immediately, for she had quite forgotten Alan, which was not surprising, seeing she had met him only once and then for a short, interrupted interview.

The jailer shut the door upon him. He foresaw a fee for a private interview and since the lady was to be such a temporary charge upon him, her value was likely to be small and this opportunity of profit must be secured.

Alan soon learned all he came for. The King's little son was, as he had expected, lodged with old Mother Schik at the wine-merchant's store in Dordrecht. Mistress Walter would be taken by water that night down river to the Pool and despatched back to Amsterdam.

'If I am able to find your ship I will accompany you,' Alan told her.

'I do not know the name of it,' she answered.

'Does Master Leslie go with you?'

'That traitor! That betrayer! They threatened me with the rack! With hanging!'

'Have a care, madam. The jailer is but just outside the door.'

She cried a little. Alan felt no sympathy for her, but only confirmation of his anger and contempt for Thurloe's spy, his cousin. He repeated that he would try to find her ship. His duty was to bring true news of the young duke to Charles.

So he left very shortly after, handing over several small sums to sweeten his path from that grim prison and ensure the lady's way thence as well. He found Tom Howard at the wharves by the Pool not far below London Bridge. The latter gave him the name of Lucy's ship and waited until both were safely on board. She had been provided with a cabin and was guarded there by a Commonwealth man until the vessel was about to sail.

So Alan fulfilled his mission. He delivered a full account of it, first to Lord Clarendon, then in private audience to the King, who was graciously pleased to commend him.

'You have shaped well, sir,' Charles said. 'Well, successfully, modestly. We are pleased with this performance and look to employ you again soon. Therefore do not leave us too readily for those learned studies in Oxford. Moreover we fear you may not be welcome in that university after your recent escapade, which seems to have caused no little stir of notoriety.'

Alan felt a cold air engulf him as the King spoke, renewing all those misgivings he had known at the house in Paternoster Row.

His fears were inevitably fulfilled. After some weeks a letter came, brought to him by special messenger from his father, who had been delivered it direct from London. It had passed from Mistress Leslie to a Dutch friend of the dead alderman and from him to the colonel. It was from Susan Phillips. It was addressed coldly to Master Alan Ogilvy and began in her well-formed writing, for all the cloth merchant's children had attended school, 'Sir, I have been made aware of your lying treachery and betrayal, not only of my tenderest feelings but of my family's safety, since you have encompassed our ruin. I must demand that you trouble me no more and I wish I may never see you again.'

The ending was abrupt, but correct. It was signed 'Susan Phillips.' It struck upon Alan's heart like a thunderbolt hurled from heaven.

CHAPTER SIXTEEN

Alan was not too shocked and horrified by Susan's accusation not to wonder immediately what she meant by it. What dire mischance had misfallen the Phillips family and how had it come-about? Some more of George Leslie's mischief, no doubt. But how could it possibly be linked with his own behaviour in any way? All of those pleasant sensible people with their various gifts and abilities had been fully aware that his political views differed from theirs. He was no cavalier like Mistress Cynthia's brothers, no rabid royalist like her old father. He stood on middle ground as far as Cromwell's government was concerned, for there was much he saw as improved and in no way more unpleasantly autocratic than Charles the First's ways of attempting to raise money. They knew this and they knew Colonel Ogilvy had always served the Stuart dynasty, though abroad, and had brought up his own children in a like persuasion.

So what could they possibly hold against him? His only services to the King had been of a strictly personal nature. Though he had gone to Devon, the rebellion there had already failed when he arrived. He had then simply helped his own kinsmen, those unfortunate cavaliers, the Mistress Cynthia's brothers. Again a totally personal matter. He was determined to find out the truth of this horrible and shocking letter.

The truth was harsher than he had imagined possible. It came to him without any effort of his own, in the person of a secretary from Lord Clarendon's office.

'My lord would know how much you can inform him of a certain Master Hugh Phillips, a cloth maker and merchant of the City of London, until lately a member of the restored Parliament, that so-called Lord Protector hath called together.'

Alan was reluctant to speak in any way about a man who was father to the girl he loved. But there was news, perhaps of exactly the kind he needed, so he said, 'Master Phillips is married to the daughter of a great-uncle of mine, the learned Doctor Richard Ogilvy of Oxford.'

'Ah, this is what my Lord Clarendon hath been informed. Can you tell me more?'

'If it concerns my family I will try,' Alan said boldly. 'But first with what purpose?'

The Chancellor's secretary smiled but answered amiably enough, 'I see you are ignorant of the position of that family. The worthy clothier has been purged from the parliament and proscribed. But he was forewarned by his well-wishers and left the country a week ago. He is now in Amsterdam, with those of his profession, his family perhaps in hiding, perhaps in prison. But they are not with him in the Low Countries.'

Alan burst into loud cursing of the Commonwealth, its narrow puritan superstitions and prejudices, its crass stupidity of putting any trust in an evil liar and blasphemer, who deserved a criminal's fate if one of his victims did not provide it first. When he had calmed himself a little he explained who he meant and why he had spoken so of him. He begged leave to see my lord, as he thought it possible the whole matter might have to come before the King.

When the man had gone Alan sat down and wrote an impassioned letter of protest to Susan, with many expressions of sorrow at the plight of her family, indignation that ill could be believed of such an upright worthy gentleman as her father and anxiety for his present welfare. The English Court had heard how ill he had been treated and were shocked and angered by it. He hoped he would be allowed to meet her father, explain all he had put in his letter and have it conveyed to her. In any case he remained her faithful, loving, humble, obedient servant –

The Chancellor sent for Alan, but he did not allow him to see Charles, nor did the King command him to arrange another audience. But he did graciously give permission for the young man to visit Amsterdam if Colonel Ogilvy took responsibility for the expedition.

Charles was very well aware of his own present unpopularity with all three nations embroiled with one another and at the same time with the English upheaval. France, Holland and Spain of the Spanish Netherlands, having all suffered from the aggressive skill of Cromwell's navy, looked with unreasonable but natural dislike upon the surviving cause of each continuing strife. The King was too poor in men and wealth to do anything as yet for himself. Indeed, as Alan had been shocked to observe, both he and his Court were still more poorly dressed and meagrely fed than when he had last attended there. So he was not surprised by the outcome of his appeal to Lord Clarendon, simply thankful for his father's kindness.

It meant confessing the depth of his feelings for Susan Phillips.

'I had not intended to confess our mutual regard,' he said, 'until this woeful state of our country be altered back to freedom, so men may live in England again as they choose, by the light of their own conscience.'

'The men of property, you mean, my son,' the colonel said dryly. 'For those without have never lived by their own will but by their stomachs, dependent upon the wills of their masters and the work of their hands.'

'You would say that under the Lord Protector that name is rightly given? There is a sort of freedom?'

'His troops show a great, an astounding difference from those among whom I served under Buckingham and others before I found a place with Gustav of Sweden and later His Highness of Orange.'

'You do not consider that God has worked this miracle for Cromwell as a sign of His personal favour?'

'I consider that meat and bread and stout clothing have

worked the miracle as they always do and that every good general knows they do. And that Cromwell is a general of genius, but as an administrator makes too many enemies.'

'So we have no hope of that return I long for? Would you approve my marriage if matters change?'

Colonel Ogilvy put an arm across his younger son's shoulders. He loved him dearly, but seldom understood his thoughts. Unlike his heir, who was so like himself in his devotion to the military life that they understood one another almost without speech. Gordon was already a fine soldier: Charles had even promised him a command when the army on paper began to assume a living form. But Alan would go farther in the end, perhaps, with the new knowledge and the new skills. The boy must not be discouraged, but nor must he become mixed in rash endeavours in his anxiety to heal his present misunderstanding. To turn his mind from the Phillips family, Ogilvy said, 'My son, I am content you go find Master Phillips in Amsterdam. I think he may refuse to see you, but you can try to discover how he lives and who are his friends and where are his wife and young Mistress Susan and the other children. And at the same time while you are in Amsterdam I would have you inquire after those two other Ogilvys, Thomas and James. I have had no news of them these many weeks and I feel very greatly Tom's wound may not have healed as we hoped.'

Alan was ashamed to say he also had no news of the brothers and had not set about getting any since Doctor Richard had refused to consider joining his sons abroad and so both helping them and relieving their anxieties for himself. So he took down a note of the last address where they had established themselves to continue the treatment for Thomas's shoulder. He determined to find them as soon as he had, as he hoped, explained himself to the exiled cloth merchant.

With Master Phillips he had no success whatever; the merchant refused to see him and when he tried again the good people he was staying with ordered him to go away and cease to pester them. He gave them his address in Amsterdam, begging them to persuade Master Phillips to allow him to explain the misunderstanding. In a couple of days a very stiff letter came that seemed to finish his hopes, for the time being at any rate, most probably for ever.

'Sir,' the letter began. 'I confess I was misled by your lying and deceitful approach, as formerly I was betrayed by your dastardly uncle, George Leslie. Your commerce with the rebel Charles Stuart and his followers hath led the Lord Protector to suspect that your growing familiarity with my family must be due to my disloyalty, both to my cause and my leader. Your part in this seems plain and confirmed by your attention paid to the said rebel's former mistress, the notorious whore, Lucy Walter. Wherefore there can be no communication between you and any member of my family. Signed, Hugh Phillips.'

'God's curse on that filthy hag!' Alan exclaimed aloud. So that accounted for Susan's cruel rejection. It was easy to understand. Most of those about her would distrust him for his apparent neutrality, his probable allegiance to the Stuart cause, hopeless though it now seemed. Susan had failed him because of her instant jealous rage! She had failed in her love, for it had not been strong enough to hold up her trust in the face of Lucy's brazen presence, the woman's bold, stupid attempt to make money out of her predicament.

All this must have been manufactured, shaped, guided by Leslie in his endless seeking for revenge. Alan swore another firm oath to turn vengeance about upon the head of the evil schemer. He tore up the two Phillips letters, father's, daughter's, and set about finding his cousins.

They had moved from the lodging where he had seen them installed after their escape from Devon. Their fortunes had not improved. James explained that though Charles welcomed his loyal approach he had been quite unable to employ him, for his so-called army consisted entirely of volunteers, unpaid, and would remain so until the King's prospects improved, which they showed no signs of doing at present. However, knowing that James was an experienced soldier, he had used him to train these raw recruits to some advantage, but on a voluntary basis.

Colonel Ogilvy had been very generous, James said, and had even found him a semi-military position with the States government that carried a small stipend. This provided a meagre living for the brothers, but they had to forgo the services of the surgeon who had been attending Thomas and it meant too removing to their present single room in a poorer part of the town, where the houses stood close to a very stagnant canal, seldom flushed out to clean it.

'But the wound?' Alan asked, looking from one to the other of the pair.

He had been shocked at once by the younger man's changed appearance. Thomas had been gravely affected by the serious state of his shoulder after his difficult and dangerous voyage, but he had improved so much, with marked healing and absence of fever, that Alan had expected after so many weeks, to find him cured. But on the contrary, he looked worse now than he had done when he arrived in Amsterdam. He was very thin, very pale, with an unhealthy yellow pallor. He was dressed and walking about, but the wounded arm was out of his jacket, held up in a sling, packed and bandaged; and it stank abominably.

'Young surgeon Alan, egad!' the sufferer exclaimed with a cracked laugh. 'Your first thought, I see. I warrant you'd have it exposed to your curiosity?'

'I know a few more facts of my profession now,' Alan stammered, uncertain whether Thomas resented or welcomed his interest.

'My lasting gratitude if you relieve me of my daily nausea,' James told him. 'I'll go fetch basin and water.'

The wound was foul, as Alan's nose had led him to expect. but he found it healed except for two small open spots, with much spreading, granulated tissue of the kind he had learned to call 'proud flesh'. This, he knew, could be controlled by touching it with a caustic stick. It should then heal if the cause of the continuing suppuration was also treated. He decided there must be a deep pocket of pus here that could be probed to allow discharge.

'Do what you can, cousin,' poor Thomas said feebly, when the first examination and cleaning-up was over. 'I am reduced to a mere skeleton, as you see. I much fear the rest of the winter and the early spring, for my cough has worsened all the time since we came to this damp place and the filthy ditch outside.'

'Cough?' said Alan, suddenly seeing Thomas's condition in a new, fearful light.

'No new affliction,' the other said, trying to laugh. 'I have been subject to it for years. In which I take after my dear, dead mother.'

Alan found no comfort in this, but he was too ignorant of the described disease to find an added alarm. He bought fresh dressings, some caustic, some vinegar and a probe and over the next three weeks produced a marked improvement in the stale wound by the discharge of a considerable pocket of pus that brought with it the final piece of dead bone that had caused most of the delay in healing. Encouraged by the end of pain, the promise of final healing and a certain freedom of movement at the shoulder, Thomas's spirits were greatly improved, also his appetite. He was delighted with himself, began to go abroad on fine days and even to get some strength back into his hand and forearm by increasing their use. But his cough did not improve.

James took Alan away from the house alone one afternoon while Thomas was resting.

'I think you have wrought a near miracle,' he said, 'for which I am everlastingly grateful. But this cough is the absolute like of that which killed my mother. An affliction, a kind of dropsy of the lungs, the physician in Oxford called it. They say it carries off its victims at any age, most rapidly in childhood, less quickly in the prime but no less certainly, and slowest of all in old age, but still fatally. None of us suffered before my lady mother died, but Tom and I were still children at the time and felt her loss most deeply. Thomas above all, except for my poor father. *He* was driven near mad by her loss and I think hath never quite recovered his wits since.'

Alan continued to visit the Ogilvys frequently while he lingered in Amsterdam, hoping to find some way of approaching Master Phillips or at least of discovering news of him. This last he did succeed, through a friendly inn-keeper whose house stood on a corner near Alan's lodgings. He knew the people who were looking after the distressed cloth maker and merchant and after Alan had explained in part his own situation, was willing to tell what he had heard of affairs in England. He did this with a certain relish and smugness, since the Dutch merchants were profiting by the sporadic war that was going on with the troubled island, so long their rival across the narrow seas and also now beyond the oceans.

'This General Cromwell now, sir,' he said, in his fluent English, for he had plenty of business with seamen of many nations and knew something of several dialects. 'This general that calls him Protector. The other generals envy and hate him. The people hate both him and the generals. His own particular army and his own followers, as it might be a bodyguard, obey him but few love him.'

'Master Phillips is still in Amsterdam?' Alan asked. He wanted simple news, not a political report of a kind he had heard over and over again.

'Still here, sir. Still waiting for his wife and family to come over.'

'But they have not yet come?'

'I have heard nothing.'

And so it went on. There was news that Master Phillips was in touch with all his former Dutch contacts in the cloth trade. But still no news of Susan.

Then, one day, loitering beside the great main canal at the centre of the city, Alan heard a cheerful well-remembered voice and felt a heavy hand clap his shoulder.

'Young Ogilvy, as I live, by God!'

It was Henry Wilmot, Lord Rochester, stouter in the body, redder in the face, greying fair hair tumbling about his shoulders, his manner as strongly confident as ever.

'What do you here, lad? I was told you had become a scholar in Oxford, studying under the great William Harvey. You that turned from the sight of blood or even a bout of sea-sickness, as I remember?'

Alan laughed.

'I do indeed study in the medical field, my lord. The interest has dispelled my squeamishness. I should be in Oxford at this present time, but His Majesty required me upon a certain service and now I attend two cousins of mine, former captains in the royal forces.'

Lord Rochester said positively, 'They will not lack employment long, nor you, either, should you seek it.'

Alan had no wish to confide his personal anxieties and disappointments to the noble lord, whose reckless attitude to events was not reassuring. But he was close to despair over Susan and his rejection by Master Phillips, so he asked for more particulars and presently found himself seated with Lord Rochester, drinking Holland's gin and hearing another new account of affairs in England.

'Cromwell's power is still absolute,' Rochester said. 'But he is more hated now than feared. Those rulers lack stability and are coming to realize the country hath no true head. A leader, yes, but they lack a symbol. I have been told they would crown this Norfolk commoner, make him king in the Martyr's place. Already he is addressed as "Lord", he wears a robe, he bears a sceptre. But he will have no truck with the Crown, which is not surprising, seeing he struck off the last head to wear it.'

Alan shuddered: the very possibility of such a thing seemed to him obscene.

'That shocks you, lad? So it does me. But it raised my spirits. For such a suggestion means the end of all the unnatural substitutes for true government that these scoundrels have attempted. It means the growing impatience of a people bound by the chains of an unfamiliar and unwanted religion of puritanical bigots. It means we may look forward to fresh rebellions that in the end must prevail.'

'Surely we have nothing ready that could prevail as yet?' Alan protested. 'I have seen the New Army's power.'

He held back any detailed account of his adventure in the west country, but Lord Rochester had heard most of it from Charles, who had had it from the Chancellor's files of Alan's full report. But the young man did not know this. He could only agree and refrain from adding anything more.

Alan continued to stay in Amsterdam. Thomas Ogilvy continued to improve and as he became less dependent upon his brother, Captain James was able to find and take more employment, which greatly improved their circumstances.

Master Phillips remained totally obdurate; his wife and family had not yet arrived. Tom Howard appeared from time to time, but he had no firm or detailed news of George Leslie. The latter, having succeeded as he imagined in ruining Master Phillips, had not pursued his victim abroad but had seemed to have renewed his persecution of the Ogilvy family in England.

Sarah Ogilvy, upon the collapse of the Phillips family home in London, had consented to return to her old father. She would not go abroad with her sister. She would stay in England, bearing her secret attachment to George close within her shrivelled heart. She would do his bidding if he had any further use for her; as she foresaw he might, for he now began to devise and pursue a fresh purpose with regard to the Ogilvy house in London. He was determined to wrest the ownership from Colonel Francis, whose claim he swore he would never recognize. Now was his chance to force his old uncle from Oxford, present him with the loan of Paternoster Row and secure as well the more valuable Oxford property for himself. With Sarah's help he might succeed.

So Alan, partly from despair over his lost love, partly from an intention to protect the legal rights of his father in London, which he guessed would be threatened, did, when the occasion finally arose, agree to go with Lord Rochester on a secret expedition to the capital, leaving no message to explain his purpose except a single remark to Tom Howard that Life no longer held a future or a plan, but Death in a noble cause was all he desired.

Tom, as was his duty, reported this to Lord Clarendon, who saw fit to inform the colonel of his son's highflown and romantic intention. Colonel Ogilvy kept the news to himself. If Alan chose to make a fool of himself over a cloth maker's daughter, that was his own business. And as for affairs of state, the lad was quite of an age to engage himself in any way he wished.

CHAPTER SEVENTEEN

During the journey to London Lord Rochester made it plain to Alan that he knew most of the detail of the young man's escapade in the west country.

'Nay, do not look so horrified, lad,' the earl told him. 'There was no breach of confidence. His Majesty, at a second interview, demanded the full story from your cousin, Captain James Ogilvy. How Penruddock brought on the action in the west with a certain initial success, but had no support save from those distant counties. The sortie of parliament troops from Exeter, trained, disciplined, well-armed men, rolled up our royal enthusiasts with lamentable ease, so that they fled away westwards, scattering in all directions.'

'To where I found my kinsmen,' Alan said bitterly. 'Led by Silas, that faithful servant.'

'I met the fellow,' Rochester answered. 'He returned again to Devon and brought back terrible news that hath grieved the King sorely.'

'The whole rising was grievously mismanaged,' Alan continued, but Lord Rochester interrupted him.

'There you are very right.' He paused and then said, 'I think you do not know I was there at the start. Do not look so appalled. The plans were fair enough, had each leader concerned assembled and produced those troops he promised. We were to attack upon Marston Moor, ill-fated plain, ill-chosen for a second defeat! Defeat! Battle scarcely joined, with troops appearing late or not at all. Paralysed it seemed and then fleeing at the mere sight of the enemy!'

So Rochester must have fled too, Alan thought, or he would not be here now, quite unrepentant, very cheerful, not exactly boasting of his escape, but ready to do so upon the slightest encouragement. Which Alan was unwilling to give him.

Lord Rochester may have been aware of this for he did not continue his story and did not revive the subject at any later time.

In London they went at once to a house outside the City near the Strand, where Alan was introduced as the earl's secretary and treated as of inferior rank, but a gentleman. The house belonged to gentlefolk called Harrington, related to landowners in Sussex, who had heard of Doctor George Ogilvy, the schoolmaster, Alan's grandfather. From them he heard much about the state of the country parts in this fourth year of Cromwell's reign as Protector. And of the growing unrest, particularly in London.

For a plot had been discovered to kill the Lord Protector, and not by a royalist group, this time, but by a Leveller, one Miles Sindercombe.

'These Levellers have been against Cromwell from the early dissolutions of the Commonwealth Parliaments,' Alan was told. 'This Sindercombe has been devising plots a long time. But Secretary Thurloe and his clever spies were too much for him. He was caught trying to set fire to the chapel of Whitehall. So now he is in the Tower, condemned for high treason.'

Lord Rochester was much occupied with meetings and consultations with various friends and bodies of men, all unknown to Alan. Although he was supposed to be acting as the earl's secretary he was never invited to join these meetings and so found much empty time on his hands, which he spent moving discreetly about the cities of London and Westminster, noting what the people were saying to one another and reading the news in the various broadsheets that appeared.

There was a feeling of tension in the town, of suspense. The hated major-generals still prevailed, but the fear with which they were regarded was turning now into anger. They knew it and it made their rule more strict, more cruel than ever. While Cromwell himself still believed the people should have freedom of conscience, the Army, particularly the Presbyterian zealots who formed its most active part, pursued a course of suppression, persecution, even destruction, wherever they met rebellious or obstinate minds. And still the people must suffer a joyless existence, which the quick-witted, cosmopolitan Londoner resented ever more bitterly, deprived as he was of his ale, his play, his masques, his gambling, his bear-baiting, his cock-fighting, his ribaldry in speech and action.

To Alan it seemed that the time was drawing very near indeed when their patience would give place to open rebellion and he wondered how Lord Rochester could go on with his fruitless meetings, presumably plotting or trying to link up plots for action that never seemed to grow any clearer or promise any but repeated failure. He had joined the earl because he hoped for action, but now he wished he had not come or that he could do something for his own part to further the work of forcing away the iron hands that were holding down commoner and highborn alike, landowner and pauper, worker and idle rogue.

At last he ventured to ask Lord Rochester if there was any work he could do for the Cause, since otherwise he thought he should make his way back to the King's Court. Rochester explained that all was still in confusion, but preparations were always being planned.

'Only for that vile Secretary fellow, Thurloe,' he said, 'whose spies frustrate our every move. I was about to tell you, Alan, when you came to me that I have news Lord Aldborough hath been placed in the Tower within this last month.'

'My grandfather! Upon what charge, my lord!'

'Not treason, so do not look so pale, lad! Some failure to pay his taxes upon his land. They'll have it from him, as like as not.'

'Should I not go to Banbury? My Lady Aldborough – '

Lord Rochester screwed up his face, but said, 'My Lady Aldborough has Villiers blood in her veins. That tribe have strong tenacity and a head for gain. Leave her to protect their wealth, boy. You had better not make your presence here known, though it may be so already.'

But Alan was very upset by this news. He was fond of his grandfather, who had often been very generous to him. He was grieved to think of the old man shut up in that grim fortress, perhaps ill-attended, even denied reasonable food and comforts. So next day, unheeding possible danger to himself, he went through the City towards the entry from the west side.

It was a cold day in February in the year 1657, with icy sleet falling from clouds blown in by an east wind. Yet the streets were full of men wrapped in every kind of dark garment with black hats on their heads, and women in dark cloaks with the hoods drawn forward and even black scarves across their faces. These crowds grew thicker the nearer he approached the Tower, until, in sight of it, he could not move any farther forward, for the mass which he saw, being taller than most of those in front of him, had been halted at the gates.

'What means this crowd?' he asked of his nearest neighbour.

'You do not know?' the man asked, suspiciously. 'Why are you here then?'

'I came to speak to one at the gate,' Alan answered. 'To inquire of the welfare of a certain prisoner.'

'We are here for a like purpose,' the man said. 'But the word came earlier that our man is dead. Dead by his own hand, by poison to escape his persecutor's sentence. Ask me no more. Rather pray for his soul.'

The man eased himself away from Alan and was soon lost in the crowd. But he had heard enough, for the name was soon on all lips about him, a name called in the high-ringing voice of a self-appointed preacher of their sect, the Levellers. Miles Sindercombe, the would-be assassin of the Protector, but here called martyr, blessed martyr, victim of oppression. This multitude was demanding his body that had escaped a more fearful, more prolonged death on the scaffold. The poison that had been conveyed to him had been very merciful, Alan heard voices about him explaining. Not a word of blame for the man's criminal intention. England had come to a pretty pass, Alan thought, when cold-blooded murder of their ruler was condoned in this way. But had not a like murder been condoned and actually accomplished nine years before? The laws of God and man flouted then as Sindercombe had intended now? He shuddered. This was anarchy once again.

A movement at the head of the crowd sent its stir back through the ranks. Alan could see the pikes of the guards and understood their meaning. He turned towards his right, where he saw an opening between two houses only about ten paces away, beyond a group of twenty people in a close knot.

He eased himself gently between them and past them, only to find that though the house walls were separate they were joined at ground level by a six-foot wall of brick that seemed to lead through a wooden door into a shared yard. He paused at the wall, waiting for the expected diversion to make his leap to freedom.

It came very soon. There was turmoil at the front of the crowd, made worse by those behind trying to press forward to see what was happening. Shouts broke out, a clash of steel, screams of terror and pain.

'They are dispersing the crowd!' Alan yelled. 'Turn back! Turn back! Back, you fools! Back!'

As those directly beside him did so, trying to force those directly behind *them*, Alan caught at the top of the wall, which was a couple of inches below his own height. He put one foot on the ringed clasp of the lock halfway down the wooden door and leaped to the top. It was a stout wall some eight inches wide. He stood there for a few seconds. Below him the space he had left was filled with a struggling mass. His good sense told him to leap down into the yard and run away, but his eye was caught by a youthful pair, a young woman and a youth with her, who both looked too frail to survive the pressures and brutalities of this mob-dispersal. He could not abandon them in their obviously great danger.

Throwing himself down across the wall, Alan yelled to the young man, 'Hand her up to me! Quick, fellow!'

His thrashing legs had found a place on the top of the door in the wall, which on the inner side jutted out a little from the bricks.

The young man grasped the situation with praiseworthy speed. He wrapped her cloak about his terrified companion and thrust her up in a tight parcel into Alan's receiving arms, who swung her over the wall and lowered her carefully by one strong hand clutching the clothes at the small of her back like the loose skin on a puppy, while he held on to the top of the wall with his other hand. The girl staggered a little as she landed on the ground, chiefly because her arms were not free to balance her, but Alan had turned at once to help the young man struggle up, and when both joined her she was firm on her feet, her gown and cloak neatly disposed, her hood covering her hair and the sides of her face.

They all leaned back against the wall to recover their breath while on the other side the mob, few of whom had noticed their action, continued to run and shout and scream as the soldiers of the Tower drove them back the way they had come marching.

'Can we leave this yard by the other side?' Alan asked. 'It is plain we must not join that riotous mob again.'

The girl shuddered but said nothing. The man looked about him and nodded.

'This way,' he said, moving boldly across the yard. Alan saw when they came to the corner of the right-hand house an extension of the yard and at the end of it another door in the strip of wall that formed the boundary at that spot.

'Is it not locked?' Alan asked.

'I think they may open if we knock,' the girl said, speaking for the first time.

'You know these people then?'

'They watched us from an upper window. They saw you pull us over.'

Alan repeated his question. This time the young man avoided the answer, but knocked three times on the door, whereupon almost at once it was opened by an elderly woman to whom the girl spoke in what seemed to Alan a foreign tongue or else a very unfamiliar dialect of English. She turned and said to Alan, 'You may pass through this house and leave by the side door by which you can find your way to Blackfriars and thence wherever you will.' He realized then that the English she used for him had a foreign sound about it.

'I am much beholden to you, mistress,' he answered, bowing politely to the girl, 'and to you, madam,' he added, bowing in turn to the woman who had admitted him.

They thanked him earnestly for rescuing them from the crush in front of the Tower entrance and from the charge of the soldiery, but it was plain they wished him gone, so he simply bowed a last time to all three and followed the elderly woman to the side door of the house. She let him out, repeated their collective thanks and shut the door upon him before he was down the four steps into the street. He heard the lock turn and a chain rattle into place.

There was a brass plate fastened to the iron rail beside the steps. It gave a name that dispersed his puzzlement. 'Julius Ritter. London and Amsterdam.'

A Jew! No wonder they had been so reticent! These were some of the foreigners, the sectaries, anti-Christians, allowed into the country by Cromwell's rule of liberty of conscience! Well, why not? Discreet, intelligent, respectable people, Alan decided, wondering why they had let themselves be exposed to a Leveller mob, bigoted at any time and rendered furious by the death of Sindercombe. They had been told it was self-inflicted, but in the shock of hearing this news, the crowd had decided he was murdered most foully. In any case they were ready to look in all likely places for a scapegoat. What better than a nest of Jews? What group more likely to murder by poison, more quick to strike, than Jews?

Alan reached the house near the Strand without any trouble. He found Lord Rochester at home and told him what had happened that day at the Tower. The earl was not much impressed; he had no regard for Levellers or any other sect. It was the army and the major-generals that mattered more. They had the power. While Cromwell could control them and did so, they need not be feared, but rather regarded as an asset, for they promoted hatred of the regime and of Oliver without being able to bring anarchy to supplant him.

'But we fail to join together for our part,' Lord Rochester said sadly. '"Sealed Knot", Trust". I have been meeting with their leaders, but to no purpose. You were wise, boy, not to pursue your intention to see Aldborough in the Tower.'

'Hardly my own decision, my lord.'

'Never mind. You were not embroiled and you made a most judicious escape. Alan, I have it in mind to leave this land again. I am not well. It is an old distemper; it saps my strength. The King is in Flanders, recruiting for his future invasion. Spain favours him now he is rejected by France and Holland. He is in Brussels. I can give him no encouragement, but I would be with him for such time as is left to me.'

Alan was both alarmed and depressed by this interview. He had noticed the changed appearance of the earl, but had decided it was due to his great discouragement. Now he understood the deeper, more dangerous cause and was at once anxious to go back immediately to Charles's Court.

All this time he had avoided trying to trace the present whereabouts of the Phillips family, chiefly to avoid the inevitable pain of another repulse. He had not visited Paternoster Row either, for fear of bringing trouble to good old Mistress Leslie. But now, about to leave England again for a lasting, further exile, he could not bear to face the grinding loneliness, the loss of a love he knew to be true for his own part, no passing infatuation. He could not go without some real knowledge of Susan's present fate.

He went first to the Phillips's house, near Aldersgate, where he was deeply grieved, but not surprised, to find it empty, shutters closed over the windows, the doors bolted and barred, the stables empty. There was an official seal upon the main door and a sentry posted outside. Putting on a foolish smile and manner and a countryfied voice Alan got into conversation with the man, but found he knew very little about the people of the house, except that the master had fled to Holland for some kind of treason and the rest of the family had left London some weeks back.

This was what he had expected to hear all along. He could not be sure the whole family had not been together in Amsterdam when he himself was there with his cousins, though surely these two would have told him of it if their sister was indeed in the town. There was, however, one source of reliable knowledge, Mistress Leslie. He must not bring trouble upon her, but he must discover from any available friend of the Phillips family their true existing circumstances.

So he beat down his misgivings and went the next day to Paternoster Row, moving carefully, not approaching the house direct, but passing it on the other side of the road, glancing carelessly across as he drew near to note the familiar appearance of curtains and shutters and furniture at the windows.

There was so much change that he had passed it by before he realized he had done so. All the windows were shrouded: the front door was varnished black and carried a new large, brass knocker of ugly elaborate design. The yard door was open wide, disclosing a new coach, standing at the middle of it, shafts facing outward, into which a pair of plump grey geldings was being harnessed. The grooms were strange, as was a kind of guard or sentry. All were in the same livery, all looked expectant, as well they might, for their master was bidden to the Lord Protector in Whitehall to receive thanks and a reward for his services, at the recommendation of Master Secretary Thurloe.

All this Alan learned from a man in the little crowd that had gathered to see the notable set forth. Alan had kept his wide-brimmed hat pulled down while the man spoke, but glancing up he saw a face he recognized as that of Mistress Leslie's stable lad grown into a man.

Their eyes met, they recognized each other and each grew wary.

'I have kept away as I half feared something of this sort,' Alan told him, in a low voice. 'When?'

'It is not safe to speak here,' the man answered. 'Nor to be seen together. 'Tis George Leslie, who hath now prevailed, may he rot in hell!'

'He will,' Alan assured him. 'Mistress Leslie?'

'At Luscombe, these three months since.'

'Thank heaven for that. You prosper?'

'Well enough, sir. And yourself?'

'You have not seen me. Nor recognized. 'Tis safer so.'

There was a stir in the courtyard. The coach was ready. Alan turned his back and moved away, bending his knees a little and stooping his back to disguise his height. He heard the horses' hooves slide and grind on the cobblestones of the yard and the coach pull out into the street and move away in the opposite direction.

Dear Mistress Leslie was safe with her daughter and her good, quiet, hard-working son-in-law. But still no news of Susan. He must have some certainty before he left the country, must know she was neither suffering for her father's supposed misdeeds, in hiding or worse still in prison. But perhaps they were really all together in Amsterdam.

Amsterdam! Master Ritter! The Dutch Jew, the jeweller near the Tower! Alan stood still as the name and the house and the well-spoken, slightly foreign people he had helped, came again into his mind's eye with a quickening hope. A vague hope, for he did not remember the name of the street where the side door of their house opened.

But he did remember the name-plate and the appearance of one or two other houses nearby. He dared not ask for help but he had plenty of time to spend on his search and he found his way in the end, went boldly up the steps to the door and knocked.

The same elderly woman opened to him. He smiled at her, not ashamed to greet her since she owed him much. But she was still very cautious, very disinclined to greet him and when he asked her if she knew a certain Master Hugh Phillips, who was in Amsterdam, she called out for help and tried to push the door against him.

'Madam, madam!' cried poor Alan, who found this behaviour confirmed his guess. 'I am his friend though he suspects otherwise. Only tell me –'

He was interrupted by a cry from the darkness of the passage behind Mistress Ritter. It was Susan herself, calling in turn for help to drive him away.

'Hear me!' he cried. 'Only hear me! Susan, you must hear me! Madam, I beseech you, I am their kinsman! I am here to help them as I helped your own kin the other day –'

'Liar! Traitor!' Susan cried. 'Madam, you must not hear him! He has destroyed us! We want none of him! Will no man in this house bring his sword against the monster?'

She was white-faced, furious, but not afraid. Alan saw Mistress Cynthia appear behind the girl and two men, with pistols in their hands, clearly unwilling to act, but determined to do so should he leave his position just inside the door to attack them.

He gave in. He raised his hands to show he had not drawn his sword nor offered fight. He bowed to Mistress Ritter and opening the door again himself, went out and down the steps. As before he heard the lock turn and the chain rattle into place behind him.

His guess, far-fetched as it had seemed, had been right. They were in hiding, they were safe at present, they would undoubtedly escape to Holland very soon. But as for himself, his lovely Susan, more beautiful than ever in her passion of rage, more desirable than ever in her fearless if absurd abuse, was lost now for ever. He felt his heart was broken, his despair had no bounds.

CHAPTER EIGHTEEN

When Lord Rochester next came upon his young secretary he was so shocked by the change in Alan's face and bearing that he at once demanded a full and truthful explanation of it.

'You are ill, boy!' he exclaimed, taking the young man's arm and drawing him into the room that he used to entertain his frequent visitors. 'What have you been up to? The price of gallantry, eh, my lad?'

This was so utterly the opposite cause of Alan's agony of spirit and so typical of the former Lord Wilmot's principles of living, that his heart overflowed and he burst into tears.

The old adventurer looked at him in astonishment, but had the good sense and long experience to wait until the other had recovered himself.

'You had best let me have the root of the trouble,' he then said, very seriously.

So Alan gave it him, withholding nothing, not even his small adventure with the young couple caught in the mob at Tower Hill, nor his discovery of the Phillips family at Master Ritter's house.

'You went there because you remembered the Dutch connection and the present whereabouts of Master Phillips?'

'Yes, my lord. I see now that the reluctance of Mistress Ritter to entertain me upon the first occasion was not because they were Jews in that household but because my kinsfolk were hiding there.'

Lord Rochester smiled.

'Your kinsfolk would not be likely to take refuge with people of the Israelite belief and practice,' he said. 'Strict Calvinists, are they not?'

Alan had not considered this. His own parents had brought him up on Christian principles and beliefs according to the episcopalian practice of the Church of England, which his mother followed. His father as a child had been schooled in Presbyterian rules in Scotland, which he had found useful in his long stay in the Low Countries. Later he had adopted his wife's views. As for himself, he was debarred in Oxford from church practices and considered the type of Protestant religion at Charles the Second's Court perfunctory, largely insincere. Charles proclaimed it, but Alan was not alone in suspecting a leaning here towards the Roman persuasion for all the King was quarrelling with his mother over his youngest brother Henry, now living with her in Paris.

'Mistress Cynthia would follow her husband in this matter as in all others,' Alan answered after a long pause. 'So they must be Dutch immigrants, just foreigners, come to set up a business here in London.'

'We will discover the truth of that for you,' Lord Rochester promised. 'In the meantime you must turn your mind to matters of more general importance. I have neglected you, my poor secretary. I must find a means to employ you.'

But he sent Alan away a few minutes later, still heart-broken but less self-pitying. He could reflect that his beloved Susan was with family friends and though not completely safe until out of the country, would probably achieve that object very soon.

His thoughts turned to George, whose success the vile rogue was flourishing with such vulgarity. The scholar's son! How grieved Sir Francis would be if he should hear of it. He thought of Luscombe, giving thanks to God that Lady Leslie had her mother there now, safe surely in that protected and favoured home. He hoped that Doctor Richard Ogilvy, in his far from safe establishment, had received regular news of his surviving children, poor old pugnacious faithful royalist that he was!

He did not know that Sarah had gone back to her father or he would have felt compelled to return to Oxford himself, in spite of his grave danger if he attempted such a move. Susan had given him many hints in the past, but without much real evidence, of her weak-minded aunt's attachment to her wicked cousin. He would have seen the awful possibility of her final betrayal of her own father to the villain's hatred.

But this knowledge came to him too late for any action on his part, rash or otherwise. For Lord Rochester's illness progressed until it reached a point where even his sanguine temper and great physical powers of resilience were overcome and he knew that he must return to Flanders and his King at once if he was ever to see either again.

Before that time, however, a month after the unfortunate but guilty Sindercombe had managed to avoid the Law's ghastly penalty by the added sin of suicide, the Lord Cromwell was again urged to accept kingship. Again he refused the Crown: instead the 'Instrument of Government' was repeated in a solemn ceremony, for which he wore an elaborate robe and was formally given the sceptre and the orb. In fact he was acknowledged king though he would have nothing to do with either crown or title. But more significant still, he agreed to the setting up of a Second Chamber in Parliament, an Upper House, to aid and balance the always obstreperous and argumentative and obstinate Commons.

Cromwell needed this creation to help him raise a sufficient revenue. For want of an aristocracy to serve in it he introduced several of his own family and such was the poverty in numbers of his truly faithful adherents, apart from his army, the question of nepotism did not at first arise.

This Second Chamber was set up in the first month of 1658 and disgust, anger and a new feeling of hopelessness, added to his growing weakness, brought forward Lord Rochester's departure. He and Alan, with two servants who had joined their old master upon his arrival in London, managed to secure a quiet passage from Tilbury in an English ship bound for Flanders. They arrived at Sluys, the small seaport connected with the ancient town of Bruges by canal. And here the earl took to his bed.

King Charles was still in Brussels, they learned. Very busy with all possible preparations for the future. Rochester wanted Alan to carry a message for him to the Master he had served so long and so faithfully.

'I am on my death-bed Alan,' he said. 'I cannot go to him but I would dearly like to see him once more. We should not have lingered so long in England. We did no good there to our Cause and found only ill for ourselves, heartbreak for you and this pestilence for me, that no physician is able to understand, far less cure. Their purgings and bloodlettings weaken without improving. So go you to His Majesty, boy, and ask him in God's name to let me see his face once more.'

Alan, very distressed now for his lordship, made preparations to go next day to Brussels, though he did not expect the King would be able to leave his Court on such an immediate errand. Though Rochester was too impetuous always to make wise decisions and had indeed done a number of foolish and dangerous things in his time, he had been a kind and considerate master to him during their rather pointless visit to London.

But his journey was postponed and there was no haste needed when he did leave. For Lord Rochester lapsed into a coma that same evening, from which he did not recover consciousness, but died quite peacefully before daybreak the next morning.

Alan made what arrangements he could and leaving the two servants to carry them out, rode off to Brussels, where he inquired first for his father and finding he was again at The Hague with the Lady Anne and his daughters, asked if his brother Gordon was with the King's new army.

'Would that be young Ensign Ogilvy?' he was asked.

'It would.'

'Then you will find him with Captain James Ogilvy,' he was told and was directed how to find them both, billeted in the town.

They were delighted to see him, but he refused to give

them any long account of his recent fortunes. Lord Rochester was dead, but Charles must have this news just as soon as he could convey it to him. So he found his way at once to Lord Clarendon's establishment and being admitted very quickly to the Chancellor himself, made a full and detailed report of the position of the Royalist Cause as Rochester had found it, the state of London and its people as he had himself observed it, the onset of Lord Rochester's last illness and its rapidly fatal outcome.

'So the noble lord is dead?' Lord Clarendon said thoughtfully.

'Yes, my lord. Very early in the morning, yesterday. He will be buried at Bruges, the authorities say. But should we not consult his family? There is a son, is there not, my lord?'

'There is indeed.' Lord Clarendon's pursed lips showed great disapproval.

'My Lord Rochester did hope to see His Majesty once more,' Alan went on. 'He sent a message I was to bring, but he died when I was about to set out, so I felt I must arrange matters before I left. There are two of his former servants with the body, my lord.'

'You did rightly,' Lord Clarendon said. 'I think His Majesty may wish to receive your message. Hold yourself in readiness for an audience.'

Alan went back to his brother and cousin, having told Lord Clarendon's secretary where to find him. This time he was quite willing to satisfy their curiosity about his recent adventures. They had been joined by Thomas, whom he was pleased to see had continued to improve in health, at least as far as his shoulder was concerned. The wound was now completely healed and though the arm did not move much in any direction at the shoulder, the elbow was much freer and the whole limb far less shrunken than it had been.

'I have the use of my hand again,' Thomas said.

'You were lucky to avoid surgeons earlier,' Alan told him. 'They would have had it off and killed you most like.'

'My cough remains,' Thomas said, sadly. 'But seeing I shall never be fit for more soldiering, that is no matter.' He added with a smile of great sweetness that would have reminded anyone who had known her of his mother Celia, 'The soldiers call me Captain, though I hold no commission. James hath that rank by right now.'

'The regiment is part of the late Lord Rochester's command, is it not?' Alan asked.

Thomas nodded.

'So we understood when we came here. But his lordship was for ever travelling away to raise money for the King among the Protestant States. And recently with you, cousin, to observe the lie of the land in England.'

Alan continued to stay with Captain James and his brother until Charles sent for him two days later. Lord Clarendon, who had given his Master a full account of Alan's report, presented the young man and then retired to a little distance in order to make the occasion less formal, less embarrassing for them all.

But Charles chose to put on his most regal manner.

'We are grieved indeed, sir,' he began, 'to hear our sometime friend and early adviser in miltary matters, hath passed to his Maker. We will have a – We will have prayers offered for his soul and his well-earned rest.'

Though the King's face did not lose its dignified and distant expression, the dark eyes caught and held Alan's grey ones with a sparkling challenge. Had the young man noticed his near slip? He had almost suggested a Mass for Henry Wilmot's soul. Almost, but not quite. Prayers, yes prayers.

Alan had noticed. He had been amused, even at that solemn moment, by the boyish challenge in His Majesty's glance. But he had learned by now to express nothing unless asked to do so. He did, however, venture to murmur 'Amen', and then stood silent, waiting to be invited to deliver Lord Rochester's last message.

After a long pause Charles said, still formal, very cold, 'Proceed, sir. Proceed. Our Lord Clarendon tells us you carry a message.'

Alan gave it word for word as he remembered it. And the hopeful, muddled, reckless, loving words brought his lost servant and friend so perfectly before the King's eyes that his kingly bearing crumbled, and the sensitive child of misfortune, the increasingly cynical man of unwilling compromise, took its place. He struck the arm of his chair with a swift gesture of helpless rage.

'I could not have reached him in time,' he said, brokenly.

'No, sire. He was never to know that. He passed into a coma believing Your Majesty would soon be there to take farewell of him in person. He had left his return until too late. He would not regard his illness seriously, sire.'

'He regarded few things seriously,' Charles said with some bitterness. 'But I could not have left here to visit him even had he lingered on.' Returning to his regal manner as suddenly and surprisingly as he had abandoned it, he said, 'We have heard of the usurper's present confusion from other sources than those of Lord Rochester and his friends at home. We are aware of plots against him, his own army leaders thought to be corruptible. Without them he would be rendered helpless and easily overthrown. We must take the leadership against him. We must follow every move from our headquarters here, to encourage or to restrain.'

The silence that followed was so prolonged that Lord Clarendon approached nearer to assist Alan's dismissal. This came with a wave of the hand, but as he began to retreat backwards after a very low bow, Charles said, 'You have done well, Master Ogilvy. You shall be rewarded.'

Alan could only bow again and remove himself from the presence and from Lord Clarendon as quickly as he could.

On his way back to the captains' quarters he thought over this audience and what it meant regarding King Charles. Was it grief he had seen, natural human grief, a warm distress at the loss of a long-standing friendship? Surely not, unless His Majesty had a greater power of hiding his true feelings than he had hitherto seen in him? There had been regret indeed, one more useful servant gone for whom replacement must be found. Was that the sum of it? Alan thought of the succession of the King's mistresses, most of whom came and went like butterflies in a garden, while a very few continued as favourites of a seemingly permanent kind, and all the time rumours of an imminent marriage with this or that princess blew up and blew away again as readily.

It would seem then that Charles Stuart had great capacity for passion but none for true love. Was he himself any judge of this? Indeed, no. For he had taken to telling himself now that his love for Susan Phillips had been simply a boyish infatuation and the sooner he buried it finally the better. Forcing this conclusion upon himself in direct contradiction of his former belief he managed to recover his spirits in his cousins' company during the next week. He then begged leave from the King's Controller of the Household, upon whose lists he still appeared as 'page to the Bedchamber', to travel to The Hague. He wished to acquaint his mother of Lord Aldborough's present incarceration in the Tower of London, he said, and also tell his father of George Leslie's seizure of the house in Paternoster Row.

Meanwhile affairs in England followed the course they had been developing all that year. Cromwell's army continued to split away from their allegiance to him. Even his own Ironsides were becoming disillusioned. He found it necessary to revoke the power of the eleven major-generals, because their harsh mis-rule was clearly driving fresh bodies of citizens to the revolt of despair.

The plot that Lord Rochester had found mis-planned was laid bare and its inventors, Sir Henry Slingsby and a Doctor Hewitt, were arrested, tried, convicted and executed for trying to subvert officers in the army, though no treasonable action had actually been made.

Cromwell's popularity, except among his immediate close supporters, sank still lower. The Presbyterians hated him for his tolerance towards all the sects, except the Roman Catholics and the Anglicans. He favoured the independents in religion, so that the growing band of Quakers began to prosper at last, few being cast into prison, though most of those already there continued to be left inside.

The Second House was found to be a failure by the restored Commons, so Cromwell dissolved it, in much the same way and for the same basic reason as the Stuart monarchs had done from the beginning of their rule.

In August the Lord Protector's much-loved daughter died of a cancer. By that time he was himself ailing, with a fever very prevalent in the capital that summer. Her death was a final blow. Cromwell's health, undermined for years by the revolution, his military campaigns, and his less successful political battles to rule the country, gave way. He sank steadily and on the third of September, accepting his death with pious conviction still of God's special regard for him, he died.

At Brussels Charles received the news with joy. The tyrant had not been a truly old man. He had expected to have to wait many more years before the usurper was swept away by death, since he was no longer risking that fate on the field of battle. He had feared having to wait until he himself was too old to have any romantic appeal to a populace starved of all such for so long that they could not rise to it. Now all was changed. That longing for the Crown! Surely –

'The Protector took the right to name his successor,' Lord Clarendon reminded Charles. 'He hath named his son, Richard, young, beloved by the populace I am told –'

'A weakling,' Charles said, standing his full height, his eyes shining, his cheeks flushed with a growing sense of his own potential, his own hardened, disciplined, proved strength. 'We must begin to move, my lord.'

'But first discover if their army accepts Master Richard, if not as a leader, then as their puppet. We must move with caution sire, with patience.'

'Have you ever known us to act otherwise, my lord?' the King asked, smiling broadly now.

CHAPTER NINETEEN

In Holland the news of Cromwell's death came as a surprise and was viewed with caution. The many refugees from the Protector's regime began by greeting it with extravagant joy, with parties, meetings, feasts they could ill afford. But this did not last very long, for the next news told of the accepted succession of Cromwell's second son Richard, who was little known by the exiles. He was as little known by the majority of his new subjects, they told one another.

And yet they seemed to have raised no objection to him. Nor had the royalists who had banded themselves together for all those years of oppression. They had not taken this unexpected crisis of government to raise their forces and seize power. Had they really lost the hearts of the people by their feebleness? Would they allow the present dismal rule to continue indefinitely?

Colonel Ogilvy had a third idea. He had never lost touch with King Charles's inner circle of advisers. Indeed they had deliberately supplied him with all significant news from England and kept him up to date with the juggling of the great continental powers, the Protestant Allies in the north; France, ruled by Cardinal Mazarin; and Spain with her still occupied base in Flanders, the Spanish Netherlands. Clarendon had found Colonel Ogilvy a most reliable, cosmopolitan gentleman who could be relied upon to form a sane judgement in every fresh turn and crisis of the King's affairs. Also a veteran soldier who could be called upon to command where military danger threatened.

So Ogilvy knew already that England under Cromwell and with the help of his trained army and his brilliant Admiral Blake had won the respect of the continentals. He knew too in spite of the fact that Spain had great possessions and had granted a small treaty with Charles that gave him leave to stay in Brussels, this country of the Great Armada was in a state of early decline, her power and wealth in the western world across the ocean diminished, while that of England in North America and the Caribbean grew by conquest and emigration, together with those of the French and the Dutch. British naval power in the Channel, reflecting this advance, could aid and confirm a change of government at home far more effectively than those ageing royalists with their ineffective plots and uncertain bands of secret followers.

'The old Protector's generals will never serve under the Lord Richard, as they call him,' Colonel Ogilvy explained to Alan. 'The people hope for an easing of the worst of the puritan rule, but there is great unrest in the army. Only in Scotland all is under control, I am told. For they have there General Monck, who knows his own mind. Which is not, I believe, for wholehearted support of this Lord Richard and his parliamentary supporters.'

'My poor father,' Lady Anne Ogilvy lamented. 'He will be in greater danger than ever if there is another turmoil, army against army, general against general and each trying to seize the old Protector's place.'

'I think the minds of the people at this present are all set upon giving the late Oliver a royal funeral,' Alan suggested. 'I heard from Tom Howard he is to be sent to observe the ceremony, embalming of the body, an effigy upon the coffin and so forth.'

'A Norfolk farmer's son!' Lady Anne was astonished.

'A gentleman farmer.'

'A yeoman!'

'His uncle – or was it his great-uncle? – was a wealthy man. Did he not entertain King James the First, when that monarch came from Scotland to London to be crowned King of both countries?'

'Sir Francis Leslie tells that story,' the colonel said.

His own father, his natural father, had told it too. He had no wish to go back in conversation to those far off times when the Ogilvy connection had begun, so he asked, 'When did you hear from Tom Howard, Alan? By letter or by word of mouth?'

'In person and only this morning. He was sailing from Ijmuiden. He brought me orders from the King. I must return to Brussels to undertake a private and personal mission for His Majesty.'

Alan's family knew he would not tell them what this was. Probably his orders held no detail. This was true, but he guessed what they must be. Mainly the King's concern for his eldest son. It never left him for long, this concern, nor was he allowed to forget it, for Lucy Walter had continued to follow her disgraceful career. Having exhausted the possibilities of Holland she had transferred herself to the wider field of Paris, where the boy's surroundings must be even more undesirable than at Rotterdam, Dordrecht or other towns in the Netherlands.

So Alan returned to his duty and was summoned very soon to hear His Majesty's pleasure.

He found Charles in a happy, carefree mood, using his unfailing charm with great effect.

'I am about to send you on a triple mission to Paris, Alan,' he began.

'Sire!'

'First to my most beloved little sister, Minette, who hath been betrothed to the French King Louis's brother, an immoral product of Gomorrah, God help her! Give her the package I shall put up for her and observe if she grieves for her fate or accepts it as something she may surmount and for which she looks to find compensation.'

Alan bowed, to show he understood the whole of this unhappy news, but he did not dare to speak of it.

'Then you are to convey my greetings and my duty to my royal mother, but by her Chamberlain, not in person, lest she should be offended by your youth and humble station. Also by the hand of her Chamberlain my request for my brothers, the Prince James and the Prince Henry, to join me here in Brussels as soon as may be. My letters to them put forward the reasons for my pressing the urgency of this action. And lastly, Alan, you are to find and bring here to me in Brussels my son, His Grace of Monmouth. The time is over-ripe for this action. I can no longer endure the notoriety that follows his mother wherever she goes. She hath done me too much harm already over the years. It must end now that our exile may not be much longer extended.'

He had risen from his chair when he began to speak about the boy and now as he hinted at the great developments he fully expected to take place in England, he returned to his royal manner, so that Alan, flattered and bemused by the former intimacy, the charm of confidence from such a source, was moved to fall on his knees before his King, to swear his full allegiance again, to ask God's blessing on his dear Master and to kiss the hand extended to him to mark that Master's acknowledgement of this enthusiasm.

'We would our faithful subjects in England showed a wit and energy to equal yours, sir,' Charles said as he dismissed the young man.

The mission to Paris proceeded without a serious mishap. The letters and packets to the royal personages were delivered to Queen Henrietta Maria's Chamberlain and friend, whom some said was now her lover. No answers were returned to Alan, but he understood they had been made to Charles direct.

It was far different with Mistress Walter. It took him some time to find the lady and when at last he did so he found her in a poor quarter of the city, much reduced in circumstances but still attended by Dutch Mother Schik. She had no steady protector, the old woman told him.

'Nor has she had one since she came here, looking to the widowed Queen for help, poor misguided creature. She hoped to have earned money for her silence, her discretion. She nearly found herself taken and hanged for such insolence, but we had hid ourselves and as the Queen dared not attract attention –'

'But surely England is in favour again with the French just now? Some of Cromwell's soldiers have fought for France against Spain, have they not? Louis's war was ended with Cromwell. The Queen is Louis's aunt, after all?'

The old woman shook her head.

'I know nothing of politics. I only know the boy should be away from her. Will you explain it to her while I get him ready? He has little enough to take with him, poor lamb.'

So Alan saw Lucy Walter again. He scarcely recognized her, for though she was not yet thirty years of age her dissolute life and her present poverty had entirely destroyed her early beauty. She appeared as she undoubtedly was, an old, experienced whore, hardened in her trade, grown vulgar, coarse, diseased and with it all despairing, resentful.

She wept when she saw Alan. His still youthful face reminded her of the boy she had spoken with in Dordrecht more than six years ago, who had then seemed to be sorry for Charles's neglect and disapproval.

She tried to revive that memory with him, even to jest about his sudden escape from being seen by his uncle. But this only brought up Alan's own persisting sorrow over his ruined love, so that he answered coldly out of his own sorrow, 'I must not delay, madam. That time is best forgotten. If His Grace is ready – '

'His Grace?'

'The King demands full control of his son's future, madam. The young Duke's further upbringing will be in the hands of his royal father.'

'And his sister?'

'Your second child, madam, is not the King's, as you very well know. She stays with you.'

Mistress Walter wept again. Alan was greatly relieved when Mother Schik brought the young James Scott to say goodbye to his mother, which he did with no show of feeling of any kind. This chilled Alan somewhat, though he was grateful for the ease of their departure.

In Brussels the boy behaved quietly and with due deference when presented to his father, whom he was meeting for the first time. He was a well-grown and comely boy, nearly ten years old now. Charles was delighted with him. Even Clarendon, who was present, could not have wished the interview to have gone better. But later, watching the King from a window walking and laughing in the garden with his latest light of love, he shook his head, murmuring to himself, 'Monmouth hath his father's heart. But how many more young dukes will spring from that source and ne'er one of them an heir to the throne? A bride, a bride, is what the new England needs, please God, to succeed.'

But the coming of the new England proceeded at a very slow pace indeed. However, proceed it did, at first with a fresh knowledge, provided mainly by Thurloe's well-managed and manned organization of the government's security. The new Protector was left in no doubt that the opposition to him was growing fast. The whole country was moving slowly into rebellion, like a heavy much-filled stew pot coming to the boil, with bubbles bursting on the surface here and there and a general tendency of the contents to heave up over the rim of the vessel.

A new Parliament was formed, mostly of the surviving members of the old 'Rump'. But, as before, religious difficulties immediately caused discord. The Presbyterians wanted their sect to prevail unopposed, with a Directory to lead it; while the Anglicans now became bold enough to demand a return of Episcopacy and the Prayer Book.

At the same time the Army grew more and more disaffected. The end of the major-generals had meant the great reduction of their forces, so by the time Cromwell died there were large numbers of soldiers, especially those conscripted in recent years, who quietly deserted and made their way to their homes and former occupations, mainly on the land. Their loss was felt and their allegiance now very doubtful.

Meanwhile those sluggish bodies, 'The Trust' and 'The Sealed Knot', gained further important recruits of fame and distinction, but made little use of them. They were urged on by appeals from the King in exile, but for the most part decided that the time was not yet ripe for military action. In this they were probably right, immediately after Cromwell's death, But a few months later, in the new year, when his son's incompetence became quite obvious, John Mordaunt, a prominent member of 'The Trust', began to urge plans upon his fellow leaders of the group for a general rising.

But the plans were muddled and Sir Richard Willis, a government spy and traitor to the Royalist Cause, who had already helped to bring about the failure of Penruddock's rising, was again at work in their midst, directed by Thurloe's office. He opposed action in August, ostensibly on account of the harvest. However, John Mordaunt did in fact go to see the King, who realized without difficulty that a further period of waiting could not be avoided.

A letter came to Captain James Ogilvy in Brussels from his father in Oxford. He took it to Alan in great excitement.

'I have this news, cousin,' he said. 'England begins to stir. The chains that have chafed her for so long begin to loosen. They expect this new Protector to fail and to resign, for he is a gentle soul, unused to military ways.'

'Which have been the Usurper's only real power,' Alan said. 'What else does my great-uncle say?'

'First that my poor sister Sarah grows daily more uncertain in her wits. This because George Leslie with whom she was ever infatuated, poor thing, hath never gone to Oxford to visit there as he promised her. This means he finds her no longer useful to him as he did when she lived in the Phillips household.'

'But it also suggests George is no longer plaguing Doctor Richard does it not?'

'Let us hope so. One more hopeful news. My father's man, that went to fight for the Martyr and never came back from the Wars, hath returned hale and hearty to serve his old master. My father writes of him thus: "The fellow has a wife and a young son he will set to school in Oxford. How thankful I am to have him with me."'

'So we may thank the good Lord that Doctor Richard will have the care and attention he has lacked for so long,' Alan said with feeling.

James answered with equal feeling and tears in his eyes, 'I shall take Thomas home to him. I have asked leave to give up my commission here where I do nothing on very short commons. If there is to be a rising I shall join it while Thomas will be safe with proper care.'

'You deem it safe to go back to England?'

'I feared Thurloe far less than George. I belong to none of the would-be rebel bodies. It is only George who could bring our name into disrepute again. And George seems to have given up his evil moves.'

Alan nodded. Thomas was no better in his general health, his cough remained. It seemed to Alan likely that he was not long for this world. After all, he was in his late thirties and had led an active, hard life since early manhood. In recent times there had been many men who had not survived their twenties from death in war or death from those twin fatal diseases, the smallpox and the plague. The Lord was merciful. He might have planned a quiet end for Thomas, without much pain, in the pleasant house and garden of a happy childhood.

Captain James's release from his commission came in the spring of 1659. His arrangements were already made: Doctor Richard, in a state of thankful jubilation, was ready to receive them. At the last James was called to an audience with the King. He gladly obeyed.

'We are much beholden to the family of Ogilvy,' Charles said to him. 'You have been faithful to our Cause. You have given much thought and time, since you joined us here, to the training of those volunteers who have come with great enthusiasm, but no military training at all. You will, we know, continue to serve, as and when you are able. But you have deserved this retreat both for the sake of your aged father and your maimed brother. It is right and just you should become their guardian for such time as they are spared to you.'

'I humbly thank Your Gracious Majesty,' Captain James said, overwhelmed by the King's words and his whole royal presence.

'In token of our gratitude, we propose to make you knight,' Charles went on. 'Come forward, sir, if you please.'

So Captain James went forward and knelt for the accolade and left the audience chamber in a daze, to be greeted and toasted by his army companions and again by his cousins, Colonel Francis and Lady Anne Ogilvy and Alan and three shy little girls, the latter's sisters.

The next day he and Thomas rode north to Bruges, where they arranged for a boat to take them to England from Sluys. It was in Bruges they heard the latest news from England. Richard Cromwell had resigned. The Protectorate had fallen.

CHAPTER TWENTY

In Amsterdam the news of the eclipse of the Protectorate and the consequent confusion in the seat of government in England was received by Master Hugh Phillips and his family with very mixed feelings. They had heard it from the good friends who had protected Mistress Phillips and her children while their escape from London was arranged. But he had learned much from his wife already. The news, when it came, was not unexpected.

'The poor Lord Richard never looked to succeed his great father to anyone's satisfaction,' Cynthia told him. 'And besides, the severity that so unjustly fell upon you, sir, was already crumbling throughout the land, for the people had grown intolerant of it.'

'I was attacked by false reports to Thurloe engineered by that young scoundrel, Ogilvy.'

'I begin to doubt it,' she said boldly. 'I begin to think the chief misinformer all along hath been your sometime friend and longtime enemy, my childhood's playmate, George Leslie.'

'We have known that his unsavoury jealousy and envy has eaten away all of his excellence, alas,' Hugh Phillips groaned. 'But since he has sedulously avoided us and our house these many years how can he have put forward those facts that Thurloe twisted into betrayals?'

'Because Sarah supplied him with them.'

'*Sarah*! Your sister Sarah? Poor witless youngest child of your parents?'

Cynthia nodded.

'She was always devoted to George, because he pampered and flattered her as a means to gain access to me, at the time he was courting me. Always deceitful was George, always ready to sacrifice others to gain his desired ends, always cruel, always an arrant liar. Did you never observe her devotion? I could not explain her feelings for George at the time you were becoming his rival, either to you or to my father, whom I feared would forbid our marriage.'

She looked at her husband with deep affection; the same assured loving, trusting confidence her mother had bestowed upon Doctor Richard and that now sustained the cloth merchant in his present trial.

He was too moved on this occasion to continue the discussion, but thinking over what she had said, he found a great deal of sense in it. Certainly George Leslie seemed to have made no progress against his cloth business contacts, nor his house in London. The latter had been sealed for sequestration, but a guard had been mounted upon it and so far the contents were safe. And this was after Sarah Ogilvy had gone back to her father's house. Well, that was where she should be, where she should always have been, but that Cynthia had felt such compassion for the poor creature whom she had befriended as a child when her nursemaid had lost patience with her slowness at walking and talking and also with her frequent tantrums.

In London the Dutch jeweller Ritter, having got rid of his dangerous guests, returned to full activity in his business, able to entertain his friends and colleagues as before. His strange retirement had been due to illness in his family, he explained, feared to be infectious at the time. By the mercy of Heaven it had come to nothing.

So Master Ritter heard all the current rumours and realized with the rest of the business world that some stronger Head of State must be found now that Richard was gone. The Parliament demanded absolute power, but was unable to wield it. The Army sought a supreme leader but there were too many contenders for that position and none was prepared to go to war to establish himself. The City of London merchants knew better than anyone else that there was no money anywhere available until the confusion ended.

But presently a fresh rumour, a new certainty grew. In Scotland, General Monck, who had put down the only promising rebellion and was in total control there, had conceived it his duty to bring back the true Head of State, the only possible Leader, the much spoken of, part feared, part admired, but deeply, universally accepted, even in disapproval, Charles the Second. King by right of birth by the will of the people rather than the will of God, the Presbyterians said, repudiating superstition. King by Divine Right the Royalists and Anglicans affirmed, moving slowly, too slowly, towards the universal rising they had planned for so long.

In Master Phillips's sound business mind and tolerant heart the bitterness began to melt, common sense to plan again for the future. His new business friends in Amsterdam, who admired him for his fortitude, told him 'King Charles is gone from Brussels to Calais. His brothers, the two Princes, are with him. Surely we may expect great things to follow, to the benefit of us all.'

And so they might. Charles had indeed gone with his principal advisers to Calais, though Prince James had moved to another position in a port on the Channel coast. Clearly they were preparing to invade England at separate points when the time was right for Charles's small army to help the royalists at home.

And now a very significant event took place that altered all the plans and promised a magnificent reward for the young King's patience and keen understanding, together with Clarendon's wisdom. A visitor presented himself at the Court in Calais. He was General Monck himself, who had left his care of Scotland in the hands of capable subordinate officers, to offer Charles the restoration of the Throne in a bloodless counter-revolution.

'It is that or anarchy, sir,' Monck said, gravely. 'The

Parliament is aware of it. They are well primed by Master Secretary Thurloe, who hath agents in those supposedly secret bodies that plot continually.'

'But they avoid action,' Charles said. 'We do not greatly admire our faithful friends, but with your help they may in the end work wonders.'

He spoke formally, because the general had not addressed him in a proper manner at any point in their encounter. But he could not restrain a half-jibe that cut both ways.

General Monck found in it the kind of wry Scottish humour he was familiar with in the northern province. He grinned, appreciating a quality in his future Master that would help to reconcile the country to a change he knew to be absolutely necessary, but that until a few months ago would have been regarded by his colleagues as outrageous treason.

The discussion continued; a rough plan was made and agreed. The general, polite but stiff to the end, made no obeisance, used no title other than 'sir', took his leave without being dismissed, but did say, as he shook the hand Charles extended to be kissed, 'The people will rejoice when you return, sir. They have a great need to be merry again.'

'They shall fill that need, we promise you, General,' Charles told him with a great laugh that rang in Monck's ears as Lord Clarendon led him away.

When the Chancellor went back to the King he found him still in a most cheerful mood.

'My lord,' Charles said. 'You must send official news to our cousin of France, suggesting that our restoration is now but a matter of months, perhaps less. And at the same time send secret news to the sly fox, Mazarin, to confirm it. And press once more our suit for the hand of the Cardinal's most desirable niece, the beautiful Lady Hortense Mancini.'

'A Papist, sire!' Clarendon protested, shocked to find the King had not forgotten this unsuitable Queen for England, already refused him when his prospects seemed to Mazarin to be quite hopeless.

'An Italian,' Charles answered. 'Loveliest of all I have sought for a wife hitherto. Warm-hearted, gay and most desirable. If you can persuade the Cardinal to agree, you may win her for me, my lord.'

Lord Clarendon did not make any more open objections but he felt fairly certain he would be unsuccessful. Had not Mazarin formed an alliance with Cromwell to fight Spain and therefore had Charles removed from France to go to his sister in Germany? Was the Cardinal likely now to reverse his alliance in the exile's favour? He would obey the King, of course, but he felt fairly confident a Catholic Queen would again inflict outrage upon the royalist aristocracy and the English Anglican religion.

Matters went as Lord Clarendon expected. Cardinal Mazarin was already conversant with current affairs in England, but he still had no confidence in the promised restoration. He favoured a great position for his niece, but was not inclined to risk a marriage with one who was still practically penniless, was dissolute, gravely immoral, a Protestant, a continuing exile. In his reply to the Chancellor he added a sardonic note. 'His Majesty's early mistress, the mother of his eldest bastard, died in Paris last year of multiple ailments connected with her irregular and scandalous way of life; in dire poverty and loneliness, her daughter having been taken into a convent and her ancient Dutch companion having predeceased her.'

Lord Clarendon delivered this message. Charles received it very calmly, saying only, 'How wise we were to rescue our son in time for him to escape such events. Pray see that the news goes to young Alan Ogilvy, my lord.'

Alan had known of Lucy's death for several months when Lord Clarendon's report came to him. When the young James Scott, Duke of Monmouth, had left Paris in Alan's care the boy had clung to him in his inevitable alarm and homesickness. He had called frequently for Mother Schik and for his little sister, but less often for his mother. So no one was surprised when he showed no grief for her death when told of it. They concluded that this was natural, since such a base character could not possibly inspire a true filial love. But Alan found the answer in the boy's character. He was wayward. He had charm, but he expected it to win him outstanding rewards; a great position at Court, and great privileges as befitted his name, with great possessions to match it. These he could not have, since they did not exist at this time. Having been fed most indulgently upon false promises and lying hopes, the poor spoilt child was quite unfitted for the change. He could not regard his clean but frugal surroundings superior to his former sordid squalor. He knew, however, who had sent Master Alan to look after him, so he clung to Ogilvy more and more closely as they travelled from Paris to Brussels and wept copiously and loudly when they parted upon reaching the Court. Alan remembered how calmly he had parted from his mother and was not in the least flattered by the boy's behaviour.

However he was in some measure sorry for the young duke, in spite of his less sentimental, less indulgent estimate of his character than that of his immediate guardians, appointed by the Lord Chancellor. He took the necessary steps to allow himself occasional access to the Duke of Monmouth's new home. One day upon an errand of this sort, he met Tom Howard, who greeted him very cheerfully, linked an arm in his and drew him along to a wine shop where they could refresh themselves and exchange news.

'To the future,' Tom said, lifting his glass.

'And may it be not long delayed,' added Alan, drinking deeply. 'May we all find ourselves at home again at last.'

He told Tom that his cousins had already left for Oxford and that Captain James Ogilvy had been honoured with a knighthood for his long service in the cavalier armies.

'Exiles begin to move,' Tom answered. 'The flow reverses. Which makes it hard for those recently obliged to leave London.'

'Such as my cousin, Mistress Cynthia,' Alan said casually, hoping for news without asking for it directly. Try as he might, recent events had stirred him out of the lethargy of his accepted grief.

Tom laughed.

'Still hankering after that fair daughter?' he said. 'You do not know then that the family were reunited in Amsterdam a month since, but no sooner had they arrived where Master Phillips was living than a letter came from the King – '

'From *our* King, from Charles *himself*?'

'Carried by a special messenger that I was to watch and guard upon his errand.'

'And the letter's content?'

Tom stared.

'You do not expect me to know *that*, I hope,' he said.

A steely look had come into his eyes; Alan hurriedly withdrew the implied insult that Tom had found in the question.

'Why no, sir, but the King is gathering support wherever he finds a hopeful source. And this unjust attack upon an upright merchant – '

'Exactly. We have disclosed a feeling in the City that

Master Phillips was condemned unfairly upon insecure evidence. Master Thurloe is clever, not easily deceived. If overborne by his Masters he seeks only the truth of any case. He does not favour unreliable agents. He drops them.'

Alan felt his excitement growing.

'You are telling me that Master Thurloe has dropped George Leslie? That Master Phillips may be exonerated, the case against him quashed, his return to his old business, even his house in Aldersgate given back to him?'

'That is what I have learned this last week.'

'Then I thank the most merciful God for it. Will he return?'

'He will return.'

'And Lord Clarendon knows all these things?'

'He does.'

Alan looked at Tom with admiration. He had unravelled the Phillips case to its very last knot. It was not difficult to imagine with fair probability what lay in King Charles's letter to his long successful cloth merchant, man of business and exporter. A conviction of his restoration before many months were passed, a reassurance that there would be no punishment for any member of the opposition over the terrible years of conflict, except for those who had taken a direct part in the murder of King Charles the First. An appeal to ally himself to the forces of law and order according to the ancient laws and traditions of England. Moreover to support the coming transfer of power from a group of muddled extremists to a new freely elected Parliament of Commons, a new Second Chamber of peers of the Realm, a new Army controlled by a great general who would shortly engineer the recall of the true, hereditary Head of State himself, Charles Stuart, third of that dynasty to rule England with Scotland, Wales and Ireland attached.

His imaginary appeal, his whole conclusion so absorbed Alan's mind that he was both startled and alarmed when Tom Howard went on to say, 'Master Phillips will return and take his family with him. George Leslie is in London still.'

'I saw him,' Alan groaned. 'Lording it over my father's house in Paternoster Row, that he hath seized, pretending some right to it as his mother's legal elder son.'

'He could be dangerous,' Tom said slowly. 'He could be dangerous as long as he lives.'

These words remained with Alan as a heavy foreboding

during the weeks that followed. If George Leslie had been discharged as an agent from his work for Thurloe he must be all the more free to pursue his vile intentions. His hatred, his so-called pursuit of revenge, was endless and by now uncontrollable. Tom was right; while Leslie lived, the Ogilvy family in all its branches was in peril. And none more so than the original cause of his disorder, Mistress Cynthia. They were in Amsterdam together still, Tom had suggested. Where was George?

Again Tom Howard relieved his uncertainty. The King's letter had seemed to Master Phillips both generous and sensible. A restoration of the monarchy, with certain safeguards, appealed to his keen business mind. He wrote back to Lord Clarendon that he accepted Charles Stuart's proposals and would act upon his suggestion that he return to England to pursue his trade, provided there be no tyranny and no intolerance of his religion. He was a Baptist, he said, and would always remain so.

Tom brought the letter to Calais; the King ordered an acknowledgement to be sent to Amsterdam. Tom sought out Alan and together they begged leave for the latter to be messenger instead of Tom.

So Alan found himself again in the street of his early attempt to see the merchant and approaching the door where he had been twice rejected. He was pausing at the foot of the steps that led up to it when a rough voice ordered him in broken Dutch to stand aside and to his horror George Leslie pushed past him and assailed both the iron bell pull and the large brass knocker.

The door was almost instantly opened by a stout middle-aged woman. Again Leslie grated out, 'Stand aside, wench! My business is with Mistress Phillips. Where shall I find her?'

The woman said courageously, 'I do not think she will receive you, sir.'

But George thrust her aside and marched into the house, whereupon Alan stepped forward, saying quickly, 'That man is mad! I know him! Where shall I find – ?'

A hand fell on his shoulder and a voice the woman knew said, 'Young villain, I *know you*! Alan Ogilvy, you shall not force my house!'

Before Alan could answer, a scream from close at hand drove both men forward. Alan leaped towards the source of the cry, loosening his sword as he did so. Master Phillips, more sure of his way, dodged past him and flung himself into the room at the end of the hall. Alan followed, his blade drawn and ready.

George Leslie stood in the centre of the room, an expression of pure, triumphant evil on his twisted face. Mistress Ogilvy and Susan, clasping one another, were cowering behind a heavy table in the window recess.

'Have at you, villain!' Alan yelled.

The would-be murderer swung round and the fight began.

Neither was highly skilled; it was a clumsy affair. George Leslie was in his early forties and had never been much interested in sword play. Alan was young and active and had learned the weapon's skill with intelligent care, but no real aptitude, nor liking. He had never fought in anger, nor ever meant to kill, but now he did both.

It was George who broke off the fight, after Master Phillips's shouts for help, relayed by the stout maid, had brought voices to the hall and sounds of steel drawing. With a final thrust that sent Alan staggering from a flesh wound in the thigh, the madman drove his sword through the window of the room, shattered a hole by which to escape and was through it and the small garden beyond and over the wall by the time the helpers had crowded into the room.

Alan, blood pouring down his leg, dropped his sword, felt in his jacket with both hands to fetch out the King's letter and holding it at arm's length towards Master Phillips said in a weak voice, 'A reply to your message, sir, from His Gracious Majesty, King Charles.'

Master Phillips moved forward towards the letter that shook in Alan's trembling hand. He had, while the fight was on, stood in front of his women folk. He was unarmed but he would have defended them with his bare hands if there had been no champion to do it for him. But the champion was here in the person of the young man who had sought his daughter's hand, whom he had blamed for his misfortunes, reviled –

'You are no betrayer!' he cried. 'I have done you a great injustice! I must plead forgiveness, I must – '

Alan wanted to say it was no matter, only a misunderstanding. But his forehead seemed to be made of ice, his eyesight was fading, a loud buzzing drowned the sympathetic voice and he collapsed on the floor at Susan's feet as she ran towards him with open arms.

CHAPTER TWENTY-ONE

Doctor Richard Ogilvy was overwhelmed with joy when his two youngest sons arrived home. They had survived, they had found their way into service with the young King, James had been honoured. Thomas would not be able to fight again, his wound had rendered him a cripple for the rest of his life. But surely a long rest in country air, English air, would soon bring back his colour and cure his cough.

The old man fought down his recognition of that cough. Nor would he accept the other symptoms, the recurrent fever of an evening when flushed cheeks gave the cripple an appearance of health that faded away by morning. But he knew in his heart that poor Thomas was treading the slow path that had led his beloved Celia to her grave. Thomas himself was not deceived, but would not alarm his father. So the pretence went on between the two and the old childhood's love drew them together again, wiping out the bitterness of that seeming neglect, while Thomas the youth, and later Thomas the young man, pursued his royalist ambition to win victory in an already lost cause.

James watched the progress of this total reconciliation with pity and a great thankfulness that events had made it possible. He was willing to suspend all plans for his own future while Thomas lived. He did not expect this to be many months, only prayed that they both might see the Restoration that was beginning to be talked of freely among the scholars at Oxford and the servants who overheard their talk. Even the country folk in the villages, who looked forward to their squires and parsons and great landowners to be restored as well. They needed them all to lead their impoverished communities back to prosperity and save them in future from the dread risk of war.

Under James the domestic arrangements at Doctor Richard's house were instantly improved. Before he left the continent his cousin Colonel Francis had managed to extract some valuable arrears of pay for his Netherlands services. There was also a gratuity for Thomas's sufferings bestowed by 'The Sealed Knot', who had over the years acquired a varied accumulation of gifts to finance battles that were never fought. With a bloodless counter-revolution now definitely in prospect the officers of that openly secret organization had felt generous.

So James got rid of the incompetent and mildly fraudulent housekeeper and in addition to Doctor Richard's former man had engaged a new one, also a fresh gardener to attend to the growing of vegetables, while he engaged such daily help in the house as they considered necessary. In a very short time the establishment settled into a modest, comfortable regime. The stables, too, under James's direct rule, were put into order, the Doctor's old coach repainted and once more fit to take him and Thomas, who no longer rode a horse, for drives in the countryside or to Luscombe, or into Oxford to see Doctor Richard's other old friends.

The only discontented member of the household was poor Sarah. Her father had welcomed her back without much show of feeling either way. He had always accepted her mental disability with fortitude, without rancour, nor with sentimental pity. He had expected her to succumb during early childhood to one or other of the fevers that usually afflicted the young. This would have been greeted as God's will, as was her whole condition, and considered a merciful release. Without hypocrisy such an event was usually welcomed as the return to its Blessed Maker of an innocent, pure spirit unsullied by the sinful world.

But Sarah had not succumbed; she had grown up into a plain, rather stunted young woman, given to long sulks or sudden fits of violent temper. But on the whole able to manage her own life moderately well, so long as someone gave her a little affection and directed her daily routine in useful directions. Useful, that is, to the guardian who looked after her welfare.

Doctor Richard knew there was no chance of finding a husband for this daughter. Nor did he think it right to attempt to do so. In the old days she might have been placed in a convent. But that, as a Protestant and a scholar, he found immoral, if not cruel. Fortunately, Cynthia had been willing to look after her sister when their mother died. She would have been willing to look after her still, but Sarah had refused to go abroad. So, Doctor Ogilvy regretted to himself, she was back in Oxford, but fortunately James, Sir James, bless the boy, would see she prospered and did not saddle him with a bastard grandchild, always a danger in the case of these afflicted women.

He did not know of Sarah's obsessive infatuation for George Leslie, nor her part in ruining the Phillips family by stoking his malice with fuel he could use to that purpose. Cynthia, had, however, confided it to James, who unfortunately had not thought it possible. He was wrong, as it appeared, alas, at the end.

Meanwhile happiness on the whole prevailed at the ageing scholar's house and spread to Luscombe. Sir Francis Leslie rode over to welcome his old friend's sons directly after their arrival and when the Ogilvy family coach was restored to use it brought Doctor Richard and Thomas and his sister to pay their respects in a return visit.

Sarah was indifferent to the visit until she recognized Lady Leslie's mother as the former mistress of the house in Paternoster Row. Her beloved George had won it for his services to the Protector. Malice shone in her little eyes as she remembered the old lady's expulsion that had followed immediately upon Master Phillips's disgrace and flight. As she had been returned to Oxford by her sister before she learned any more or had now forgotten it, she felt considerable satisfaction in finding Mistress Leslie was now wholly dependent upon her son-in-law.

Mistress Leslie, however, showed no sign of discomfort. She had no need to. The alderman had left her very comfortably off, with funds invested where they could scarcely be touched. She greeted Sarah kindly and then paid her no more attention, a kind of treatment so very familiar to the afflicted one that she took it for granted. So the general reunion of the two families was altogether a happy one.

'I think we have seen the end of all this sad strife,' Sir Francis said. 'If only those loyal souls who have plotted and planned for so many years can be patient at the last.'

James said, 'I fear they will not. His Majesty expects to have their support for his coming back. He knows there will be an army at his disposal – but I should not speak of this, perhaps – '

Sir Francis smiled.

'We do nothing but discuss it in the town, in the colleges. Loyalists and parliamentarians alike. We hear the ports are guarded by government troops. We are told that lists are made of all available horses and they will be impounded at the first sign of rebellion.'

'So!' Thomas exclaimed. 'That is why a fellow came to our stable last week to know if we had a horse for sale. I showed him our four, but denied he should buy any one of them and he went away.'

On the whole James was right. 'The Trust', urged on by John Mordaunt, had demanded action more than once, but the Army was still paramount and the various branches of 'The Trust' were not fully prepared nor all agreed. In Wales they were willing, but hung back, fearful of Ireland, obedient to the iron fist that had destroyed disobedience. In the Midlands there was a small force under Lord Byron; in Staffordshire under Sir Charles Wolseley. In Kent Sir Thomas Peyton longed to rise, in Sussex Willoughby of Parham, in Surrey Mordaunt himself.

As the weeks passed without incident, the Government ordered certain precautions to be put into practice. Many of the listed horses were in fact impounded. The English ports were more closely guarded still. Some important people were arrested, some of them held, others released on parole. The Navy patrolled the Flanders coast and the northern Channel and North Sea. Secretary Thurloe's knowledge and powers of anticipation seemed to be endless.

Not that he expected to succeed. He knew too much for that. He knew that General Monck held the future of the country in his capable hands; the general had full control of his Ironsides, he had a clear view of his country's need for the return of the King. And the Government knew that Monck had seen and approved the man who could fill that post. Not perfect, in fact in some ways most scandalous; but possessed of a keen brain, a tolerant outlook, a most royal manner and an iron determination to take back the throne.

'Charles will be back,' Thurloe told himself. 'And if he do not hang me for my work since Worcester, he may find that work so valuable to him I may barter my life for my files.'

Which in some sort he managed to bring off, for he did not suffer, but did indeed survive the change.

There was only one rising, in the north-west, led by Sir George Booth, who had kept all his plans secret, especially from Willis. Being unexpected it was at first successful as other attempts had been, with in this case a published appeal against tyranny, a reminder of Magna Carta and the Petition of Rights.

But the general response was poor. The 'Rump' Parliament, governing shakily, sent General Lambert against Booth. With easy trained competence the government troops defeated an amateur force and Sir George Booth was captured and put in the Tower. But events were moving fast. The rebel was never brought to trial and suffered no punishment.

Events were indeed moving fast. In Calais, in Holland, in London, Thurloe's agents were being recalled, sent upon new missions or discharged. Among the latter was George Leslie, who, though unemployed for some time, had never been formally discharged.

His failure to kill the entire Phillips family had only increased his murderous intention, which soon became obvious to Secretary Thurloe when he made his next report and which prompted that astute manipulator to end his services for good. The man was now become mad, he judged. If a restoration was on the way and who, other than himself, was in a better position to know the detail of it, then assassination must not appear anywhere in his recent files. Particularly such blatant family quarrels as this affair must not seem to have been fostered, even promoted from his office.

So George found himself out of employment, out of friends, out of funds, except for a rather meagre gratuity. But with his occupation of the house in Paternoster Row to solace him for what he continued to think were his eternal wrongs and frustrations. His thirst for revenge was unquenchable.

General Monck had already begun his march south to establish the Restoration when George Leslie took horse for Oxford. He knew by then the whole situation at Doctor Richard's house there.

Sarah, who could not write nor read, had given him all the detail by word of mouth she had sent by the regular messenger her family shared with Sir Francis Leslie's establishment. The messenger, who knew of her affliction, was ready enough to indulge the poor creature, seeing her message was to Master Leslie, Sir Francis's son. It made little sense, but Master George would understand it. He made no inquiry about it, though the young lady had delivered it to him herself with a degree of secrecy he might have questioned had he not been so long acquainted with her state.

George came a few days later, rode into the Ogilvy stable yard, dismounted and flung his reins to the boy who came forward to greet him.

He said arrogantly, 'My uncle is at home, I suppose?'

It was dusk, the boy did not remember him, but to save himself the trouble of inquiry answered, 'Doctor Richard is at home, sir.'

'See to my horse. Give it drink but leave it saddled. I shall not be staying long.'

'This time,' he told himself, 'I shall not argue as I did so mistakenly with the Phillips women. This time my argument will be death.'

He had forgotten his cousins; Sarah he totally disregarded. It was the uncle who had given his Cynthia to the cloth merchant, Uncle Richard, the old villain who had destroyed the hope of his youth, who must die now, at last. Die with his sins upon him.

But he had forgotten his cousins. He had not even remembered the servants, though Sarah had tried to describe all the new staff in her muddled, excited message. He found the heavy door of the house fastened; he had to knock. It was opened by a young maidservant, by which time his patience was ended so that he pushed past her as he had done in Amsterdam, drawing his sword as he did so.

She screamed and when he turned and threatened her screamed again and called for help so lustily the sound echoed through the quiet house.

Doctor Richard heard it, sitting dozing in his library, with an open book on his knee.

Thomas heard it, sitting in the ground-floor parlour, trying to amuse Sarah with a game of backgammon. He leaped up, made for the door, pulling out a dagger from its sheath at his waist. He had given up wearing a sword because he knew he would never be challenged to a duel. But George, plunging forward from the house door, was beyond such considerations.

'The old miscreant!' he yelled, seeing Thomas but not recognizing him. 'The old villain!'

Thomas knew him and knew what he had already done. He backed towards the parlour door he had left, hoping to draw the madman away from the library, but Doctor Richard had been roused by the screams and shouts. He got up quickly and went to the door of the library in time to hear the single clash of steel as Thomas leaped aside from George's first thrust and tried to disarm him as they clinched.

'You first then!' George yelled, twisting away.

But James was on the stairs, hurling himself down, drawing his sword as he came. He pushed his father back into the library with a sweep of his arm at the moment George's sword drove into Thomas's side.

'Down, murderer!' he shouted and before George could withdraw his weapon and turn James had driven his blade into the assassin's chest.

The servants came running, but too late. Sarah came, adding her demented screams to those of the other women. Disregarding George, except to kick his sword from his hand, he went to Thomas, who had pulled himself to his knees and was trying to stand.

'Where?' James asked.

'My side.' The voice was faint and as a manservant came forward quickly Thomas collapsed again on the floor.

It was Doctor Richard who gave the orders to the staff. Thomas was carried to his bed where James undressed him and bound up his wound. It looked small on the surface and bled little. But they both knew it had gone deep.

'It will be the end of me,' Thomas whispered. His face was grey and pinched, but he was not in much pain. 'Better so, brother. I shall not have to wait so long as I feared.'

They both knew this was true and accepted it. They had been ready for many years to die in battle; had hoped for it. It had come so now for Thomas and he was glad.

Doctor Richard directed that the murderer, who still lived, should be taken to another bedroom and laid upon the bed. At the same time one stable boy was sent into Oxford with a message to the family physician to bring a surgeon at once and the other to Luscombe to bring Sir Francis to his dying son.

The men of healing arrived first, but there was little they could do. They attended Thomas at once, until they were disturbed by the arrival in his room of Sarah, wild-eyed and distraught, demanding succour for George Leslie, who would not answer, she said, when she asked him how he fared.

Her cries were so frantic and so insistent that the surgeon went with her, but came back almost at once to report he could do nothing, the man was unconscious and dying. James then went to take his sister downstairs to the female servants, but he found she had locked the door against all comers and refused to unbar it, telling him to leave her with her beloved, who had fallen into a healing sleep.

Leaving her to her sad delusion and his brother to the men from Oxford, James went downstairs where he found his father still in a state of unnatural agitation and energy, refusing to rest, refusing all sustenance, though clearly needing both.

It was several hours later when Sir Francis Leslie rode into the yard. He dismounted quickly and made his way at once towards the house, whose great door stood open, while candles seemed to shine from every window.

As he reached the porch another, angrier flame shone in one of the upper windows and through the open door a great billowing cloud of smoke poured over him, while through it he heard cries and shouts as those in the bedroom with Thomas became aware that fire had seized upon the house, coming from the room where Sarah had shut herself.

The former pandemonium broke out more strongly than before, but this time it was Sir Francis who gave the orders and began the rescues, for Doctor Richard was no longer capable. He had given way at last to his son's pleading and had allowed himself to be seated in his big chair in the library, with his feet up on a footstool. He had sipped a little wine, he had given way to his utter exhaustion and raging anxiety for Thomas; he was not able to rouse himself again.

But his friend of a lifetime was with him, helping some of the servants to carry him out of the house and lay him upon a long garden seat. They brought rugs to cover him and when James with the physician and surgeon carried Thomas from the now blazing upper storey, they laid the injured man beside his father.

Only then Sir Francis demanded, 'And George? Where is George?' His voice grew to a shout as his fear mounted.

James heard him, turned and fled into the hall. Useless to bring the villain out, for he must be dead by now, but Sarah?

He began to climb the stairs, wrapping his waist sash about his mouth. The staircase creaked ominously, as the whole upper part of the house began to sway from the loosening of the great tie beams.

'Sarah!' he yelled again and again, but the sound did not carry far through the muffling about his face and head. He could see that the door of the room where she was with George was still shut. He managed to reach it, still calling to her to come out, he would save her, to open, to come *out*! But either she was already overcome by smoke or obstinately determined to die with her beloved, there was no telling. All was silent inside that locked door.

James heard a voice behind him. Sir Francis from the stairs ordered him back. He gave up the hopeless struggle. Useless to be killed, Sir Francis told him again and again, as they stood together on the edge of the grass, coughing and wiping their eyes and shaking away the burning sparks that showered upon them after the roof fell in.

All round them servants and neighbours poured and pumped water from the well, made chains with buckets, beat down flames. Farther back lay a pile of furniture, books and objects from the ground-floor rooms that these same servants had run in and fetched out while the feeble inmates had been rescued.

At the edge of the lawn, when James and Sir Francis had recovered their breath, the latter said, 'You must come to Luscombe – all of you. Nay, James, my son's death he brought upon himself. He has wrought a great evil and now paid for it. But Thomas – and your dear father, who hath suffered – '

He could not go on; he was blinded by his tears as well as by the smoke. In fact James had to guide him towards the spot where Doctor Richard and his son lay upon the bench, hand clasped in hand.

The coach was ordered to be got ready, but in the end it was not needed. Thomas's wish was fulfilled. He had died in a fight – a true fight. He died quietly, rejoicing at the end of pain, clasping his father's hand.

But the old man had seen James dash back into the burning house. He had concluded that he too, together with the poor feeble daughter, had perished. Shock, together with despair, brought the final hammer blow to break a heart that had endured too much.

'But James lives!' Sir Francis whispered, as he knelt beside his friend. 'See, he is here! He lives!'

Doctor Richard heard his friend's voice, tried to open his tired eyes, but could only manage a smile to show he understood. Sir Francis tried again to rouse him, but the overwrought heart had stopped: the tormented spirit was free.

'God rest them both,' Sir Francis said, kneeling, deeply moved.

James Ogilvy, soldier of the King's Army, stood staring before him, while the fire-fighters, continuing their task, poured water and beat flames to contain the ruin of his once happy, carefree home.

CHAPTER TWENTY-TWO

They found the charred bodies of Sarah and George Leslie close together when the fire was out and the ashes cool enough to make a search for them possible. It was thought she must have overturned the candles in her frenzy when she realized the man was dead. Sarah was buried in the family vault, together with Thomas and their father. In due course all three names were cut in the stone slab that recorded the family deaths.

James stayed at Luscombe for several months. He showed little outward sign of grief, but the haggard look on his face did not lift and though he made obvious efforts to join in the life of the Leslie family circle their interests and pursuits were so different from his own accustomed way of life that his appearance among them led more to awkwardness than pleasure.

However, matters in general were now fast coming to a head. General Monck was on his way from Scotland to London to make arrangements for the actual return of the exiled King. In principle Charles had been accepted throughout the country. The sad risings, so passionately meant, so feeble in execution, were no longer needed.

Not that the remains of the former government, after Richard Cromwell's resignation, did nothing. It continued to work as if great uprisings might cast the country into confusion. Universal orders for mobilization went out to the army in all parts. All horses in private hands must be impounded, lodgers in country houses must be listed and notified. The navy continued to patrol the Flanders coast and the Channel ports. Important people everywhere continued to be gathered in and examined before being released. Even Sir

Francis Leslie did not escape the net. It was well for James that he counted as a lodger at Luscombe and apart from being ordered to stay there was not troubled.

At The Hague Alan Ogilvy, nursed with grateful care by Mistress Cynthia, recovered quickly from his wound, which was neither wide nor deep. At first the surgeon spoke darkly of the dreaded gangrene and even hinted at amputation, but as the initial fever subsided almost at once and it was clear no vital organ in the leg, no major nerve or artery had been cut, these gloomy prognoses were no longer heard, a healthy suppuration led to a slow healing and though much weakened in his general health, the young man began to make steady progress.

All this time Susan, though constantly offering to help her mother, was forbidden the sick room. It was only when Alan, pale but no longer haggard, was allowed to put on a warm fur-lined robe and sit by a comfortable fire of logs that he saw her at last.

He did not know, for he had fainted at the time, that she had caught him in her arms to break his fall and held him, weeping bitterly for shame and shock and fear that he might be dying, while others stopped the flow of blood and bound up the wound before they took him from her to carry him to a bed.

So now, with their misunderstanding lying a dead corpse between them, she was tongue-tied, shame again overcoming her. And Alan, suffering from the natural depression of a convalescent, waited, equally at a loss.

It was not until Susan in a choking voice managed to say, 'Forgive me! Oh, forgive!' that Alan took both her hands in his and drew her into a shaky but fervent embrace. Whereupon they both wept and Alan clasped her again and then collapsed back into his chair by the fire and Susan fussed over the footstool for the wounded leg, that did not yet bend fully at the knee and had given him a sharp twinge as he struggled to do justice to his passion. The knee never did fully bend again but they were not to know this at that time.

The misunderstanding and the mutual despair it had caused them both, was forgotten. Alan explained the two missions he had fulfilled to Lucy Walter.

'She died in Paris last year,' he finished. 'Poor woman, it was a sad fate, but her own doing, alas.'

'You mean Charles Stuart's doing,' Susan cried, indignantly.

'Nay, I do not,' he answered. 'A pair of innocents, maybe, at the start, but poor Mistress Lucy must soon have understood the King's nature. Indeed I found she had long accepted it. Alas, it was very like her own. But where His Majesty keeps these matters apart from affairs of State and inferior to them, as is right and proper – '

'Lucy became a plain whore,' said Susan, bluntly, 'and suffered for it as women always must.'

Alan laughed at her rough speech but loved her the more for her honesty. Where his mother would have been shocked and his grandfather Aldborough surprised, his father would admire the merchant's daughter for her sense of reality while deploring her puritan prejudice.

Alan's mother had visited her son twice during the early days of his recovery. Finding him in such good shape she had suggested, but not insisted, upon taking him away to her own house. But the distance to travel was clearly too great for safety at that time. Now that the move back to England was almost certain to take place soon, it was very likely that the two families would find themselves in London and a move could then be made very easily by coach, even if Alan could not yet ride.

The tragedy at Oxford affected them all in varying degrees. It did much to reconcile Master Phillips to the Ogilvy family and particularly to the idea of allowing his eldest daughter Susan, now nineteen, to marry Alan. He had had a good many grave talks with the young man and found him serious, intelligent, and set upon following a noble profession, with enough good contacts in high places to satisfy the cloth merchant that Alan's commercial prospects were good.

Colonel Ogilvy had no objections either. If he had ever hoped that Alan too might eventually take to soldiering, this wound had put an end to the idea. As for himself, he foresaw an early retirement from his service and that of his wife to the House of Orange. King Charles had already offered him promotion and a title. He knew he had little time left for active military service. Gordon could continue the family tradition in the field.

So the colonel and Lady Anne set about making a permanent move from the Netherlands where they had spent so much of their lives. The actual move could not be made just yet, but Colonel Ogilvy was granted a very friendly audience by the King, who fully understood his position, confirmed the title, a barony, that he would bestow in honour of his coming Restoration, and gave him indefinite leave until that actual event.

In the meantime Captain Sir James Ogilvy arrived back at Court, ignoring the order against leaving Luscombe, which he rightly found to be ridiculous. He was anxious to lay his own plans before the King. He went first to his cousin with the full and accurate story of the disaster at his father's house. He had recovered from his early despair, but his grief for his beloved brother Thomas would never be fully healed. He explained to the colonel that he could not bear even to visit the ruins of the house where his father, brother and sister had died. He had no need for remorse for slaying the villain who had brought about their tragic end. Only regret that he had not done so earlier.

'There is no work for me here now,' he said. 'Certainly the wars in Europe are not yet over. But Englishmen will go back to England when the King comes into his own. I would not be a courtier, perhaps with some pretence of a command about the Royal Person.'

'But you have a purpose, none the less,' Colonel Ogilvy said, smiling kindly. 'I see it in your face. Will you let me hear it?'

'Willingly, sir. I plan to join those forces in the north part of America that have made settlements along that coast of the great ocean. They need escorts for their pioneering, to guard them, to fight the treacherous native, to explore for the wealth that lies hidden there. A new life. Maybe a welcome but honourable death.'

'A new life,' said Lady Anne, 'and a new hope, I pray to God for you, James. You well deserve it. Perhaps a time of reasonable peace, with a wife and family at last.'

Sir James shook his head vigorously.

'No family for me, my lady,' he said in a harsh voice. 'I have had enough of family love, family loss, family death.' He turned to Colonel Ogilvy. 'Those ashes, sir, those stones at Oxford, they shall be yours as head of the family now in England. I resign my whole right in them. Do with them what you will. It shall be sealed legally before I leave this side of the world for ever.'

They argued with him off and on for some weeks, but nothing would alter his purpose. Only, since Colonel Ogilvy refused to take the property as a gift or by right of succession, Sir James consented to sell it to his cousin. The colonel had been thrifty all his mature years and the Lady Anne had brought him a good dowry, so James, with his knighthood and a substantial sum assured him, was able to make much more definite arrangements for his future, even consenting to take Master Phillips's advice in these matters, since he was reconciled at last to his elder sister and her husband.

Master Phillips, interviewed by the shrewd Clarendon, had received a free pardon from the King, both on account of his unjust expulsion from Parliament and his forced exile from England. And more particularly on account of his undoubted future usefulness to the English economy when the throne was restored.

This great event took place in May 1660. A fleet from England came for Charles, filled with all manner of notables, army, navy, church, chapel, the law, the nobles. With documents for the King to sign, concessions, promises, rules to follow. To his particular joy, money to spend.

He sailed from The Hague with his Councillors, his chief friends and a guard chosen from his small army, including Colonel Ogilvy, now Lord Folliot. The ship was the *Naseby* but later was re-christened *The Royal Charles*.

He was welcomed at Dover by General Monck amid great rejoicing among the people in general. He rode by way of Canterbury, Rochester, Blackheath and Southwark to the City of London and on to the City of Westminster and from there by Charing Cross to Whitehall.

His long exile, his terrible penury, was over at last. He had enough to eat; he could indulge his fancy for rich, elaborate clothing, beautiful surroundings, gay courtiers. Though Cardinal Mazarin had still refused him the hand in marriage of his lovely niece, Hortense, he could now look forward to gaining a royal princess for wife. Meanwhile he could enjoy his mistresses and reward them suitably with fine jewels.

In all this easement of his condition he did not neglect the very important affairs of state that followed his restoration and preceded his full acceptance of the throne and subsequent coronation. He proved himself to be a king unlikely ever to become a tyrant. Lord Clarendon understood he was a king fully and competently determined never to lose his throne again, far less his head in defending it against a sternly successful body of puritan rebels.

Moreover he showed himself ready to restore and reward all those who had supported him in his exile, particularly those who had engineered his escape from England after Worcester.

Among them Captain Tettersal and his crew came into prominence and won great rewards. The ship *Surprise* was honoured, to Tettersal's great gratification, by having her name changed to *King's Escape* and to being used as one of His Majesty's yachts. Charles also kept his promise to the mate of the vessel, Richard Carver. The imprisoned Quakers were freed and Carver himself was given a sum of money to help him and his body of co-religionists to emigrate to the newly established colonies on the eastern seaboard of America. As Carver told Alan Ogilvy, 'The King was pleased to inquire of me why I would leave my native land so soon after it was made good to live in again. So I told His Majesty, "It is good just now, sire, seeing Thy Majesty's heart is overflowing with gratitude and goodwill and will remain so, God willing. But lesser men may well change again towards us for our way of life and I think we have suffered enough of late to wish to be done with persecution." So the King smiled and said, "You speak boldly, my man. But you do not offend us, for we know your worth. Go and prosper." So he gave me his hand to kiss. And later there was a fair sum at my disposal. And so we go hence when we shall find a vessel to take us.'

'God be with you,' Alan said, almost envious of the man's simple purpose and great faith in the complete rightness of his beliefs.

Lord Aldborough, with many others, was released promptly from the Tower and rejoined his wife in his home near Banbury, where he continued his vague existence in harmless country pursuits, to the satisfaction of his neighbours and the peasantry of the district. He had no wish whatever to attend the new King's Court. He had sufficient news of it from his sons, who had survived the war, chiefly by using very loyal inaction in one or other of the gentler plotting, wholly inefficient, secret societies.

Colonel Ogilvy, Lord Folliot, decided to rebuild the Ogilvy mansion at Oxford. While the work was going forward he and his family lived in the dower house on the Aldborough estate. This freed the house in Paternoster Row for Alan, who, after his marriage to Susan, lived there while he continued to study for his profession at Saint Bartholomew's Hospital, following in the footsteps of Sir William Harvey.

King Charles did not forget him, but since there were so many of greater social importance than himself, and many who had risked their lives both in England and abroad to serve him during his exile, it was nearly a year before the call came from Whitehall, by which time Alan was married and Susan was expecting their first child.

Lord Clarendon greeted him warmly. This in itself was an honour Alan did not fail to appreciate, for the great man had no need now to arrange nor attend the King's audiences. His Court was fully organized, with a plethora of eager men and women seeking to establish themselves there either as representatives or descendants of the former aristocracy or as members of a new one. Charles was very careful to preserve a certain power for the always argumentative and critical Commons, while surrounding himself with men and women of culture, wit, beauty and even learning, all of which qualities he had missed sadly for so long.

Alan found His Majesty changed in appearance but not, after a few overwhelming minutes, in his behaviour. The King's dress was magnificent, rich in design and material, elaborately decorated with bows and ribbons, the jewelled orders blazing. His hair, black, curled, hung lower than ever, well below his shoulders. Between the two dark rippling falls, his face with a quite new expression of content and well-being, was Charles the Second at his most kingly, Alan thought. Time would never fill the hungry furrows in each cheek, nor remove the cynical set of the wide mouth. But as the young man rose from his obeisance the eyes that could wither a liar or a villain were gazing at him with all the old friendly interest.

'So we have come to you at last, my page,' Charles said. 'Did you think we had forgotten you?'

'I never did think Your Majesty had any reason to remember the small missions I was graciously entrusted with,' Alan managed to say, stumbling a little over the words, for he found the occasion very moving.

The King spoke a little of their very first encounter on *Surprise*.

'Poor Wilmot,' he said. 'He was no sailor, was he? He suffered for me, then, and many times before that. I would he had seen the outcome of his service.'

He went on in his old familiar strain, recalling incidents at the Court in Paris or with his sister at Spa, in Brussels and The Hague and Calais. But he did not once speak the name of Lucy Walter nor of the young Duke of Monmouth. He demanded to know how Alan was faring in his profession; he suggested a pension. But it was plain his attention was wandering and the young man was relieved when the audience came to an end with fresh regal condescension and formal grand manners.

The pension did not materialize. But Alan did not hold its non-appearance against the King. He continued to admire him, though he no longer actively loved him now as he had done as a boy.

In this he copied the general mood of the country. Released from the iron hand of the bigots, the people rejoiced in their long-lost freedom. Even Master Phillips saw the advantage of a moderate indulgence in the pleasures of life, so that the long quarrel in the two parts of the Ogilvy family was completely healed.

'Just as the wars are now over for ever, my love,' Susan said to Alan, on the occasion of the christening of their son in Saint Paul's church.

'In England for ever, I pray God,' answered Alan. 'But it was the strife in our land brought war into our two families and brought you to me, at least, my dearest. But that war, I hope and trust, is well and truly over.'

So they kissed across the cradle of Arthur George Francis Ogilvy and turned to welcome the guests they had invited to celebrate the occasion.